MW01141287

Tanya

MICHAEL PARLEE

Bloomington, IN Milton Keynes, UK

authorHOUSE®

AuthorHouse™
1663 Liberty Drive, Suite 200
Bloomington, IN 47403
www.authorhouse.com
Phone: 1-800-839-8640

AuthorHouse™ UK Ltd.
500 Avebury Boulevard
Central Milton Keynes, MK9 2BE
www.authorhouse.co.uk
Phone: 08001974150

First published by AuthorHouse 1/10/2007

ISBN: 1-4259-3299-1 (sc)

Library of Congress Control Number: 2006903514

Printed in the United States of America
Bloomington, Indiana

This book is printed on acid-free paper.

DEDICATION

TO MY FAMILY

Pauline my wife of thirty-seven years

Shane my son and Juanita my daughter

Edith my mother and Rob my father

Both now enjoying their eternal rewards

ACKNOWLEDGEMENTS

I would like to acknowledge and thank the many people who have assisted me in writing this book.

At the top of the list is my wife, Pauline. In addition to being my sounding board and mentor, she has spent hundreds of hours on the computer assisting me in the endless task of editing. Pauline and I have been so closely tied to Tanya that I now think of it as our book.

My editor, Barb Baer: Tanya has evolved for the better from her professional, honest and occasionally frank suggestions. Barb's sensitivity in handling what I had strove so long to create, meant a great deal to me. Soon we'll be working together on my second book.

My daughter Juanita: She managed the painstaking task of transcribing my longhand manuscript onto the computer. This was no easy task, as at times neither one of us could decipher my hen scratch.

Judith Kozub, dear friend and intuitive counselor: After reading the book, she envisaged the layout for the cover.

Henriette Greidanus, friend and journalist: Her critique of the first and last chapters was very helpful.

All of the forty-odd proof-readers of my draft version of Tanya: Not only did they help me realize that I'd written something of interest, but their critiques helped immeasurably in fine-tuning the story.

INTRODUCTION

"Tanya" is a forthright, emotionally charged figment of my imagination. It is an occasionally earthy, occasionally violent, passionate love story of a pioneer couple, Tanya and Tom Parker. From the nineteen twenties to the mid-nineteen seventies, we follow them through all the joy and pain that life brings their way.

As my first attempt at writing, "Tanya" has been a growing experience for me. Like many authors, I have learned much about myself in creating my own story. Although "Tanya" is fiction, a fair amount of it is true to life. Any direct comparison though between the characters in Tanya and people I know or have known is strictly of the reader's making.

As you begin "Tanya", you are back in the mid nineteen twenties in the Westview Valley of mid- western Alberta. The western end of the valley is forested and melds into the foothills of the Rocky Mountains. Some thirty miles to the east the valley flattens out and becomes parkland.

This is homesteaders' country. Being born in this era myself and having brought several thousand acres of bush land under cultivation, I can vouch for the struggle of these hearty pioneers as they attempted to turn forest primeval into productive farm land. Along with the hardships though, there were plenty of good times.

But first, before you start, a few words of caution. Undoubtedly there will be those who will take issue with the occasional bit of coarse language used by some of the more earthy characters. In addition, there are some scenes of graphic violence and a few sexual encounters that will be shocking for some. If my words of caution don't faze you, read on.

CHAPTER
1

Betty Collins sat at the kitchen table, sick with worry. At the sound of an approaching vehicle she jumped to her feet and went over to the window. She watched apprehensively as her neighbour Jed Osmond's car pulled up their driveway and stopped at the back gate. Her husband, Aaron was slouched over in the passenger seat, his head resting against the side window. Jed went around to the passenger side to help him out.

"Oh my God, he's drunk again!" Betty cried out, fear welling up in her chest. "I've still got bruises from the last time he was on a bender. How much more of this can I take? Please God, don't let him beat me again," she whispered. "Why can't he treat me better now that there's a baby on the way?"

Jed supported Aaron down the path and up the porch steps. At six foot four and two hundred thirty five pounds, he towered eight inches over Aaron. Jed was lean and hard, while Aaron was getting quite a beer belly from all his drinking. Jed's ebony complexion sharply contrasted with Aaron's chalky white face.

Betty went out on the porch landing to meet Aaron, but he stumbled by without acknowledging her. After a couple of tries, Jed got Aaron through the kitchen door. Jed steered him over to the kitchen table, helped him into a chair and then went back out to see Betty.

"You don't know how horrible it is having my husband brought home drunk," she said, without making eye contact.

"How could a man treat such a beautiful woman this poorly?" Jed wondered as he glanced at Betty. She was petite, dark, with haunting brown eyes, jet black hair and a trim figure that would turn any man's head.

Jed rested his big hand on Betty's shoulder. "There's fear in your voice. I'd better take the drunken idiot home and sober him up."

Betty struggled to regain her composure. "I think it will be O.K.," she replied, her voice shaking, "but thanks just the same. Thanks for bringing him home."

"Now look here, Betty. I remember that black eye you had a few weeks ago. If this guy is ever rough with you again, promise you'll let me know. I've a sure cure for anyone who's violent with women." Jed clenched his big fist. "This here is the best cure there is. I know it works because I've used it before."

"Thanks a lot," Betty said hesitantly. "Your support means a lot to me. Unless Aaron smartens up, things will soon come to a head."

Jed took his hand off Betty's shoulder and turned to go down the porch steps.

The fight began the second Betty stepped inside.

"You low-bred bitch," Aaron slurred, lurching forward and hitting her hard across the face. "I'll teach you to screw with that black bastard. I saw his hand on your shoulder."

Betty cried out in pain and backed into the corner.

Aaron lunged at her, but never quite made it.

Half way down the porch steps, Jed was having second thoughts about leaving Betty, with Aaron as drunk as he was. He quickly re-climbed the porch steps and waited at the door. When he heard Betty cry out, he barged into the house.

Jed grabbed Aaron by the shirt collar just before he reached Betty again.

"I've no use for woman beaters," Jed roared. "I'm going to thrash you but good."

Jed hit him a good backhand across the face. Aaron's head flopped like a rag doll. Jed hit him several times, alternating the back of the hand with the flat of the hand.

"That's for beating on your wife," Jed snarled. He paused for a moment then belted him another good backhand. "And this one is for calling me a black bastard."

Aaron's face was a bloody mess. Still grasping him by the collar, Jed dragged him to the wash basin and poured a couple of dippers of water over his head. As Aaron regained consciousness, there was terror in his eyes. Jed lifted him clear of the floor and pinned him against the wall.

"I'll let you off easy this time with just a good thumping," Jed said, glowering at him. "If it ever happens again though, I'll hit you with my fist, not the flat of my hand. If I have to do it again, you'll be in the hospital for a long time. There's no excuse what-so-ever for abusing your wife, especially now that she's expecting. You get the message?"

Aaron attempted to nod. As Jed released his grip, Aaron slumped to the floor.

Betty followed Jed back out onto the porch landing.

"Are you O.K.?" he asked

"Yes, I'll be alright," Betty replied, on the verge of tears. "Thank you so much for protecting me and the baby."

Betty fought hard for composure, but sobs were soon racking her body. Jed pulled her close and held her until she finally stopped crying.

"It's been getting steadily worse," she finally blurted out. "I can put up with the drinking and doing most of the farm work, but I can't take the abuse. I'm so scared for the baby now."

"I'm sorry I had to work Aaron over the way I did, but if you're to continue your marriage, he must learn that he can't abuse you and get away with it. You're going to have to make up your mind whether or not you can stay with this drunken moocher. Only you can make that decision. Maybe the thrashing I just gave him will bring him to his senses, maybe it won't. At any rate I'll take him home, sober him up and bring him back tomorrow."

Jed half carried Aaron to his car. After cleaning him up, he decided that a couple of the lacerations needed medical attention, so drove him to the hospital in Milden, fifteen miles east of his farm. Milden was a small town located in the middle of the Westview Valley in west central Alberta seventy miles north west of Red Deer.

Gordon Stuart, Milden's Doctor, was aware of Aaron's drinking problem and how it was impacting on Betty, especially now that she was pregnant. Jed told the doctor about Aaron's attack on Betty and the trimming he just gave him.

Stuart was a Scot with the tendency of being blunt. As he was suturing up Aaron's cuts, he said. "Well laddie, it looks like you finally got what you deserve for abusing your wife. If you're wise you'll smarten up. If you don't, I'll guarantee you one thing, your marriage won't last long."

Aaron slept for eighteen hours straight, finally waking at eleven a.m. the next day. Aaron and Jed didn't have a great deal to say to each other. After making him something to eat, Jed drove Aaron home and followed him into the house.

"Now listen here, Aaron. This is to be the last time you raise a hand to Betty. As I told you yesterday, if you ever abuse her again, I'll put you out of commission for a very long time. That's not a threat, Aaron, that's a promise. The arrangement you and Betty make is none of my business. If you decide to carry on, I'll support both of you in any way I can, but remember Aaron, no more abuse."

Over the next few days Aaron refused to talk to Betty. He made no attempt to help with any of the chores, choosing instead to lie around nursing his sore face. He kept contact to a minimum by sleeping on the couch in the front room. Betty tried in vain to get things back on track, but Aaron maintained his surly attitude. He refused to apologize for his actions and was soon cursing Jed under his breath and mean-mouthing him for interfering in their marriage.

Betty was doing the chores when she heard Aaron's old pickup truck pull out of the yard. There were no words of farewell, just a brief note on the kitchen table that read:

Can't stand this BS anymore. Got to take some time to think things out.

The day after Aaron left, Betty borrowed Jed's car and drove into Red Deer to talk things over with her folks. They wanted her to move in with them, at least until after the baby was born. Betty thanked them for the offer, but said she would wait to see what would happen with Aaron.

"I haven't made up my mind yet whether or not to give him another chance. If he tries to come back, though, he'll have to change drastically. At any rate, if he doesn't show his face, I'd still like to look after the cattle until maybe a month before my due date. Jed has offered to help me."

As the months slipped by, Aaron made no attempt to contact her. The longer he stayed away, the more Betty realized that any feelings she once had for him were dying.

As Betty's pregnancy approached the eighth month, she was depending on Jed for help with all her chores. Near the end of January, Betty contacted a cattle buyer to give her a price on her young stock. Once the young cattle were sold, Jed offered to take her cows up to his place until Betty had her baby. Betty hadn't made up her mind whether she'd return to the farm after that.

On the morning of January twenty sixth the temperature dropped to -40F and only recovered to -35F by late afternoon. That evening, after supper, Betty was checking on her cattle. Despite the stillness of the night, she heard the distant unmistakable roar from the west, the familiar sound of the warm chinook wind on its way.

On returning to the house, Betty made herself a cup of tea and turned in early.

She awoke with a start to the howling of the wind in the pines and the hissing sound of snow blowing against the bedroom window. Above the roar of the wind, she heard the banging of the shed door.

"The Chinook must have blown in," she thought. Betty snuggled back under the covers. Suddenly a feeling of panic swept over her. "Dear God, I can't be going into labour! I'm not due for another five weeks. No, the wind must have woke me," she said aloud.

As Betty tossed and turned, her thoughts returned to her estranged husband, Aaron. "Never should have married that drunken bum," she muttered.........

She was awake again. This time there was no mistaking it. She definitely felt a contraction. "Oh dear God help me!" she cried, wild fear gripping her chest.

She looked at the clock. It was 3:30 a.m. "I must get help but how?" she said frantically.

She climbed out of bed, put on her housecoat, lit the coal-oil lamp and began pacing the floor in a frenzy.

"Damn it!" she cried. "No phone and my old car broke down. Why didn't we get hooked up to the party line? What a mess I'm in! Oh dear God, what can I do now? I've got to get to Jed's place for help."

Betty was breathing heavily as she put on her coat and boots. When she stepped outside, a sobering thought occurred to her.

"It's drifting so badly it's like a blizzard out here. I just can't afford to do something foolish like trying to walk to Jed's. It would be disastrous if I had my baby in a snow bank somewhere on the way. Oh my God, what am I to do now?"

"I've got to calm down, I must," she kept repeating to herself as she stepped back inside. "It's not going to do me any good to panic. I'll time the contractions. That will tell me how much time I've got left."

When her next contraction came, she glanced at the clock. "I'm okay for now. They're still forty minutes apart. Jed will be here by eight-thirty to do the chores. I'll just have to try to relax and wait till he gets here."

Betty slowly regained control of her emotions. She pulled the old arm chair up to the table, covered herself with a blanket and dozed off between contractions.

Betty awoke to the sound of harness bells coming with the wind. She looked out the kitchen window and saw a single faint light coming up the drive way.

"That's Jed with the horses and sleigh. Why did he come with them?" Then she shuddered. "The Chinook must have blown the roads in and made them impassible for the car."

Betty greeted Jed at the door. He stomped the snow off his boots and stepped inside.

"Boy, am I ever glad to see you! I went into labour about five hours ago."

"Damn it, this is all we need with the roads drifted in. How long do you figure it will be?"

"Well, the doctor told me the first birth can be a bit unpredictable. If all goes by the book though, I expect I should have at least four hours or so. The contractions are still pretty far apart."

"I guess our only option is for me to go and get Mrs. Weiss. We could try to make it to her place with the team and sleigh, but the last one and a half miles is cross wind. It's likely drifted solid by now. If we bogged down somewhere along the way with the sleigh, it would be disastrous. I'm not up to delivering a baby in a sleigh box and you're in no shape to go bareback. I may have to drop the sleigh and ride the horses if the roads get impassable. I'll do a quick job on the chores before heading out."

Jed was back in the house in twenty minutes.

"I'll stop at Crawfords' and get them to come and stay with you." He went over to Betty and put his hand on her shoulder. "You holding up O.K.?"

"Yes, I guess so," she replied, her voice breaking. "I really don't have any other choice, do I?"

The road to the Crawford place was nearly impassable and Jed had to stop several times to wind the horses. He pulled into the Crawfords' yard, jumped from the sleigh box and loped to their back door.

"Son of a bitch!" he exclaimed. A note on the door read: We've gone to my brother Ray's for a few days. Be back on the twenty-eighth.

Jed went into the house and got Olga Weiss on the phone. "Betty went into labour at three this morning. We'll need you to help deliver the baby. I should make it to your place in half an hour if the roads aren't blocked. If they are, I might have to leave the sleigh and come with just the horses."

"It won't be the first time I've gone on horseback to deliver a baby. Before the hospital was built in Milden, I delivered a number of babies during blizzards. Whenever you get here, I'll be ready to go."

At that precise moment, eighty miles to the south-east, Betty's mother bowed her head at the kitchen sink. Mary had been awake since two a.m. with a feeling of foreboding for Betty and the baby.

"Why does that girl of mine have to be so headstrong?" she pondered. "If only she had moved in with us. All I can do is keep on praying."

"I don't know what it is," she commented to George as they were eating breakfast. "I just have this strong feeling that Betty desperately needs help right now. I've been praying for her and the baby most of the night."

As Jed's team swung out of Betty's driveway, fear again welled up inside her.

With tears streaming down her face, she cried out, "Dear God help me! Help Jed get through. Let my baby to be born healthy. Oh God, I'm so scared! Please help me."

As she continued praying, her sobbing gradually subsided. Slowly at first, but then with growing intensity, she felt a blanket of peace and well-being descending on her. It was like the warmth, love, and security she felt as a small girl when she would become scared at night, come into her folks' bedroom and climb into bed with them. The sensation completely enveloped her, making her feel secure. With God's shield of protection around her, her worry vanished. She felt confident that Jed would get through to the Weiss place and was sure that the baby would be born healthy. Once again she was able to cat nap between contractions.

As Jed suspected, the last mile and a half into Weiss's was badly drifted. Coming to a huge drift right across the road, he turned the sleigh around and unhitched the horses.

Jed climbed on King and let the mare Darkie follow. The horses bounded like deer to get through the big drifts and they were soon turning in at the Weiss driveway. Anticipating that she might have to go on horseback, Olga Weiss had all her midwifery paraphernalia on two pack boards. Jed tied the pack boards to King's hames and helped Mrs. Weiss up on Darkie.

Once under way, Jed decided not to pick up the sleigh as it was still drifting badly.

Betty awoke from one of her cat-naps to the sound of the horses' harness bells. Jed helped get everything into the house, then took the team to the barn. Mrs. Weiss went right into rotation and within a half-hour, everything was ready for the birth.

Betty's water broke at two p.m. and the contractions became more severe. Jed relentlessly paced the floor, worry and fear playing across his face. Betty had never seen him so agitated.

"What is it, Jed? You look like you're about ready to come apart."

Jed quit pacing and quietly replied. "Well Betty, some years back......." He stopped in mid-sentence as a sad, far away look came into his eyes.

"Never mind now, Betty. This isn't the time to go on about my past. I'll tell you about it some other time. Right now, all I want is to see you and the baby doing well."

As Betty's contractions became more intense, Jed was confined to the kitchen and front room. He all but wore a path in the kitchen floor with his incessant pacing and was constantly calling out to Mrs. Weiss for an update.

"Honestly, Betty, at times, these men are more of a problem than the babies."

"Well, I've known Jed for years, and there's something quite odd about his anxiety. It's just so out of character for him."

And so it was that late in the afternoon of the twenty-seventh of January, Nineteen Twenty-Seven, in a sparsely furnished bedroom in a small homesteader's home, Betty gave birth to a baby girl.

When Jed heard the baby cry, he shouted out for the umpteenth time, "Everything O.K.?"

"Everything's under control," Olga replied. "Betty has a beautiful baby girl. They're both doing well and as you can hear, the young one certainly has a good voice."

"Thank God," Jed sighed in relief. "Thank God."

While Mrs. Weiss was cleaning up, the baby started nuzzling Betty's breast. Although slightly smaller than normal because of being born a month early, the baby was healthy.

"If you'd like, you can come in now," Betty called out.

Jed stepped into the bedroom and stood quietly watching the baby nursing contentedly. He slowly reached out his hand and gently laid it on the baby's blond little head.

"Thank God you and the baby made it," he whispered, wiping the tears from his eyes. "Praise God for a healthy baby girl."

Again his expression changed to a sad, painful one and he whispered quietly to himself.

"Tanya, my little Tanya."

As he turned to leave, Betty reached out her hand to him, her eyes now soft and full of relief.

"Well, we all made it, Jed. I could never have managed without your help. Thank you for being here for me."

After supper, Jed rode his team home and phoned Betty's folks. They were relieved that all had gone well and overjoyed that they had a healthy granddaughter.

"I knew there was something amiss last night," Mary said. "I had this overwhelming feeling that Betty was so in need. All I could do was pray. We owe you so much for taking care of Betty."

"Never mind, that's what neighbouring's all about. You folks were always there for me when you lived on the farm. I'll call you again when the roads are plowed out. I think we all agree that Betty and the baby should stay with you, for now, anyway."

The next morning, Jed took Olga Weiss to his place so she could phone Dr. Stuart. Because the baby was a month premature, the doctor suggested that she stay an extra day or two, just in case there were some complications.

When Jed returned with Mrs. Weiss, he started building Betty a new cattle loading chute. Several times in the afternoon he looked in on Betty, the baby and Mrs. Weiss. "Just checking to see that everything is under control," he'd say.

Olga was not to be fooled though. She observed the closeness between Jed, Betty and the baby and knew that he just wanted to be near them.

"I'd swear that Jed acts more like a father than most fathers I know," Olga said, when Betty and she were alone. "It's very obvious that he likes to be near you and the baby. It's probably none of my business, but you sure could do worse for yourself than him. Mind you, you'd have to straighten out your own affairs with Aaron first. I know Jed is black, but I can tell by the way you look at each other that there's something more than just friendship between you."

Betty blushed. "Yes Olga, you're right. When I was fourteen I had a crush on Jed. I remember feeling so frustrated. I wanted him to treat me as more than just a close friend. He's so handsome, so kind and so strong. Who cares what color his skin is? But you're right. First, I have to start working on my divorce."

With Betty and the baby doing well, Mrs. Weiss got Jed to take her home. She was put out by his offer of payment for delivering the baby and staying with Betty.

"Here in homesteader country, we need to lean on each other. You've been a tremendous help to Betty. Just continue to look out for her and the baby and I'll be well paid." She smiled and added, "If my intuition is right, I won't have to worry too much about that request."

Jed looked away, deep in thought. "Yes Olga, they're both pretty special to me."

As Betty sat in the rocking chair with her little girl sleeping peacefully on her lap, her mind drifted back over the tumultuous events of the last three years............

She recalled how shocked she was when she learned that her parents, George and Mary Benson were both infected with tuberculosis. With her folks spending eight months in a sanitarium, Betty jumped right in and took over the operation of the farm. Although she did well in the secretarial course she took after finishing high school, her first love was still the farm.

When her folks were released from the sanitarium, the Doctor suggested that they'd be wise to quit farming because of their weakened lungs. George and Mary talked things over with Betty and she volunteered to take over the operation of the farm. Their neighbour, Jed Osmond work-shared with George over the years and offered to help Betty out as needed. George and Mary reluctantly left the farm, moved into Red Deer and went into semi-retirement.

Shortly after her folks left the farm, Betty met her future husband at a local dance. Aaron Collins had blond hair, blue eyes and an athletic build. His good looks and charm swept Betty her right off her feet and they were soon talking of marriage.

Betty's girlfriend cautioned her about being in such a hurry to marry. She knew Aaron from high school and was not at all impressed with him. Her folks suggested she wait until they got to know each other better.

Even though Aaron was fired from his job two weeks before their wedding for reporting to work drunk, Betty would not change her mind. She was confident that getting married and being in a new environment, away from his drinking buddies, would turn the tide for him.

Once they were married, Betty started lobbying for them to move to the farm, but Aaron was dragging his feet. Despite his reluctance, Betty prevailed until he grudgingly agreed.

At first things were working out well, as Aaron hadn't touched a drop of alcohol since their wedding day. However, his resolve soon began to slip and by the end of two months, he was drinking heavily again.

Betty was very disheartened. The more she pressured Aaron, the more he turned to the bottle. As if his drinking problem wasn't bad enough, Aaron showed little interest in farming. Betty found herself doing almost all the farm chores.

The physical abuse started six months into their marriage. At first, Betty paid little attention to it as it seemed so insignificant. It took the form of a small shove or the like, when they had a disagreement while Aaron was drinking. He would always apologize for getting physical, once he sobered up.

As the abusive behavior escalated, Aaron began an insidious scheme. Although still apologizing, he would shift the blame to Betty, saying that forcing him to move to the farm caused him to start drinking again.

In desperation, Betty decided to get pregnant. Before they were married, Aaron seemed as eager as she was to have a family. With the news of the baby on the way, she thought the drinking and abuse would stop. She felt her pregnancy would also motivate Aaron to take over most of the farm work.

When Betty broke the news to Aaron that she was expecting, he stormed out of the house without saying a word and went on a three day drunk.

Betty was at wits' end. She was constantly worrying that the physical abuse would injure their unborn child. When she suggested they get outside help to resolve their difficulties, Aaron adamantly refused, maintaining that she was blowing things all out of proportion.

Betty finally contacted her parents and family doctor for help. They encouraged her to get counseling, even if Aaron refused to go.

Betty could still hear her mom's voice. "Remember, he is responsible for his actions, not you. If things don't improve, you might have to cut your losses and leave Aaron for both yours and the baby's safety. Maybe it will take that to make him realize how serious his drinking problem is."............

The sound of an approaching vehicle brought Betty back to the present. As she watched Jed's car coming up the driveway, she mused, "It hurts that Aaron doesn't even have the decency to see how his own daughter is doing. Why couldn't he be responsible like Jed?"

Betty was still in the rocking chair nursing the baby when Jed stepped inside. He filled the kettle with water and made tea.

"Jed, I wonder what I should name my little girl? I've gone through as many names as I can think of and nothing seems quite right."

"Do you fancy the name Tanya?" Jed replied, that far away look again coming into his eyes.

"Tanya," Betty repeated several times. "Tanya....I like that! Tanya it will be!"

As Betty glanced up at Jed, she wondered about his quick reply, and what significance the name Tanya held for him.

Betty's folks arrived late in the afternoon to pick up Betty and the baby. As the roads were poor, George thought it wise to spend the night and leave in the morning. He helped Jed with the chores while Mary prepared supper.

The next morning, as they were leaving, Jed told Betty he'd bring her the cheque as soon as the cattle buyer issued it.

"I'll be looking forward to that. Maybe you could stay for a few days when you come."

As they were pulling out of the yard, Mary turned to Betty. "If you ask me, Jed must be more than a little interested in you and Tanya. He could deposit your cheque in your account in Milden without making a special trip to bring it to you. When you were in your late teens, Dad and I wondered if you and Jed would get together someday. He was a bit older than you but such a kind, industrious sort."

Betty smiled. She paused a moment, reflected some, then chose not to comment.

In the afternoon, the cattle buyer came and looked over the young stock. Betty asked Jed to do the dealing on her behalf and after a bit of friendly haggling, they settled on a price of $2500 for the lot. Jed assisted with the loading and as soon as the young cattle were trucked out, he walked Betty's cows up to his place.

That evening, Jed sat alone in his little house, reflecting on the past. He recalled the first time he met Betty and her folks. Shortly after he arrived in the community, they dropped in to welcome him. For the first few years, Betty was like a younger sister to him. By the time she turned fourteen, though, Jed realized by the way she dressed and acted when she was around him, that her feelings were becoming deeper than just friendship. Since he was still dealing with the loss of his wife and baby girl and was more than ten years older than Betty, he put the brakes on things.

Sitting in the twilight, Jed's eyes filled with tears as he thought of the losses he suffered in the past. He hardly dared hope that Betty, the baby and he would all be together someday, but with the warmth he felt for them, he wanted it so. As the twilight turned to winter darkness, it occurred to him how much helping Betty out had helped him heal.

"Is God in his mercy giving me another chance?" he mused. "Maybe the little baby I'm coming to love so much is a replacement for the little girl I lost. Is Betty a replacement for my wife now dead twelve years? I'm so grateful that Betty and baby Tanya made it through the crisis. I miss them so."

Jed was up at the crack of dawn and on his way to Red Deer. Even though they'd been apart for only a few days, whenever he thought about Betty and Tanya, he got a warm feeling in his chest. For the last four or five months, there was hardly a day that he hadn't seen Betty, eating dinners at her place most of the time.

Jed stayed in Red Deer for a couple of days and made arrangements with Betty to rent her land. She in turn agreed to return in the spring to help him out with the housework so he and his hired man could concentrate on the seeding.

"It's sure going to be lonely without you," Jed said as he was leaving.

"Yes, it will be lonely for me too. I'm so looking forward to coming back to the farm in the spring."

CHAPTER
2

As a husky eighteen year old, Bill Parker came west from eastern Canada on a harvest excursion. He fell in love with the Westview Valley in west central Alberta and stayed on. He homesteaded one quarter section of land and took over another quarter section from a neighbour who became disillusioned with clearing land. As was the case with many young men in this era, Bill worked the winters in the sawmills and the summers bringing his land under cultivation.

Before the advent of modern equipment, the brush was cleared by hand. Once the breaking was done with horses, steamer or tractor, the roots were picked manually. It was all back-breaking labour.

When Bill was asked about homesteading he'd quip, "You don't have to be a fool to do it, but it sure makes it a lot less painful if you are one."

Shortly after his twenty-first birthday, Bill joined the Army. World War I was still grinding away and Bill was seeking adventure. While on leave from his basic training, he married his girlfriend, Ema Miller. Ema's folks' land adjoined Bill's.

Bill made arrangements with Ema's dad to rent his land while he was in the Armed Forces. As a homesteader's daughter, Ema had already picked her fair share of roots and rocks. She and her dad would break a bit more of Bill's land as they were able to.

Tragedy befell Bill shortly after his posting to the front lines. For some time, the fighting was at a standstill with both sides well dug in. Sporadic artillery fire from both sides kept everyone pinned down. Finally the Allies' artillery laid down a blistering barrage that devastated the enemy. Bill and his company experienced little resistance as they moved forward.

For the first time in months, Bill felt elated that they were on the move and then it happened. With a thunderous roar an artillery shell exploded, hurling Bill upwards. He felt the sting of sand in his face, excruciating pain in his legs and then darkness.

As Bill drifted in and out of consciousness in the field hospital, his first sensations were a severe headache and cold feet. Finally, the feeling in his feet turned to throbbing pain.

"Must have crushed my feet some," he thought. When he looked down at his feet, Bill became nauseous. There were just two big bandages around his knees. To his horror, he realized that his legs were gone from the knees down.

It was a slow, painful recovery for Bill. The physical pain was hard enough to bear, but the emotional anguish he experienced was even greater. He constantly cursed his fate and was having great difficulty accepting that he was now a cripple and would be dependant on others for the rest of his life.

Ema and her folks received the grim telegram a week after Bill was wounded.

Regret to inform you: Bill Parker wounded in action.

Hospitalized: Condition serious but stable. Will notify if condition changes.

Ema was heartbroken. She anguished and prayed for her man all her waking hours. Most nights she cried herself to sleep. Bill and she had only been married eight months.

After a few days in the field hospital, Bill attempted to write Ema a letter. He struggled for over an hour, but it seemed an impossible task.

One of his roommates was an older soldier whose right arm had been blown off at the elbow. He noticed Bill was having a rough time. "Having trouble lad?"

"Yea, I guess so," Bill replied disconsolately. "I'm having a hell of a time writing to my wife about losing my legs."

"I know all too well what you're going through and how difficult it is. I had to write a letter to my wife with my left hand. I know it's not easy, but you must tell your Mrs. It's the only way you'll start healing, healing your spirit, that is. Best get right at it, lad. Even though it's painful, it will do you a world of good."

Finally, in desperation, Bill started his letter.

Dearest Ema,

I love you and miss you so much. No doubt you've been notified that I was wounded. I was hit by an artillery shell and both of my legs were amputated above my knees.

Tears streamed down his face and he cried uncontrollably. It was Bill's first show of emotion since being wounded.

"That's it," said his roommate. "Let it all out, lad. You're finally facing it. I know it's pretty rough stuff, but you're dealing with it now."

When Ema read Bill's letter, she burst into tears. Although relieved and grateful that Bill's life had been spared, she was concerned how he would handle the loss of his legs.

After a week in the field hospital, the Army returned Bill to England to convalesce. Shortly after his arrival in the Rehabilitation Centre, Harvey Burke, a young Canadian Chaplain, dropped in for a visit.

Extending his hand to Bill, Burke saw a clean cut, handsome young man with reddish hair. There was a tortured look in his steel blue eyes.

"Good day, sir."

"I can't think of too much that's good about it," Bill retorted.

An uncomfortable silence ensued. Finally, Burke replied. "Feeling a bit peed off with life, I imagine?"

"Well, how would you feel if your legs were blown off?" Bill said angrily. "How would you like to live the rest of your life like this? How in the world will I manage now?"

"It would be foolish for me to say I know what you're going through, but I can appreciate some of the pain you feel. My youngest brother was killed in action three months ago."

"I'm sorry to hear that," Bill said, subdued. "This bloody war is so senseless."

"I don't think any of us know why these tragedies happen, but I've had a great deal of help handling the loss of my brother by asking for God's assistance. For what they're worth, Bill, here are some thoughts. Try to be thankful that your life was spared. Ask yourself, 'Is it better to have lost my legs, or my life?' You can still live a productive life, Bill. The doctors say you will be around for another month, so I'll check in on you in a couple of days."

Burke ended his visit by offering a humble prayer asking God to help Bill through the hard days that lay ahead. Over the next few weeks the Chaplin visited several times and did his best to help Bill adjust to his loss.

It was a very trying time for Bill. He experienced periods of rage, periods of depression, times when he gained some control, times when he would again slip into the pit of self-pity. Even though Bill was often surly with the Chaplain, he always looked forward to his visits.

Having done all they could for Bill in England, the Army returned him to Canada for a pension assessment and his medical discharge from the service. The doctors advised him that since both legs were amputated above the knees, he would be confined to a wheelchair for the rest of his life.

Once discharged from the hospital, Bill boarded the train for his four day trip out west to Milden. As the miles slipped by, he pondered his physical disability and tried to project how his loss would impact on Ema and their family. His talks with Chaplain Burke helped Bill in evolving his own simple philosophy. It would be his staying power for the rest of his life.

"I vow before God that I won't burden others with my pain. Like Burke said, I have two choices: be thankful that

God spared my life, or rail on God for my misfortune and be bitter and resentful to the Almighty. I know it's going to be hard, but I'm going to do my best to try to stay thankful."

When Bill's train pulled into Milden, Ema, her folks and several of Bill's neighbours were at the station to give him a hero's welcome home. Bill suffered a lot of pain as they drove the rough road to the farm, but there were no words of complaint. Ema and her mother had prepared a feast and invited a few of the neighbours to join them in their celebration.

By ten-thirty, Ema could tell by Bill's eyes that he was in a lot of pain. Finally she spoke up. "Bill's getting tired, so if you'll excuse us, we'll go over to our place now so he can lie down and rest."

"Let me have another good look at you," Bill said, once they were inside their house. "When I was lying in the trenches in the battle zone, I often tried to picture you in my mind. I saw your long black hair blowing back into my face as we rode together on horseback. I'd gaze into your beautiful hazel eyes. Then my hands would be on your breasts again and I'd be on fire. You know something? You're even more beautiful than I pictured you'd be."

There, in the privacy of their bedroom they laughed together, cried together and talked of their future. After making passionate love, they drifted off to sleep, snuggled close to each other.

The adjustment that Bill faced in trying to get back into the farming operation was trying for both him and Ema and fraught with many setbacks and disappointments. Bill's vow never to complain also caused problems.

"I know your intentions are good Bill," Ema began one day, "but honorable though it is not to complain, sharing your frustrations and hurts with me helps both of us. If you won't share with me, I'll just have to keep prodding."

Years down the road, Bill realized that it would have been wiser to pursue a vocation other than farming, but at the time, it seemed the only way to go. Straight grain farming was out of the question, since it was so labour intensive. Although there was the odd tractor about, most farmers still relied on horses. Any work that involved horses proved nigh unto impossible for Bill.

After a lot of deliberation, Bill and Ema finally decided to raise sheep, as there would be less heavy labour involved. The next spring, Bill used his soldier's grant to buy a small flock of sheep and some haying equipment.

Bill soon found that a wheelchair was totally useless for doing most of the farm work. The ground was far too uneven and he had to use his hands for propulsion. He desperately needed a rig that would go through mud and snow, something he could use in the barn and go out to the field to help him with his flock. There was nothing like this on the market, so he set out to design his own self-propelled four-wheel vehicle.

Bill lay awake many a night, designing the cart in his mind and soon had a rough drawing on paper. He started with two balloon-tired bicycles, an assortment of old scrap iron, a car starter, a variable speed pulley and a number of six volt batteries. Using his gas welder, cutting torch, a set of tools and a whole lot of ingenuity and perseverance, he began his project. It took a month to build the rig and another week to test and revamp it as necessary. The end result was a battery powered four-wheel vehicle with a top speed of ten miles per hour. It would go through a foot of snow and was hard to stop in mud. Bill sat mid-ship and used one set of the bike handlebars for steering. He kept the batteries charged up from a generator run off the wind-mill.

The invention of the self-propelled cart made many impossible tasks possible. He kept it in the porch and transferred himself to his regular wheelchair while in the house. "This rig is my equalizer," he'd always say.

In hunting season, Bill's neighbours loaded his cart into their wagons or sleighs and took him hunting. With its narrow gauge, it went right in among the trees. It was a good hunting rig, except when encountering dead-fall. Over the years, Bill took his fair share of tumbles, but all in all, the cart helped him immeasurably.

After Bill got his cart mobile, things started going better for the Parkers. Ema not only looked after the house, but helped Bill with the farm work. When there was a job that required extra help, Ema's folks or the neighbours were always there to lend a hand. Bill was good with a cutting torch and gas welder and welded for them on a work exchange basis. Despite his handicap, he and Ema were not only holding their own, they were making small gains and enjoying life.

In the first years of their marriage Ema suffered many miscarriages. Finally, she carried a pregnancy to term and on January tenth, a dark haired baby boy was born. The delivery was difficult and due to complications, it would be their only child. They named their boy Tom, after Tom Chomick, a close army buddy of Bill's, killed in action. Tom had a sturdy build like his dad's and his mom's black hair.

When Tom was two, tragedy struck. Ema's father suffered a debilitating stroke. He eventually learned to walk again, but his left side remained weak and his speech was slurred. As he was incapable of doing much in the way of farm work, Ema's folks retired and moved to Red Deer.

It was hard for Bill and Ema to manage without their folks' help. With the assistance of their neighbours though, they were still holding their own.

By the time Tom was three, he was his dad's constant companion. Bill built a small seat for him on the cart and in summer they spend most of their days together. As Tom grew older, he became a tremendous help. Bill used to say that Tom was his dad's legs.

When Bill occasionally needed to discipline Tom, he never resorted to corporal punishment. He'd just tell Tom that he couldn't ride with him for a day. This would leave Tom heartbroken. Usually a few hours after levying his decree, Bill would recant and invite his buddy back on the cart.

Once Tom started school, things changed somewhat, but Tom and his dad still spent a lot of time together. By the time he was eight, Tom began to realize how much his parents depended on him. Now, when the neighbour kids came over to play, he worried that his dad couldn't manage without him. Bill invariably did a bit of lying. He'd tell Tom to go play with his friends because they were nearly caught up and he also needed a break.

"I worry about Tom," Bill commented to Ema one day. "All the work and responsibility we put on him is pretty heavy stuff for such a young guy. What other choice do we have though? I guess feeling guilty won't help any."

The extra responsibility that was laid on his shoulders made Tom mature before his time. By the age of eleven he was already doing a major share of the farm work. He was not only adept at running the small tractor, but felt equally comfortable with a team of horses.

Still having traces of shrapnel in his legs, Bill fought an ongoing battle with infection. With poor circulation, gangrene was always a threat.

Although he never mentioned it to Tom and seldom to Ema, Bill was in constant discomfort while working. He knew he was slowing down.

"Both of us know I'm starting to spin out," he said to Ema one day. "Thank God Tom's getting to the age where he can make up for my slack."

Even though hurting a lot of the time, Bill refused to allow Tom to stay home from school to help them out.

Tom did well in school, his maturity being a factor in him applying himself more than his peers.

Every school has their bully and Westvale School was no exception. Manville had a big mouth and a mean streak to go along with it. Like many bullies, his home life was rough. He thought the only way he could get even with life was to take out his frustrations on smaller kids at school.

At thirteen Manville was two years older than Tom and a bit bigger. Since the first of September, he had constantly picked on Tom and made fun of his dad. Over the last few days, the ribbing intensified and Tom felt he was nearing the breaking point.

Although it hurt to be made fun of, it bothered Tom most when Manville made sport of his dad. Tom always enjoyed attending school, but now dreaded recesses and noon hour. He was sorely tempted to light into Manville, but his dad's rules on fighting were always in the back of his mind.

In his early years, Bill was a real scrapper. He held the Amateur Boxing Champion Title for Alberta in the Middle Weight Class when he was nineteen. He had a set of old boxing gloves and although Ema was not all that enthused about it, he often sparred with Tom and coached him on boxing techniques. He taught Tom to walk away from fights and only to resort to fisticuffs to defend himself or others from physical attack.

It was Friday and school was out for the day. Manville had been tormenting Tom during the noon hour and last recess. Now there was an audience at the school barn. As Tom approached him, he began to jeer, "Here comes the Son of Old Man No-legs! Your old man's a lazy bum, too."

Tom rushed to get past him and on his way home, but Manville reached out, grabbed him by the coat and spun him around. Having an audience made him extra cheeky.

"Know what, everyone?" Manville leered. "The other day I saw Tom's old man sitting on that cart of his, screwing a sheep."

A few in the audience snickered, but not for long. With a cry of anguish, Tom lashed out with a stinging left hook to Manville's nose. The suddenness of the attack stunned Manville, but only for an instant.

With blood oozing from his nose, Manville roared, "Try this," and threw a real haymaker at Tom.

Unlike his rival, Manville didn't know the basics of boxing techniques. Tom ducked low and the punch only grazed the top of his head. His dad's coaching now came into play. Manville was completely off balance, with no guard up. Tom sprang upward and at the end of his lunge, threw a right, hitting Manville square on the jaw. Even though Tom was smaller than his rival, he was solid and strong. The blow, properly executed as it was, had a lot of impact. Manville's legs buckled and he went down on his butt.

"That will be enough of that!"

It was Mrs. Johnson, their teacher.

"Both of you get into the school this instant! Needless to say, I'm not all that impressed with you two," she continued once they were back inside. "Even though school is out for the day, I'm still responsible for your behavior until you get home. I can assure you I'll be getting to the bottom of your fight come Monday morning. In the meantime, I'm sending notes home to your parents. This type of behavior is just not acceptable." Mrs. Johnson hurriedly wrote a note for each boy. "Take these notes home directly and make sure your parents get them."

It was a very subdued, worried Tom that started out for home. The Neufeld kids waited for him at the edge of the school yard. Cheryl Neufeld was twelve, her brother Richard, ten.

"Well, did you and Manville get into trouble?" Cheryl began.

"Yah, I think so. Mrs. Johnson was pretty upset. She said she'd wait until Monday morning to settle it. Anyway, she sent notes home with us. I just know Dad is going to be tore up with me. He doesn't go for fighting except in self-defense."

"I heard what Manville said to you and it was just awful. If you'd like, Richard and I could tell Mrs. Johnson what happened."

"Yah, that might help," mumbled Tom. "Hope so anyway. I just know Dad is going to be mad at me."

Tom was still very upset when he got home. Although in his own mind, he felt that fighting Manville was justifiable, he was very worried what his dad's reaction would be. His parents were in the kitchen and knowing that his mom had a cooler head than his dad, Tom handed her the note. As Ema read the note, she looked most apprehensive. Fighting a fellow classmate was completely out of character for Tom. She was also worried what Bill's reaction would be. Although very fair, he had a rather short fuse and at times could be quite reactionary. Ema finally handed the note to Bill. He read and then re-read the note very slowly.

"Want to tell us what happened?" Ema began.

"Oh, Manville's really been on my back for about a month or so," Tom replied, his voice shaking. He bit his lip to keep control. "He was really bugging me after school and I just couldn't take it anymore, so I hit him."

"You threw the first punch?" Bill questioned, after reading the note for the third time.

"Yes, but he was really bugging me."

"There will be no ifs ands or buts," Bill roared, cutting Tom off short. "You know our policy on fighting. You'd better go to your room and spend some time thinking about what you did."

"Please Dad, let me explain," implored Tom.

"To your room now!" Bill bellowed. "I'll do the chores myself."

Tom bolted to his bedroom, threw himself across his bed and sobbed uncontrollably.

Ema followed Bill to the barn. Half-way through the chores, she stopped. "Bill, you know it would have been fairer to Tom to allow him to explain his side of the story. At least we could have asked him a few more questions. I'm going back to talk with him now. It's just so out of character for him to get into a fight with another student." Ema jabbed her pitch fork into an oat bundle and headed to the house.

When she stepped into Tom's room, he was still crying.

"Can you tell me what happened?" Ema asked, placing her hand on his shoulder.

Between sobs, Tom blurted out: "Manville told all the kids at the school barn that he saw Dad screwing a sheep. I just couldn't take it anymore, so I hit him."

"Did he hit you back?"

"Yes, he did, but I ducked and he just grazed my head. I caught him a good right and knocked him down. That's when Mrs. Johnson caught us."

"I'll go talk to your dad," Ema said with a sigh. "It's hard at times living with two hotheads."

The chores were only half done when Ema got back to the barn.

"Bill, you're a thick-skinned, stubborn old mule," Ema shouted. "Do you want to know why Tom fought Manville?

It's because Manville told everyone at the school barn he saw you screwing a sheep."

Bill was dazed. Finally, he responded. "You're right, Ema. I did act like a real arsehole. I guess I am a thick-skinned, stubborn old mule. Let's go to the house."

Bill transferred himself to his wheelchair in the porch and wheeled himself into Tom's room.

"Tom, I'm truly sorry for being such an ignorant old arse. Your Mom just told me the whole story. I should have let you say your piece."

Bill reached over and gave Tom a bear hug.

"You did right, Son. I'm damn proud of you for defending my honor. It might not be quite the same as protecting yourself or others from being physically attacked, but its close. I suspect I'd have done exactly what you did if I'd been in your shoes. By what Mom said, it sounds like our sparring paid off. I wonder if you might give me a hand to finish the chores, so Mom can start making supper."

As Ema looked out the kitchen window, there was joy in her heart. She saw her two hot heads, now buddies again, heading for the barn.

After supper, Ema phoned Mrs. Neufeld. She drove over to their place and asked Cheryl and Richard for their accounts of the fight.

"Manville is a real bully," Cheryl began. "He's always picking on anyone who's smaller than he is. When we were at the school barn, he started picking on Tom. He grabbed him by the coat and told everyone that he saw Tom's dad having sex with a sheep. Well, Tom hit him and Manville hit him back. Tom knocked him down. That's when Mrs. Johnson caught them."

When Richard recounted the incident, he chose to use the vernacular in retelling verbatim what Manville said. Both Cheryl and Richard's accounts corroborated Tom's version of the incident. Ema asked them both to write out their accounts of the fight. Ema dropped in on another two students who witnessed the fight and also got them to write out what they observed.

By nine p.m., Ema arrived at Mrs. Johnson's place and told her what her sleuthing turned up. She handed Mrs. Johnson the four notes that substantiated Tom's version of the fight.

"I can't thank you enough for all the footwork you've done, Ema," Mrs. Johnson began after carefully reading the notes. "You see, Manville is a real problem. If it wasn't for his horrible home life, I'd be a bit firmer with him. You can be sure I'll be handling this incident very carefully on Monday."

After a long pause, she added, "I know Ema that we ladies are brought up to abhor fist fights, but you must be proud of your son for defending his dad's honor."

Ema nodded, and a trace of a smile crossed her face. After having tea, she returned home and gave Tom and his dad a detailed account of what she accomplished.

Monday morning, Mrs. Johnson took Manville aside. It wasn't every day that a teacher had the opportunity to legitimately use blackmail on a problem student.

"I know the whole story of your fight with Tom," she began.

Manville looked most apprehensive as he stood there studying the floor.

"You've been doing a lot of bullying of the younger children of late haven't you?"

Manville shrugged his shoulders and kept looking at his feet.

"Let's make a deal. I won't tell your parents what you told Tom, if you lay off bullying. If you behave yourself, I'll keep these notes of what you said to Tom in my desk." Mrs. Johnson flashed the four notes in front of Manville's nose. "If you continue bullying the smaller students, I go straight to your parents and show them these notes. Do we have a deal?"

"Yah, I'll go for that," replied Manville, giving Mrs. Johnson a fleeting glance.

It was quite a relief for Manville. His dad promised him a good going over, if it turned out that he started the fight. Mrs. Johnson penned a note to Manville's parents, explaining that the whole incident had been resolved.

Before Mrs. Johnson dismissed Manville, she reminded him of the four incriminating notes that she would be keeping in her desk. That threat of blackmail may have been enough incentive to make Manville change his ways, or perhaps it had something to do with the shellacking he got from Tom. Whatever the reason, his behavior improved a whole lot.

CHAPTER
3

Betty hated city life with a passion. Even after being abandoned by Aaron, she still enjoyed the rural life style. She missed Jed a whole lot and anxiously looked forward to returning to the farm in the spring to help with the seeding. When she was in a logical frame of mind, she thought of Jed as a compassionate, supportive friend, loving him like a brother. Being an incorrigible romantic though, she did a fair amount of thinking with her heart. Her childhood crush on Jed only added fuel to the fire. As winter wore on, her fantasies and dreams continued in earnest and at times were quite erotic. She occasionally tried to purge her mind of these thoughts, but it was a losing battle.

When Jed came to visit Betty in early March, Mary observed the chemistry between them. Like all mothers, she was concerned for the welfare of her daughter, especially with Betty's track record of being impetuous.

"I couldn't help but notice that Jed is really special to you," Mary commented to Betty when they were alone one day.

"You noticed?"

"I'd have to be blind not to notice," her mom replied, with a smile. "Remember, even though I am your mother, I'm still a woman. I know about those looks you give Jed because I used them on your dad when he was courting me."

"You're right, Mom. We're becoming very close, but I'm still hurting so much. Unless you've been walked out on, you can't appreciate what it does to your self-esteem. It's just so awfully confusing. Although I'm really attracted to Jed, I'm scared to try again in case I fail."

"Well, I'm glad you're thinking this one through some. Maybe in time the two of you will get together, but as you said, it's more complicated now. Tanya is only two months old and you haven't even started on your divorce. I certainly can understand your feelings toward Jed, though. I may be your mother, but there's no question in my mind of his attractiveness. I just hope you won't do anything on the spur of the moment, like you did with Aaron."

"If it looks like there could be a chance with Jed, I promise you I'll go a lot slower this time. One foul up is quite enough."

Towards the middle of April, Jed came for Betty and Tanya. On the way back to the farm, Betty said, "I don't think I'm quite ready for a new relationship yet. Tanya is still only three months old. Please help me wait."

"There hasn't been anyone since my wife died. A man gets so damned lonely. Still, you're right. There are lots of things to consider."

Although the next six weeks were exhausting, Betty enjoyed herself immensely and even found time to plant a garden. She did a thorough house cleaning, with the exception of Jed's bedroom. She felt it an intrusion of his privacy to go into his room, as there were still memories he was uncomfortable in sharing. She knew little of his past other than he was a widower and came to Alberta from the states after his wife died.

Just before they finished seeding, a gentle rain started late in the afternoon and continued overnight. Jed's hired man left when it got too wet to work in the fields and wasn't expected back for a couple of days.

As it was still raining in the morning, Betty slept in. When she and Tanya arrived at nine-thirty, breakfast was on the table.

"Would you like me to clean up your room?" Betty asked Jed after breakfast.

Jed nodded. "Go ahead. I'll be out in the machine shed. I have a couple of hours of fixing to do on the seed drill."

Although Jed's bedroom was stark and small, he kept it remarkably neat. For want of a clothes closet, he stacked his clean clothes on one end of a large table. There was a small bed and an old wooden box for a bed-side table, with two portraits on it. The one she recognized as Jed's wedding picture. She picked up the other for a closer view. It was another wedding photo of his wife, a beautiful black girl about twenty years of age. At the bottom of the portrait was neatly written: To my darling Jed   Love Tanya.

Betty gasped. The pieces were starting to fit together. Jed never mentioned his first wife's name before, but when she asked him for help in naming her baby, she remembered the sad look on his face when he said, "Do you fancy the name Tanya?"

Betty gazed at the picture with tears in her eyes. She'd named her baby after Jed's beloved wife.

While she cleaned the room, she was preoccupied with Jed's past. Now she wanted to know the whole story.

They finished dinner and were having tea, when Betty said. "It's really none of my business, but I couldn't help noticing the portraits on your bedside table."

There was an uncomfortable silence. Finally Jed went into his bedroom, returned with the picture of his wife and handed it to Betty.

"I guess it's time I finally told my story," he began softly. "I was born and raised in Tennessee. My grandparents were slaves. My folks had a small farm and dad was a lay minister in our little country church. My parents were always after me to get as good an education as possible. I did well in my studies and after graduating from high school, went on to an all black college to take teacher training. I was nearing the end of my third year when dad's health gave out. His arthritis got so bad he was forced to use canes to walk. When he couldn't look after our small farm anymore, I dropped out of college, against his wishes, and took over from him. Dad became our full-time pastor."

"Tanya and I were childhood sweethearts and we married when she turned nineteen. As you can see she was such a beautiful girl. We made so many plans for the future."

"A year and a half after we married, Tanya was expecting. We were so looking forward to our firstborn. When Tanya started into labour, I fetched Mrs. Baxter, the local midwife. She delivered scores of babies in the community and was well respected. Tanya's pregnancy was trouble-free. She saw a doctor a couple of months before delivering and he said that everything was normal. It was he who recommended that Tanya get Mrs. Baxter to help with the delivery."

"All went well until she delivered. It was just so horrible. The baby was stillborn. Mrs. Baxter couldn't get the baby to breathe. She worked frantically, but nothing she did seemed to help. Then Tanya started hemorrhaging. Mrs. Baxter tried absolutely everything to control it", Jed continued, his voice trembling. "Mrs. Baxter and I fought for over an hour, but just couldn't stop the bleeding. I went to our neighbour and phoned for the doctor. Tanya grew steadily weaker. I was beside myself with fear and kept calling out to God for help."

"Towards the last, Tanya took my hand and whispered, 'help me sit up dear.' I helped her up and she continued, 'its O.K. Jed. I love you so, but I must go now. Grandma's come for me.'"

"I held my darling wife and begged her to stay. Then her breathing stopped."

Tears streamed down Jed's face and he was unable to continue. Betty put her arms around him and they wept together.

"I held my beautiful Tanya in my arms for some time before it finally hit home that she was gone. When the doctor arrived he said nothing could have been done to save her. He mentioned something about there being hemophiliacs in Tanya's family."

"I became so full of anger and bitterness that I gave up on the farm. My brother-in-law bought out my interest in the land and I came up here to Alberta. I've been running from myself for all these years. To tell you the truth, I only stopped running when I started looking out for you. You've helped me find myself again, Betty. I hope I didn't go too far by wanting my wife's name remembered."

"I'm honored beyond words," Betty replied, wiping the tears from her eyes. "When Tanya's old enough to understand, I'm sure she'll be honored too."

Throughout Betty's stay, she and Tanya slept in their old house. While it was inconvenient to get her baby ready every day and drive up to Jed's place, there was just no room at Jed's with the hired man sleeping there. Jed fixed up her old car, so she was able to commute between the farms.

Spending the evenings alone with Tanya gave Betty the opportunity to sort through her thoughts. After hearing Jed's story, she was glad that they were separated for the nights. The recounting of the death of his wife and infant daughter moved her so deeply, she no longer trusted herself around him. Now she understood why he suffered so much anguish when Tanya was born.

On the completion of seeding, Jed, Betty and Tanya headed back to Red Deer. Betty packed a big lunch and at noon, they pulled off the road for a bite to eat.

Betty's mind was in a whirl. She dreaded the thought of spending the summer back in the city and being separated from Jed for another three months.

"Since you told me about the horrible loss of your wife and daughter, I can't stop thinking of how much pain you've suffered," she began. "All those lonely nights. All your anger and hurt."

Suddenly she reached down, took Jed's hand and placed it palm down on her upper thigh, leaving her hand on top of his. Through her light dress, Betty felt the warmth of his touch spreading over her body. Her leg was on fire. Her heart raced wildly with the realization of how daring she was. All she could think of was how much she wanted and needed him physically.

"Damn it! What are you trying to do, girl?" Jed exclaimed. "You know you're playing with fire."

"I care for you so much," Betty pleaded.

"I haven't touched a woman since Tanya died. God only knows how I want you now."

Jed knew he would lose his resolve if he made eye contact with her. Fighting to maintain control, he looked down at their hands.

"Look at our hands and tell me what you see."

Betty glanced down. "I just see our hands."

"And what's different about them?"

"Well, mine is small and yours is big."

"Yes, and mine is old and yours is young, mine is black and yours is white," Jed added.

"Well, so what?" Betty said, after a few moments thought.

"So, my dear girl, I think we need to use our heads a bit, I now have the same feeling for you that I felt for my first wife. Still, you're not even divorced yet and your little girl is only four and a half a months old."

Betty slowly lifted her hand off Jed's. As Jed removed his hand from her leg, he put a bit of pressure on his fingertips as he trailed them across her thigh.

"God only knows how I long to make love to you," Jed whispered, "so please Betty, don't do that again."

"Thanks for being so strong," Betty whispered back, after a short pause. "I guess we've got to think things through carefully. It's just that I need you so much."

Jed reached over, cupped Betty's face in his hands and kissed her on the lips. They drove the rest of the way to the city in silence.

Before Jed left for the farm on Sunday afternoon, Betty's folks looked after Tanya so she and Jed could spend a few hours by themselves. Betty made a picnic lunch and they went down to the river.

"I'm going to start on my divorce right away," Betty said. "I think we should wait until the divorce has gone through before we make plans for ourselves. I hate the thought of being separated from you for the summer, but I guess I'll have to manage."

As Jed was leaving, he held Betty close and whispered, "I'll come and get you to help with harvest. I'm sure everything is going to work out for us. Always remember, I love you."

"I love you too," Betty replied and then Jed was gone.

CHAPTER
4

Time moved at a snail's pace for Betty. In early June, she went to see a lawyer to begin divorce proceedings. He contacted Aaron, but a divorce was the last thing he wanted. Aaron feared that once divorced, he'd be shackled with a court order forcing him to support Betty and the baby.

When Betty and the lawyer met again, he stated, "Aaron was an alcoholic and physically abusive, but it would help us if we had proof that he was unfaithful to you."

Betty learned from an acquaintance that Aaron lived with an old girlfriend from Red Deer for three weeks after moving out. When the girlfriend started putting pressure on him about his drinking, Aaron pulled the abandonment caper again, leaving the young woman high and dry. Understandably, she was most upset with him and cheerfully signed a statement for Betty's lawyer stating that she and Aaron slept together for two weeks.

Armed with this evidence, Betty filed for divorce on the grounds of adultery and abandonment, but Aaron was still dragging his feet. On Jed's advice, Betty withdrew her request for support for herself and Tanya, just to be rid of him.

Now eager to expedite the divorce, Aaron showed up to sign the divorce papers with a fair shine on and proceeded to make a capital ass of himself. Betty was glad that it was all over, or so she thought.

In late August, Jed was gearing up for the grain harvest. He picked up some supplies in Milden and before heading home, stopped at the hotel for a cold beer. He just ordered a draft when his friend, Carl Stohler, came over and sat at his table. Every town has at least one gossip who knows of all the comings and goings in the community. Carl was Milden's gossip.

"I hear your old neighbour, Betty Collins just got divorced."

Jed nodded, "Yes, that's right."

"That dumb husband of hers had it made, with Betty's folks giving her the land and cattle. I guess he just couldn't keep off the sauce, or for that matter, get off his lazy ass. I hear you gave him a damn good licking last summer for beating on Betty."

Again Jed nodded. "Yes, I guess you might say that."

"Good for you. He's hanging out with his old drinking buddies Fred and Andy. He was here in the bar the other day, shooting off his mouth about the divorce to old Pete Larue. The idiot blamed you for the divorce and claimed you were screwing Betty whenever he was away. He said you couldn't trust blacks around women. Pete told Aaron that you were ten times the man that he was and if he didn't shut his mouth he'd shut it for him. Aaron's one of those assholes who figure if a man isn't white he ain't worth nothing. I'd watch him, Jed. No telling what that drunken fool will try to pull off. He's spouting off about getting even with you."

"Thanks for the tip, Carl. We all know why Betty and he split up. We all know he's trash. Just the same, I'll keep my eyes peeled. As long as he doesn't try to mess with Betty or the baby."

For the next few days Jed worried constantly about Carl's warning. "Would Aaron be low enough to harm Betty or Tanya to get at me? I'm sure there's little to fear from him if he's sober, but get him drunk, then what? "

Before harvest, Jed drove into Red Deer to pick up Betty and Tanya. They were elated to see each other. On the way home, Jed told Betty about Aaron being around and his mouthing off in the bar.

"I'm not all that fussy about you and Tanya staying alone in your old house with Aaron on the prowl. I just worry. We could fix up the old bunkhouse for the hired men. It would probably only take us three or four hours and then you and Tanya could stay in their room."

"I'm sure Tanya and I will be safe enough. Now that the divorce is through, he's not to have any more contact with Tanya or me. Still, it's awful nice to be cared for."

Betty reached over and took Jed's hand. "If you'd rest easier, I'd be happy to move in. It would save me the hassle of traveling back and forth between the farms and besides, I love being close to you."

The sun was setting when they pulled into Betty's yard. Seeing it was so late, Betty decided it best that Tanya and she spend the night there. The next day they would clean up the old bunkhouse and she and Tanya would move in with Jed.

Even with Betty's assurances that they would be safe, Jed still felt uneasy about leaving them behind. He would live to regret not going by his gut instincts. At nine, Jed bade Betty goodnight and headed for home. Betty was bone-tired and she and Tanya were soon asleep.

A few miles down the road, Aaron and his drinking buddies, Fred and Andy were driving along in an aimless fashion. As they drove, they were nipping on a bottle of moonshine. The three were on a real tear and hadn't drawn a sober breath for several days. Fred and Andy heard Aaron's woeful, blow-by-blow tale of his marriage break up time and time again.

Aaron's drinking cronies, being losers themselves, could sympathize with his plight. Fred and Andy didn't know much about farming, but they did make excellent moonshine and derived most of their income from peddling it. Aaron gravitated to them because of their lax lifestyle and the availability of large amounts of cheap over-proof spirits.

As they were coming up to the old farm, Aaron was going on again like a broken record. "I'd sure like to even accounts with that black son-of-a-bitch. He's the one who caused our marriage break up. I'll lay odds he was shagging Betty whenever I was gone. I'll get even with him, just you wait."

Both Andy and Fred were apprehensive that Aaron might do something stupid, given he was so bitter over the failed marriage. They encouraged him to keep moving on. Despite their objections, Aaron stopped, backed up and drove into the approach. As Jed and Betty hadn't lit a fire, there was no sign of life in the house.

Being in the old yard site precipitated more bitterness and Aaron's rhetoric towards Jed and Betty became even more abusive. Suddenly, a vengeful idea popped into his head.

"I'll show you guys some real fireworks," he said as he yarded the truck door open.

Aaron walked to the back of the truck and began rooting around for something in the box.

"Hey, you, what are you doing?" Fred called out.

Aaron made no reply so Andy and Fred went back to sipping on their bottle of hooch. When Fred looked up, he saw Aaron heading to the house with a small pail of gas. Suspecting what he was up to, Fred stuck his head out the window.

"Hey Aaron, don't be a dumb ass hole!" he hollered out.

Aaron made no reply and kept on walking. He was none too stable, but managed to climb up the porch steps without spilling the gas. He opened the door and threw in the container of gas. Stepping back a few feet, he tossed in a lit match.

Fred's yell woke Betty. Seconds later she saw the flash and heard and felt the explosion.

The fire was spreading fast. Just a blanket hung over the bedroom doorway separating them from the flames and the room was filling with smoke. Betty tried to open the window but it was stuck. Quickly she grabbed a pillow and broke the glass. She scooped Tanya up, placed her out on the ground and then wiggled through the window opening. Terrified, she clutched Tanya close and staying in the shadows, ran for the small shed behind the house.

"What's going on?" she cried in a panic. "Somebody started that fire. Did they know that Tanya and I were in the house? Are they trying to kill us?"

When Betty finally regaining her composure, she peered through the crack in the door and saw that the flames were now shooting out of the window she'd broke.

Her heart nearly stopped when she saw Aaron and his two drinking chums, Fred and Andy, standing back in the shadows at the side of the house. They were watching the fire and passing a bottle back and forth between them.

"It serves Betty and her old man right," Aaron gloated. "I never could stand that old jerk. It feels good to get even."

"I still think you're an asshole for not checking to see if there was anyone in the house," Fred shouted. "If there was, what chance would they have?"

"Get off my back. I told you it's abandoned. Betty lives in Red Deer with her folks. I drove by their place a week ago and saw her and the baby out on the front step."

On arriving home, Jed checked in with his hired men and told them of the plans to move them out to the bunkhouse. After a bit of friendly ribbing, they all went out to start on the clean-up.

About twenty minutes later, Jed discovered Tanya's baby bag in his car and decided to run it down to Betty. As his yard was completely surrounded by a huge spruce windbreak, he could not see the fire from his yard.

When Jed got past the windbreak, he saw the glow from the fire and opened up his car to the max, terror gripping his guts. Were Betty and Tanya safe? Had Betty started a fire in the cook stove that got away? Had there been an explosion? Could it have been Aaron?

In jig time, he covered the three-quarters of a mile to Betty's place. Jed wheeled into the driveway, flung his door open and in panic, started running towards the house. Above the roar of the fire he heard a cry. He looked in the direction of the shed and saw Betty, clutching Tanya close, running towards him.

"What the hell happened here?" Jed shouted. "Are you and Tanya okay?"

"Yes, we're alright," Betty cried out. "I'm so glad you came!

"Aaron, Fred and Andy are here! They started the fire while Tanya and I were sleeping."

"Thank God you're alright," Jed said, wrapping his arms around them.

Aaron had parked his pickup a fair distance from the house. Hearing a vehicle approaching, the threesome ran back to the truck and hid behind it. When Aaron saw Jed hugging Betty and Tanya, he lost it. He reached into the back of his truck box, found a short length of steel pipe and snuck up behind Jed.

Jed caught a movement out of the corner of his eye and pushed Betty and Tanya away. He tried to duck, but went down to his knees from a blow to the side of the head.

Although Jed realized he was fighting for his life, he bellowed at Betty. "Get to the car and lock yourself in. Go for help if you have to."

Jed staggered to his feet, just as Aaron swung the pipe again. Aaron was pretty well inebriated and none too coordinated. Jed side-stepped and Aaron missed him completely. With a roar, Jed threw a solid right to the side of Aaron's head and he went down like he'd been pole-axed. Without pausing, Jed grabbed Aaron by the crotch with one hand and the front of his jacket with the other. He lifted him over his head and brought him down hard on the ground. There was a sickening snap as Aaron's back impacted on a half-buried rock.

Andy and Fred didn't come running to their buddy's defense. Even in their drunken state, they did not condone the torching of Betty's house, let alone Aaron's attack on Jed. In addition, they had no desire to mix it up with Jed. Both knew of his remarkable strength and his ability with his hands. They waited until the action stopped before approaching Aaron and Jed. When Aaron regained consciousness he was able to talk, but was unable to move his legs.

Recognizing the seriousness of Aaron's injuries, Betty took Jed's car to his place and got Dr. Stuart on the phone.

"I'm afraid Aaron's been hurt pretty bad. He attacked Jed and they got into another fight. He's conscious, but can't move his legs."

"Make him as comfortable as possible. I'll be there as soon as I can with the ambulance."

Despite the rage Betty felt towards Aaron, she couldn't bear the thought of him lying on the cold ground, so grabbed a couple of blankets before heading back.

"Why did you burn my house down?" Betty screamed as she covered Aaron with the blankets. "Why did you try to kill Jed? You've been spreading stories around that Jed's been screwing me. Well, you're dead wrong! Jed wasn't screwing me before you left me and he isn't screwing me now. Why are you trying to destroy me? You're so low, Aaron, so low!"

Tanya was sleeping in the car, but the sound of her mom's voice awoke her and she started to cry.

"I think that's enough, Betty," Jed said. "Tanya's crying. Maybe it would be best if you went to her."

Betty burst into tears and headed for Jed's car.

"Better stay with your buddy until the doctor arrives," Jed said, turning to Fred and Andy. "The crack I got on the head made me a bit woozy so I'm going to go sit in the car. For God's sake though, get rid of the moonshine, just in case the police come with the doctor."

Betty put Tanya in the backseat and tried to cradle Jed's head on her lap. As she looked down at him, she whispered, "I love you, Jed. At first I was terrified that someone was trying to kill Tanya and me, and then afraid that Aaron would kill you. I'm so glad you came when you did. Right now, all I want is to stay close to you."

Dr. Stuart arrived within the hour and gave Aaron a preliminary check over.

"I'm afraid you may have broken Aaron's back, Jed. He has no feeling in his legs and can't move his feet. We'd better get him to the hospital. If you could follow me to town, I'd appreciate it. This old ambulance is none too reliable."

"I just can't lay charges against Aaron for attacking me," Jed said to Betty, as they trailed the ambulance to the hospital. "I know he was trying to hurt me, maybe even kill me, but he was drunk and now the poor bastard may have a broken back."

"I know what you mean, Jed. I'm still enraged with him for attacking you and lighting the fire, but he said he didn't know that Tanya and I were sleeping in the house. After all, we have each other, but Aaron has lost everything, and now, he may be a cripple for the rest of his life."

When Jed and Betty arrived at the hospital, they asked Dr. Stuart about Aaron's condition. "The hospital in Red Deer is better equipped to handle this type of injury. We'll be leaving for Red Deer within the hour. I hope I'm wrong, but I rather doubt that Aaron will ever walk again."

Just before Aaron was put in the ambulance again, Jed approached him. "Betty and I have decided not to report you for arson and assault. I'm sorry I buggered up your back, but I was just fighting for my life. I've already told Fred and Andy to keep their mouths shut about the fire."

Aaron was in shock and a lot of pain. He nodded, but made no reply.

Before he left for Red Deer, Dr. Stuart briefly examined Jed. "Take it easy for ten days or so and check into the hospital in Red Deer for an X-ray if the headaches don't subside. Level with me, Jed, Aaron's hand isn't that hard. Did he hit you with something?"

"Yes, you might say that, but I won't be laying assault charges as it sort of back fired on him."

When the specialist in Red Deer examined Aaron, his prognosis was the same as Dr. Stuart's. The X-ray showed a broken vertebra and he assumed his spinal chord was damaged.

Good fortune was smiling on Aaron though and his story took a positive turn. The doctor's original assessment that he would be permanently paralyzed below the waist, proved wrong. By the end of three weeks, he started to get the occasional twinge of feeling in his toes. Aaron was transferred to a rehabilitation centre in Edmonton. By the end of six months, he was able to walk unassisted and regained full range of motion with his legs.

Before Aaron was released from the rehabilitation centre, he met with the Doctor. "Well, Aaron, I think we've done everything we can for you here. It looks like you've been given a second chance. For God's sake, though, try to stay off the bottle."

As the Doctor glanced out his window, he saw Aaron climbing into a cab. "Well we've given him another lease on life," he mused, shaking his head. "Will he take advantage of it, or will he go back to boozing? God only knows."

CHAPTER
5

After the fight, Betty did her best to mother Jed, but it was none too easy a task. He was in the harvest mode, and his headaches were not as severe and becoming less frequent.

In a few days, harvest was in full swing. Betty was right in her glory, happy to be back, working with friends and neighbours. When she was preparing and serving meals, or bringing lunch out to the fields, Tanya was always with her. Everyone made her most welcome, recognizing that she had been through some rough times.

Although harvest was a very busy time, Jed and Betty spent the evenings by themselves. They now talked openly about spending the rest of their lives together, but as yet, hadn't picked a wedding date.

Finally, the last bundle was pitched and threshing was over for the year. Supper was like a banquet to celebrate the completion of harvest. It was a happy occasion since the crops were good. The neighbours were glad to see Jed and Betty together and knew that wedding bells would be ringing sooner or later.

Jed only worked four days on his fall plowing when the weather closed in. Rain started late in the afternoon, continued through the evening, and turned to snow by midnight. Winter blew in with a vengeance and by morning there was eight inches of wet snow on the ground. Although Jed chaffed some at not being able to complete the fall fieldwork, he was happy that the harvest was completed.

Jed was still getting the odd headache, so early the next morning he, Betty and Tanya were on their way to Red Deer to see the specialist Dr. Stuart recommended. The heavy snowfall made for slow going, but they still managed to arrive early for Jed's appointment.

While Betty took Tanya into the ladies room to nurse her, Jed stepped out for a few minutes. He was a man with a mission. Unbeknownst to Betty, he had made arrangements with a jeweler to pick up her engagement ring after harvest. Jed paid for the ring and was back in the doctor's office before Betty and Tanya returned from the ladies' room.

The specialist sent Jed to the hospital for tests. The x-rays showed a hairline fracture on his scull. The doctor chided Jed for engaging in heavy work and recommended that he slack right off the farm chores for at least a month.

As they drove to Betty's folks' place, Jed told Betty he'd reserved a hotel room for them for the night. She was delighted! Grandpa and Grandma were happy to have Tanya stay with them. She was now occasionally using a bottle, so feeding would pose no problem.

Jed tried hard to control his excitement while they were eating supper with Betty's folks. He was dying to give Betty her ring, but was waiting for just the right moment. After supper, they went to a movie. Jed made sure to sit on Betty's left side. As movies go, it was a real bummer and Jed spent most of his time playing with Betty's hand. Finally he took the engagement ring out of its case and slipped it on Betty's ring finger. She was so intent on trying to follow the plot that she didn't notice anything different for a few moments. Suddenly, it occurred to her that her left hand felt odd. She reached over with her right hand and discovered the ring.

"Is this what I think it is?" Betty exclaimed, grabbing Jed by the hand and heading for the lobby. Betty cried out with delight when she finally saw the ring!

They decided to forgo the rest of the movie and began the celebrations immediately. After a couple of drinks in the lounge they retired to their room. This was their moment. Their long wait was over. They slowly undressed each other. Although Betty had been married before, she had never reached such heights of passion and release. Jed, though strong as two men, was a most romantic, skilled lover.

They drifted off to sleep in each others arms.

When they returned to the house the next morning, George and Mary congratulated them on their engagement.

"I can't remember seeing you this relaxed before, Jed," George quipped, with a twinkle in his eye. "You must have slept well."

Tanya was doubly glad to see her mom and was soon nursing contentedly.

After breakfast, they discussed the doctor's recommendation for Jed to slack off all the heavy farm work. Mary and George offered to accompany them back to the farm. George would help Jed with the chores, while Mary and Betty worked on the wedding plans.

Jed was as poor a patient for George as he was for Betty. He allowed George to do most of the heavy work, but insisted on being with him all day long.

They would often stay up till midnight, laughing and shedding the occasional tear as they relived the old times.

One night Mary began reminiscing about the past Christmases they spent together.

"Jed would come with a box full of gifts for Betty and me. George's gift from Jed was always a bottle of Jack Daniels in a plain paper bag."

"That does bring back fond memories," George added. "Not only did Jed religiously remember my bottle of Jack Daniels, he religiously helped me drink it!"

"I remember my first silk stockings," Betty remarked, turning toward Jed. "The year I turned thirteen, you gave them to me as my Christmas gift. Mom and I sang Christmas carols while you accompanied us on your guitar. Do you still have the guitar?"

"Yes, I still have it, but it's been quite awhile since I've touched it."

"Play us some tunes, Jed," Betty suggested.

Jed went into the bedroom and got his guitar. He dusted it off and slowly tuned it.

He strummed a few chords and then to everyone's amazement sang several old Negro spirituals and a few folk songs. There were tears in Jed's eyes as the old songs brought back a surge of emotion.

"I guess this is the first time any of you have heard me sing," he said with feeling. "I vowed when my wife and daughter died that I wouldn't sing again until I'd found lasting happiness. It's been a long wait, but Betty and baby Tanya have finally brought me the happiness that I was longing for. I know that my first wife would be pleased for the both of us. You see, Tanya had a beautiful voice. We used to sing together in church and occasionally at parties."

Betty and Jed chose the fifteenth of December for their wedding date. As Mary and George had no real rush to get home, they stayed on to help with the wedding preparations.

As was the custom in most rural areas during this era, few formal invitations were sent out. It was just assumed that all their neighbours and acquaintances would attend.

Jed's folks were delighted with the news that he was getting married again and came up from the States by train to attend the wedding. Over the last year or so, Jed's mother, Grace, had learned a lot about Betty from Jed's letters. When Grace met Betty, tears ran down the old lady's face.

"The Lord finally answered Dad's and my prayers. We now have a happy son, a beautiful daughter-in-law-to-be and a wonderful granddaughter."

Their wedding dawned clear but cold. They held it in the Westview Community Hall, as the local Baptist church was just too small.

"This is a happy day for Betty and me," Jed said as he began his wedding speech at the reception. "Betty and I are honored that all of you have come out to help us celebrate our day. We've both been through some rough times, but now we're together. Betty and wee Tanya helped mend the tear in my soul that the death of my first wife and baby girl made. They've filled that awful gap in my heart. Baby Tanya has".....

Jed paused for a moment to compose himself, then continued. "She's satisfied that longing I've had for all those years to be a father again."

"Thank you Betty, for loving me and becoming my wife: A big thank you to Mom and Dad Osmond for raising me: I don't know what I would have done without the love and support you gave me through these difficult years. Thank you George and Mary for being a brother and sister to me: Finally, thank you baby Tanya, for becoming my second daughter."

Jed rubbed his eyes with the back of his hand and sat down. There was a moment of silence. Spontaneously, everyone leapt to their feet and gave him a standing ovation.

With the wedding over, Jed's kinfolk spent several days with Jed and Betty before returning to the States. Betty was back on the farm with her new husband and Jed had the helpmate and baby daughter that he so longed for. It was a constant struggle for Betty to keep Jed from spoiling Tanya rotten.

The first summer they built an addition on the house and soon Betty was expecting. In the later stages of her pregnancy, it became obvious that she was either going to have an elephant or twins. The doctor could only detect one heart beat, but most of the older women in the community concurred that single heartbeat or not, twins it was going to be.

Jed did his best to remain calm, but the haunting memories from the past were always with him. It would be difficult to say who endured more during the labour, Betty or Jed. The birth took place in the Milden hospital with Dr. Stuart assisting with the delivery. In the end, Jed was such a pain to the medical staff that they let him into the delivery room. The labour proceeded without a hitch and at eleven-thirty p.m., a dark curly haired baby boy was born. Jed was elated, but came close to needing medical attention himself when the doctor announced that baby number two was on the way! At eleven forty-five, a baby girl was born.

Dr. Stuart delivered scores of babies. He was used to mothers shedding the odd tear, but he was not used to fathers breaking down. There stood Jed, all two hundred and thirty-five pounds of him, weeping with real fervor. Once he regained some control he began thanking the doctor and medical staff over and over again.

Jed moved back a few steps and glanced upward. "Thank you Lord for being so good to me," he whispered quietly. "You saw fit to take my first wife and child, but you've given me another beautiful wife and three healthy young ones."

Within a week, Betty and the twins were back at home. Jed took great delight in holding Tanya on his knee while Betty nursed the twins in the rocking chair. They named the babies Ben and Beth. Sister Tanya was ecstatic about her new brother and sister. She soon became the twin's second mother, an arrangement that lasted until the twins were well into their twenties.

Betty couldn't have been happier with the closeness that was developing between Tanya and her dad. By the time she was four, Tanya had Daddy pretty well under her spell. When acquaintances would ask the inevitable, "Whose little girl are you?" she'd flash her big green eyes and reply, "I'm Daddy's girl, and Mommy's too."

Although Tanya and the twins loved to have Mom read them bedtime stories, Tanya much preferred her dad's ad-lib tales of his early years. Like all kids, she had her favorites that she wanted told over and over.

"Tell me the King story," she'd command, as she bounced on her dad's knee in anticipation, "when there was deep, deep snow."

"Back before you were born," Jed would begin, "back when King was still a very young horse, there was a bad snow storm. The snow was very, very deep."

At this stage of the story Tanya would invariably hop off her dad's knee and with eyes full of wonderment ask, "How deep was the snow, Daddy?"

Jed would put his hand on top of her head and whisper, "This deep, Tanya, as deep as you are tall."

Tanya would climb back on her dad's knee, and the story would continue.

"Late in the fall a bunch of hunters got caught in a snow storm, way back in the foothills. Three of them made a shelter and spent the night there, but the fourth hunter decided to try to walk through the bush to the main road and got lost. Late the next morning, my old friend, Joe Manyfingers, stopped by and asked me if I could help him look for the hunter. We started out after dinner. Joe was on snowshoes, I was riding King. The snow was so deep King would have to stop quite often and puff. Finally late in the afternoon we found the hunter, just about frozen."

"Was he glad to see you?" Tanya would interject.

"Yes, he was so glad that he started to cry. He said we saved his life. I put the half-frozen hunter up on King with me and we finally got to a farmer's place just as it was getting dark. While Joe and the farmer took the hunter into the house to thaw him out, I put King in the barn. I rubbed him down and gave him some hay. Do you remember what kind of a treat I gave him then, Tanya?"

"Yes, a snuff treat," Tanya would chirp enthusiastically.

"You're right. And do you remember if King was tired?"

"Yes he was," Tanya would cry out. "He was so tired he went to sleep standing up."

"That's right, so you better go to bed and sleep just like King did." Jed would conclude. Dad would hug his little girl good night and Mom would tuck her into bed.

As Tanya was growing up her favorite farm pet was King and it wasn't long before he, like Dad was also under her spell. She loved watching her dad giving him and Darkie their weekly snuff treat and soon had King addicted to sugar lumps. Mom provided the sugar and had to religiously monitor the sugar rations. Tanya had King spoiled and he was constantly nuzzling her for his sweet treat.

By the time she was ten, Tanya was spending many hours riding King. When King wasn't working and the weather permitted, Dad let her ride him to school. To the onlooker he may not have been the handsomest horse in the world, but to Tanya, King was her dashing steed.

CHAPTER
6

Over the last few years, Bill's health steadily deteriorated. The year Tom turned fifteen, his dad had a major setback. When the infection in his legs failed to respond to medications, Bill was referred to the veteran's hospital in Edmonton. The gangrene in his left leg was so advanced that the doctors were forced to amputate another six inches.

With Bill in the hospital, Tom and his mother did the haying by themselves. By late summer, Bill was back on the farm, but not doing all that well.

Ema and Tom watched helplessly while he suffered. After stubbornly refusing painkillers for years, Bill finally was forced to resort to them. In addition to the problem with his legs, he was getting chest pain whenever he exerted himself. True to form, he did not tell Ema or Tom about his heart problems.

By Thanksgiving weekend, Bill rallied enough to ride his cart about and help Tom with the chores and felt well enough to accompany Ema and Tom to church on Sunday. It did Bill a world of good to visit with his neighbours again. They all wished him a quick recovery from his surgery.

After finishing their Thanksgiving meal, Bill called a family conference. Over the years they had numerous family councils, usually to discuss some urgent matter. Tom and his mother were apprehensive. Bill looked at the floor for a moment and then locked eyes with Ema as if to gain courage.

"I was hoping by now to be right back in the swing of things. Back in the saddle so to speak, but my recovery is so slow this time. I'm really worried," he added, growing more morose. "You know, my grandfather knew when he was going to die and was only out by one day. He was a full blood Mohawk. I remember saying, 'Grandpa how do you know you're going to die?'"

"'Well Billy, we Natives are closer to our spirit helpers than whites,'" he said. "'We believe the spirits tell us about our future when we dream. My first wife died many years ago. Last night I dreamt of her for the first time in thirty years. In my dream she said that I would soon join her.'"

"Although he was in his mid-seventies, Grandfather was still in good health. I was very shocked when he said, 'Billy, I will soon die, maybe tonight.' The next morning he was still going strong. I thought, so much for old Indian beliefs. That afternoon, while he was weeding in the garden, he had a heart attack and died."

"I sincerely hope that in this day and age you don't believe in Indian folklore, Bill!" Ema replied testily.

"I don't know. Explain how my Grandfather predicted his own death? As you probably guessed, I had a frightening dream last night. I dreamt about my old army buddy, Tom Chomick. I was just ten feet from Tom when a sniper's bullet killed him. In my dream he was waving for me to join him, but there seemed to be a creek between us. He hollered at me, 'see you soon, Bill,' and then I awoke. I'm only one quarter native and I'd like to say it's all rubbish, but part of me is scared."

"The dream aside, we need to discuss our plans for the future. How long do we keep on farming? What happens if I can't get back enough of my strength to handle the work again? I sure don't want Tom staying out of school to help us out. Maybe we should think about selling the farm and moving into town so Tom can get his high school."

After some thought, Ema replied. "Let's not make any quick decisions, Bill. Even though I like the idea of leaving the farm and moving into town, for now, as long as we can hold out, I think we should stay on. Tom can still take his grade nine here. Remember, of late, Tom and I have been managing pretty well by ourselves. Maybe it would be best if we wait till next summer before we make any decision about what to do with the land. I know you love the farm so if you're better by then, you and I could stay here while Tom boards out in Milden and takes his high school. Right now we've got to concentrate on getting you better."

"Sounds fair to me. What are your thoughts, Tom?"

"I'm with Mom. I love it here on the farm. I don't fancy living in town unless we have to. I'm sure we can manage till next summer."

"Well, O.K., I guess what I've got to do is to try to get my strength back and not think about that damn dream," Bill concluded.

Bill's chest pain continued unabated whenever he exerted himself. A week after Thanksgiving, Dr. Stuart summoned Bill to his office for an appointment.

"I see by your medical reports from Edmonton that you're old ticker is in rough shape," Stuart began, getting right to the meat of things. "I don't suppose you ever considered telling your family doctor about your heart problem?"

Bill shrugged his shoulders and looked down.

"I know you're a tough old character who hates sympathy, but keeping this information from me is just plain dumb. I don't imagine you've told Ema either."

Bill shook his head.

"Now look here, either you tell her or I will. The last twenty years have been hell on your body. Poor circulation, gangrene, stress, who knows, maybe heredity plays a part. Your prognosis isn't all that encouraging. I'm going to prescribe nitroglycerin pills for your heart, and you'll have to keep taking the painkillers for your legs."

"If I were you, Bill, I'd be thinking seriously about getting rid of the farm and taking it a whole lot easier. If you continue to force yourself, I can guarantee you won't last long. So will you tell Ema or will I?"

"Yes, I guess you're right," Bill replied after a moments thought. "I'll tell her and Tom myself."

Stuart nodded. "I suppose I shouldn't be pushing you like this, but I wouldn't mind seeing your ugly old face around a bit longer."

Bill didn't have a great deal to say to Ema as they drove home from the doctor's office. He didn't mention one word about his condition to either Ema or Tom that evening. He now knew he must tell them, but was waiting for just the right moment.

The next day Bill attempted to help Tom with the chores, but despite the medications, his shortness of breath and chest pains made it hard. Tom noticed that his dad was having a down day, but Bill adamantly maintained that he was alright. That evening, Ema went to a ladies' meeting and Bill and Tom were home by themselves.

As Tom started washing the dishes, Bill was sitting in his wheelchair looking disconsolate. Finally he looked over towards Tom. "I've got a few problems with my health that we should talk about, Son. I haven't told your mother yet. She has enough worries as it is. I've been getting chest pains and shortness of breath for about the last two years. They get worse when I try to force myself. The doctors say that my heart's in poor shape. I guess it's got something to do with poor circulation, the gangrene, infection, or who knows. At any rate, Stuart gave me some nitro pills to take when the pain gets bad. I took a couple today and they helped some, but the pain is still there. I guess the old ticker is about worn out."

The news shook Tom to the core. Up till now, he just assumed that his dad's only problem was with his legs.

"It's been getting real bad of late, more so since I had the operation," Bill continued. "That's why I have to stop so often when I'm helping you. The doctors said there wasn't a whole lot I could do other than taking the nitro pills when the chest pains got bad. They also told me I'd have to start taking it a lot easier."

Tom had sat down while his dad was talking. Suddenly he leapt to his feet.

"Son of a bitch! It's just not fair that you've had such a rough life."

Tom walked to the window so his dad couldn't see his tears, but it really didn't matter since Bill was still studying the floor.

"You're a damn fine son, Tom. I know you'll take good care of your mother when I'm gone."..... Bill couldn't continue.

Tom went over, put his hand on his dad's shoulder and they both wept.

"We've got to tell Mom," Tom whispered. "We've just got to. She's strong. She's had to be. If it's too hard on you, I can do it for you."

"Yes you're right, Son," Bill replied after a long pause. "It's time I told your mom. I'll do it when she gets home."

Ema returned from the ladies' meeting in good spirits and launched right into some choice piece of local gossip. She went on for a minute or two before it dawned on her that both Bill and Tom were looking disconsolate.

"Is there something wrong?" Ema asked, cutting her story off in mid sentence.

Bill again locked his eyes with hers. "Yes, I guess so," he said hesitantly, and told her of his heart problems. "I'd have told you and Tom before, but I felt you both had big enough burdens to bear. Yesterday Dr. Stuart told me it was high time I told you. He was a bit upset with me for keeping it to myself. I've just finished telling Tom."

"Isn't there anything that the doctors can do?" Ema cried out.

"Nothing really, other than trying to control the pain with nitroglycerin pills. Dr. Stuart said I'd also have to take it a lot easier. He suggested that we should think about selling the farm."

"Oh my God!" Ema blurted out after a few moments of stunned silence. "Why didn't you tell us before? I'm so shocked I can hardly think. I had no inkling your heart was bad and I'm sure Tom didn't either. You're a wonderful man for never complaining, but why couldn't you have shared this with Tom and me? I just don't know if I can handle it."

Ema could not hold back the tears any longer. She rushed over to Bill and dropped to her knees. As he held her in his arms she sobbed uncontrollably.

"All the heartaches we've been through, all of your suffering and now this," she wailed. "Life's not fair! Why couldn't God give us a bit of a break? Look how you've suffered since the War! I can't see how things could get any worse."

"I've never shared this with anyone before," Bill responded quietly. "After I lost my legs, there was plenty of time for me to do a lot of thinking as I was on the mend. At first, I was supremely peed off with the hand fate dealt me and was well on my way to becoming bitter. Finally, with the help of my Chaplain, I found peace."

"As I saw it, there were two ways I could handle the rough breaks I had. I could be right tore up with God, bitch, yell, froth at the mouth and become a bitter old creature. On the other hand I could look for the positives. After all, I could have been killed in the war, but God spared me. God gave me you, Ema. How can we put a price on all the beautiful love we've shared over the last twenty years? God has given us such a fine son. I'm so proud of him. He's going to make a great man someday. Come to think of it, I guess he already is a man. Finally we've had happiness as a family and even a bit of prosperity. I'm plain thankful for all the good things that God allowed me to experience. I'm just going to keep on being thankful for as long as I'm alive."

Two days later while Bill was in the barn helping Tom with the evening chores, he collapsed with a heart attack.

Tom and his mom managed to get Bill into the house and helped him to the couch.

Ema phoned Dr. Stuart and he advised her to give Bill a nitroglycerine pill and some pain killers. "I'm on my way. I should be there in twenty minutes."

Bill got the nitroglycerine pill under his tongue, but was vibrating in such pain that he had difficulty swallowing the pain killers. Slowly he opened his eyes.

"It's O.K., Mama. It's O.K. Son. I guess this is the end of the trail for me."

Ema grasped Bill's right hand, Tom his left. Gasping for air, Bill carried on.

"I'm so proud of you Tom. You've done so well by Mom and me. Promise me you'll treat yourself well and look out for your Mom."

"Yah, Dad, I will," Tom whispered.

Turning to Ema he continued, "Thank you Mama for being so strong and for supporting me and Tom. Thank you for all these wonderful years you've shared with me. I love you so much, Ema, I love you so, but I'm hurting something awful. I know it won't be long for me now. I kind of feel like an arse. Feel like I'm leaving you both in the lurch."

Bill shuddered as another attack hit him. Slowly, his hands relaxed and a trace of a smile crossed his face. "Granddad," he whispered. Then his head sank back into the pillow and the life light slowly faded from his eyes.

As Ema cradled Bill's head in her hands, she sobbed, "We've lost our dear brave soldier."

Tom and Ema were still crying when Dr. Stuart arrived. For all his gruffness, he was kind hearted. There were tears in his eyes as Ema wept in his arms. After comforting Ema, he walked over to the couch and patted Bill on the forehead.

"Goodbye, my friend, goodbye," he whispered. Then turning to Ema and Tom, he added, "Now there is one hell of a man."

Dr. Stuart phoned Lester Corbit, a traveling minister who lived in the community. Les took his ministry to the farmers in isolated areas, sawmills, forestry towers and mines. He was a genuine man of God, heavy on the help and light on the haranguing of his fellow man. He was as often seen working alongside people in need, as holding services. He often dropped in on the Parkers, staying for a few days, assisting them in whatever project they were working on.

When Lester heard the news, he asked to speak to Ema. He expressed his sympathy and said that his wife Beulah and he would be right over to give them a hand.

The Corbits stayed a week. Lester assisted with the farm chores while Beulah took over the housework. The funeral was large and although Jed and Betty were only casual acquaintances of the Parkers, they attended. Jed and Betty offered their condolences to Ema and Tom and said they would be honored to help them out.

True to Bill's wish, Ema and Tom stayed on the farm till the next spring with Tom completing grade nine. It was a rough time of adjustment for them, but they had each other for support.

After school was out, Ema suggested they sell out and move to town so Tom could complete his high school. Tom balked at the idea. He was now sixteen, stood five foot ten and weighed one hundred and ninety pounds.

"I've been pretty well doing a man's work for the last two years, Mom. I just can't stand the thought of leaving the farm and moving into town. Move if you must, but count me out."

"But what about your education?"

"I know, but you see Mom, although I have a few school friends, I really don't have that much in common with guys my age. Besides, school doesn't interest me anymore. I forced myself to hang in there for grade nine. You and Dad did the best you could by me, but now I have to do my own thing."

After a lengthy discussion, Ema reluctantly accepted Tom's decision. In the light of this new development, they talked about what to do with the farm.

"If you're in agreement, Mom, I think we should sell all the sheep and haying equipment. For the last few years, we haven't made much money off the sheep. I think it would be best if we worked up the grassland and got into grain farming."

"Maybe so. Of late we're not even breaking even on the sheep. Without Dad's pension, we couldn't have managed."

With the proceeds from the sale of the flock and their old equipment, they bought a larger tractor, a bigger plow, a disk, a cultivator and a seed drill. Tom plowed up all the grassland and worked it down. By late August, their land was in seedbed condition.

Once their own work was completed, Tom started looking for an off farm job. He contacted Jed Osmond for work, but was a few days too late as Jed just hired Blain Kostick to help with harvest. Jed phoned around on Tom's behalf and got him a job with Tim Blakely, his neighbour.

The evening before Tom was to start his new job, the clutch went out of their old car. Tom didn't want to bother Tim for a ride so at six a.m. the next morning, he began biking the twenty odd miles to Blakelys'.

Tim gave Tom instructions on how to get to their place, but Tom forgot the directions at home. When he came to the last intersection, he couldn't remember whether to turn north or south. On a hunch, he turned north. He only went two hundred yards down the road when he got a strong feeling he was heading the wrong way. The farther he went, the stronger the feeling became. Finally he gave in to his gut instinct and turned back south. Immediately the strange feeling left him.

He was definitely on the right road even though it wasn't the road to the Blakely place.

CHAPTER
7

The summer Tanya turned twelve, a horrifying incident occurred that traumatized their family. They learned that their small community, remote though it was, still wasn't immune from undesirables.

Bill Rosser, a close bachelor neighbour, helped Jed with the farming. For harvest, Jed would often hire an extra hand. A week before harvest started, Jed hired Blain Kostick through an agency in Red Deer that placed harvest excursion workers from Ontario.

Although Jed found Blain to be a conscientious worker, Betty took an instant dislike to him. "Say what you like, I just don't trust that man," she said to Jed one evening when they were alone. "There's something about him that's so oily and have you noticed the attention he pays Tanya? It's just not natural for a man who must be thirty or more to dote on a twelve-year-old girl. I don't like it, Jed. What do you know about his past?"

"All I really know is that he comes from Ontario. He claims he worked on a farm before and is certainly familiar with farm work. I really haven't noticed him being all that friendly with Tanya. I guess I could ask him about his past, but if he's the unsavory type you think he is, he'd only lie. I'll be on the lookout, but remember, Betty, you can't fire a man because you think he's oily. That wouldn't be fair."

Betty went over to the china cabinet, returned with a small piece of paper and handed it to Jed. "When I cleaned the bunkhouse yesterday, I found this under Blain's bed. It probably fell out of his pocket or suitcase. It's got a name and an out of province phone number on it. Could we check it out?"

"O.K., Betty, O.K.," Jed replied in an agitated tone. "I'll take the phone number to Constable Blake when I'm in town tomorrow, and tell him you're a bit leery of Blain. It seems like a wild goose chase to me though. I know you're only looking out for Tanya's safety, but I think you're overdoing it."

Blain Kostick, alias Ruben Kostich, just finished serving seven years in Kingston Penitentiary for molesting small children. One of his victims had been his eight-year-old step-daughter.

Once released from prison, Blain was placed on probation for a year. After reporting faithfully to his probation officer for a three month period, he broke probation and headed out west on a harvest excursion.

When Jed introduced Blain to the family, Betty noticed him staring at Tanya.

As a skilled manipulator, Blain made a concerted effort to befriend Tanya. Being a young impressionable girl, Tanya drank in all the attention he showered on her. Blain could feel Betty's coolness and knew he'd have to be extra careful not to antagonize her.

"Sometimes adults act strangely," he told Tanya one day when they were alone. "If you tell your folks what we talk about, your dad might become upset with me and I'd lose my job."

"I've really had some rough breaks," he continued sadly. "Last year, my wife and three-year-old daughter died when our house burnt down. I was away working, but I still feel guilty that I wasn't there."

Tanya felt sorry for Blain and went along with his plan of not sharing their conversations with her folks. Being naive, she had no idea that Blain's friendliness was a guise and that he had ulterior motives.

Blain's planned intimate encounter with Tanya was an all-consuming passion with him and he fantasized about it constantly. He was patiently waiting for the time when Jed and Betty would be away.

Betty's suspicion of Blain would prove valid. Her reticence to warn Tanya of her concerns would always haunt her, but she felt awkward about broaching the subject with Tanya. If her suspicion proved ungrounded, it would make for a difficult situation if Blain were to stay on.

As Jed was getting ready to leave for town, Betty reminded him to make sure he stopped at the RCMP detachment to have Constable Blake check out the phone number she found. Betty and the twins were going to the Laffarty place to help Rose plan the church harvest supper. Tanya was to bike to the Crawford place to spend the day with her friend Nelly. Until things were resolved with Blain, Betty was just as happy to have Tanya away when she and Jed were gone.

Tanya was a quarter of a mile down the road when she heard a loud bang. "Drat, a flat tire," she exclaimed in disgust.

She looked back to see her mom pull out of the driveway and head the other direction. Tanya frantically waved her arms, but her mom didn't notice her. "I'll have to push my bike back to the house," she muttered. "Maybe I can get Blain to fix it."

Tanya dropped her bike off at the garage and headed the two hundred yards out to the pasture, where Blain was repairing the fence.

When Blain looked up and saw Tanya walking towards him, he whistled softly and his heart began beating wildly. "This is what I've been waiting for," he said under his breath.

"I was wondering if I could get you to look at my bike," Tanya began. "I was on my way to Crawford's and got a flat tire."

"I'm sure I can fix it for you," Blain replied, eyeing Tanya over. "First, though, come and sit a spell. I'd like to show you some pictures of my wife and daughter." Blain pulled out his wallet and Tanya sat down beside him.

While Tanya was studying the pictures, Blain was studying her, his heart racing in wild anticipation.

Tanya was wearing a pair of shorts and a light top. She was a cute girl just starting into puberty, but to Blain's warped mind, she was a turn-on. To him, her clothes advertised her sexuality. When Tanya glanced at Blain, she was perplexed by the strange look in his eyes.

Suddenly his hand flashed out and rested on her bare thigh.

"If you let me, we can do things together that will feel very good and make you very happy," he blurted out. "It will be our secret, just yours and mine."

"No, please Blain!" Tanya cried in shock. "Leave me alone!"

"Oh dear God!" she thought, wild fear gripping her heart. "Is this why Blain has been so friendly with me?"

Instantly Blain's arm was around her shoulders holding her tight. Tanya frantically struggled to free herself, but was unable to move. With his free hand, he lifted her top and began fondling her breasts.

"Blain, don't do that," she cried out again. "You're hurting me!"

Blain stopped but only for a moment. He forced one of his legs in between her knees, pulled her shorts and panties aside and started fondling her again.

"I'll bet that feels good," he whispered hoarsely.

Tanya had never been so terrified in all her life.

"Oh no, Blain," she sobbed, "don't do that to me. You're really hurting me. If you let me go, I promise not to tell my folks."

"This is going to feel very nice for both of us," Blain continued, disregarding Tanya's plea.

Still holding Tanya firmly around the waist, he kicked off his rubber boots, unzipped his fly with his free hand and wiggled out of his pants and shorts.

"I'll help you take off your shorts and panties now."

Tanya was terrified when she glanced down and saw Blain's bare stomach and erect penis. Realizing her only chance to escape was to fight, she started screaming for help at the top of her lungs, biting, scratching and kicking for all she was worth. She managed to escape Blain's grasp, but before she could run, he grabbed her again from behind.

"You know you want this," he leered.

With one hand on either side of Tanya's hips, he gave a quick tug, ripping her shorts and panties down to her ankles. Tanya lost her balance and fell over. Blain gave another pull and her shorts and panties came off. Tanya continued fighting and screaming, but despite all, was no match for Blain's size and strength. She was now on her back on the ground. To her horror, she felt Blain fall on top of her, nearly crushing her.

"DON'T DO THIS TO ME!" she screamed in desperation. "PLEASE, SOMEONE HELP ME! HELP ME!"

As Tom was biking down the south road, he heard someone screaming. Looked up, he saw an altercation going on about a quarter of a mile to the east at the far side of a pasture. Tom quickly lifted his bike across the fence and peddling furiously toward the action. As he got closer he saw a man push a small girl down, then fall on top of her. Both of them were naked from the waist down. A well-aimed boot to the side of the head dislodged the attacker. A more seasoned street fighter would have immediately pursued his advantage in initiating the attack. Instead, Tom turned his attention to Tanya.

"Go for help. Get your dad," Tom yelled as he helped Tanya to her feet. She snatched up her clothes and ran for the house with every ounce of strength she had.

Blain scrambled to his feet mouthing a volley of expletives and threw a wicked roundhouse that grazed the top of Tom's head.

"Better save your breath, you lowbred dog," Tom bellowed, connecting with a bone rattling right to Blain's mid section. "You're going to need all the wind you've got."

Not being able to culminate his dastardly act and being caught red-handed and bare-assed only added to Blain's rage. He fought like a demented animal. Tom was throwing some good punches, but Blain was a much bigger man and used of brawling. He had connected with several good blows and was starting to get the upper hand. Tom tried hard to remember his dad's boxing lessons.

Finally, in total desperation he cried out, "Please, Dad, I need your help!"

Instantly, he heard the calm voice of his dad behind him.

"I'm here, Son. I'll coach you. Pace yourself, keep up your guard and don't throw any unnecessary punches. The fancy stuff he's trying to throw is alright for the circus, but he's wearing himself out. Remember, Tom....jab duck... jab weave... jab dance... bob your head... guard with your right... jab with your left... The jabbing will keep him off balance. Keep your right rested, we'll use it later."

The coaching gave Tom the confidence he needed. Blain was throwing too many punches that weren't connecting and wearing himself down.

"You're doing well, Son. Now give him a stiff left hook to the nose."

Tom followed through and folded Blain's nose flat. Blain roared out several oaths and threw another wild haymaker. Tom ducked low and the shot sailed harmlessly over his head.

"Now, the right overhand!" Bill's voice boomed.

Tom was still crouched low. He sprang upward with all the strength his legs had and at the end of his lunge, threw his right hand straight out overhand. Blain was off balance with no guard up. Tom's blow caught him square on the jaw. There was a loud smack and a sickening snap as his jaw broke. Blain went down in a heap.

"Get on his chest and hammer the living pee out of him," Bill's voice roared. "Remember what he tried to do to the little girl."

Tom straddled Blain's chest and flailed away on his face for a few seconds. As he climbed off him, Tom noticed that Blains family jewels were left unguarded. Almost as an after thought, Tom grabbed an eighteen inch piece of fence picket and administered three good cracks to Blain's unguarded crotch.

Tom's face was not a pretty sight, but by comparison, Blain's face looked like he'd been fed head first into a hammer mill. Both of his eyes were swollen shut, there was a myriad of small cuts and bruises all over his face and his nose was flat and oozing blood. His teeth, or what was left of them, looked like a dentist's nightmare and his jaw was broken.

When Tanya got to the house, she phoned her mom at the Laffarty place. "Come quick, Mom!" she sobbed. "Blain tried to do something awful to me...I'm so scared...My bike had a flat tire...so I came back to the house to get Blain to fix it... When I stopped to talk to him he attacked me...Tom Parker knocked Blain off me...They're fighting out in the field right now."

Tanya was sobbing and nearing hysteria. "Try to calm down," her mom broke in. "We're on our way."

By good fortune, Mark Laffarty was working in the yard. Rose, Betty and the twins jumped into Betty's car and sped for home. Mark followed them in his truck, but first stopped at the wood pile and picked up his double-bitted axe.

"I'll bash that bastard's brains in," he muttered, "and maybe nip off his sack too."

When Tanya heard her mom's car pull into the yard, she ran out to meet her. As Betty held her daughter close, Tanya sobbed uncontrollably. Mark pulled right by them and headed out to the field.

Betty was wild with rage, her mind a whirlwind of thoughts and emotions. She was horrified and outraged with Blain for violating her daughter, upset with herself for not warning Tanya of her suspicion of Blain and angry with Jed for trusting people so completely.

When Betty phoned the police in Milden they told her that Constable Blake and Jed had left some fifteen minutes before.

Tom was guarding Blain when Mark arrived in the field. Blain was just regaining consciousness.

Mark addressed Blain with a few choice words, then went back to his pickup and brought back an old blanket and his axe. He threw the blanket at him and brandished his axe.

"Make one move, you bastard rat and I'll use the axe on you," Mark growled. "For two cents I'd lop off everything that dangles between your legs. Anyone who molests a small girl is lower than a snake."

Mark turned to Tom. "Well, you sure as hell worked the snot right out of this creep. Job well done! You must take after your old man. Your dad and I used to chum together. He knew how to use his hands when it came to scrapping and by the look of this creep's face, you do too. Take my pickup and go to the house. My wife Rose is there. She's a nurse and will be able to check you out. I'll watch this character to make sure he doesn't try to make a run for it. When you get to the house, make sure the women have phoned the police."

Meanwhile, Jed was having his own trials. As soon as he got to town he stopped at the police station and spoke to Constable Blake.

"Betty's been bugging me about the farm worker I just hired. She thinks he has eyes for our young daughter. Anyway, she found this phone number under his bed. I'd check it out myself, but we have party lines. I'm sure it's all in Betty's mind, but could you check the number? It will get the wife off my back. His name is Blain Kostick. He's a big guy, just about my size."

"I can appreciate the bind you're in," Blake replied with a smile. "I guess all mothers are a bit over protective. I'll check the number for you. Drop back in before you head for home."

Jed was stepping out of the station when Constable Blake pulled up in his car.

"Better get in, Jed," he called out. "We hit pay dirt. I never thought one phone call could cause such a commotion. The phone number was a probation officer in Oshawa. Your description fits that of Ruben Kostich. He was released on probation four months ago after serving time for molesting children. He didn't report to his probation officer last month. There's a nationwide warrant out for his arrest."

"Oh my God!" Jed exclaimed as he jumped into Blake's car. "We're in deep trouble. Let's hit it! Your car is faster than my pickup. I can get the truck later. God, I hope Tanya is alright. You see, this morning Blain, or Ruben, was fixing the pasture fence close to our house. Betty and the twins were headed over to the Laffarty's place and as near as I know, Tanya was staying at home. What an idiot I am for being so naive and trusting! Betty's been on my case about how much attention Blain's been showing Tanya. God, I hope she's okay!"

On their way to the farm, Blake was constantly trying to reassure Jed that everything would be alright.

As Blake and Jed pulled into the yard, Betty ran out to the police car.

"Blain attacked Tanya and tried to rape her!" she blurted out. "I told you he couldn't be trusted! If it hadn't been for Tom Parker, I'm afraid to think of what would have happened to our little girl. Tom was biking past the pasture and heard Tanya screaming for help. Tom and Mark are out there with Blain."

Jed came completely unglued. "That low bred bastard!" he roared, vibrated with rage. "I'm headed out to the pasture to break every bone in his body!"

"Jed," Blake hollered, "you stay here and comfort your daughter and wife. That's an order! I don't need you out there to make the arrest. I know from experience how you react when you lose your cool. It would take all our manpower and then some to keep you from killing him. I'll arrest him, then come back to get Tanya's statement."

On the way out to the pasture, Blake met Tom coming to the house in Mark's truck. "It looks like you've been in a hell of a fight. What happened? Are you alright?"

"Yeah, I guess I'm O.K.," Tom replied, blood still oozing from his mouth. "I was biking down the road and heard someone screaming for help. When I got there this rotten bastard was trying to rape Jed Osmond's daughter. I managed to knock the crap out of him. Mark Laffarty is out there guarding the character with an axe."

"Good work, fellow, good work. We've just found out that the guy's name is Ruben Kostich. He's spent several years in prison for molesting children. I'm going to arrest him, then I'll come back and get statements from you and Tanya."

As soon as Blake left for the field, Tanya ran out of the house into her dad's arms and cried uncontrollably. Jed was shaking with rage as he held his daughter close.

When Tom pulled into the yard, Jed hurried over to the car.

"Thank you so much for saving Tanya from that monster. How can we ever repay you?"

"That's alright," Tom replied slowly. "Any man would have done the same thing."

"We'll never be able to repay you as long as we live. I hope you worked the asshole over good."

"I suppose I did. His face is none too pretty. I think I broke his jaw and I imagine his crotch is a little tender."

Betty phoned Tim Blakely about Tanya's attack and he and Les Corbit arrived while Blake was getting statements from Tanya and Tom. Once the paper work was attended to, Blake took Ruben to the hospital in Milden to be patched up a bit before transferring him to the jail in Red Deer.

Rose Lafferty checked Tom out. Except for a black eye, cuts and bruises on his face, a few loose teeth and sore ribs, he came through the fight in pretty fair shape. She wrapped Tom's chest snugly with a roll of gauze that Betty had.

"The ribs will be pretty sore for a week or so, but this tight bandage will help a lot." As she placed her hand on Tom's shoulder she continued. "Thank God you were there for Tanya."

Like the others, Tim was most concerned over Tanya's attack. "We all can thank our lucky stars that you took the wrong turn this morning, Tom. We live two miles north of the intersection, not south of it."

Tom nodded. "I'm feeling pretty shook. I wonder if I could go home for a couple of days."

"Take off as many days as you need to. Your job will be waiting for you when you come back."

"Tom, you take Betty's car home," Jed interjected. "Tim can drive me back into town for my pickup."

Before Tom left, Betty hugged him gingerly. As Jed shook Tom's hand he thanked him repeatedly. Finally, Tanya stepped forward hesitantly.

"Thanks a lot," she said in a quivering voice.

"That's O.K. Tanya," Tom replied, placing his hand on her shoulder. "I'm glad I got there in time."

Tom climbed into the car and headed out the driveway. The emotional trauma of the fight and his dad's coaching was taxing him far more than the physical pain he was enduring. He felt the need to be by himself so drove to the cemetery. Since his dad's death, he often visited his grave when he was lonely or feeling down.

As he walked into the cemetery he was fighting hard to keep control and act like a man. Fifty feet from his dad's headstone, he broke down. He ran the last few feet to the grave, sank to his knees and sobbed uncontrollable.

"Hope I did O.K., Dad," he cried. "I did the best I could. Thanks for helping me out. I know you were there, Dad, I just know it."

Suddenly a feeling of tranquility came over Tom. It was so awesome that he just sat on his dad's headstone for some time relishing the feeling. Finally, he got to his feet and headed home.

When Tom left, Betty phoned Ema to let her know about Tanya's attack.

"I would be so happy to have a son like your Tom. You certainly can be proud of him. He was willing to risk his life to save our Tanya from that monster."

Ema met Tom at the door, her eyes brimming with tears and her face aglow with love and pride.

"Betty Osmond just phoned me about the fight. I'm so proud of you, Tom. Your dad would have been proud of you too."

"Dad was there coaching me when I was fighting that creep," Tom replied quietly. "Don't ask me how it happened, but he was there."

Shortly after Tom left, Jed and Betty took Tanya to the hospital in Milden to be examined by Dr. Stuart. In addition to bruises on her lower abdomen, the doctor discovered a few pubic hairs and some dried semen. He confirmed that she had not been entered. While they were still in the hospital, Dr.

Stuart contacted the RCMP in Red Deer about his findings. His statement would be used as Crown evidence when the case came to trial.

"You have gone through an awful ordeal, Tanya," Dr. Stuart began. "It could have been much worse, though. The brute could have raped you, or even killed you. Thank God Tom came to your rescue. Try to remember, most of us men are honorable."

"Your young girl is going to need a lot of help over the next while as she works, or tries to work this horrible incident out of her system," Stuart continued, turning to Betty and Jed. "I know that both of you will always be there for her. Remember, if any of you need help, I'm just a phone call away."

Tanya was so frightened and troubled that she asked her mom to sleep with her. As Tanya drifted off to sleep, Betty held her daughter close and offered a simple prayer of thanks to God for sparing her girl from a worse fate.

Difficult times lay ahead for Tanya. She was haunted with nightmares for a long time. Jed moved her and Beth's bed into their bedroom, as Tanya was terrified of sleeping without her parents near.

The attack made her suspicious of most men. It would be close to a year before Tanya would feel confident enough to go anywhere by herself.

Fate was not with Ruben, as he did not live long enough to stand for trial. Shortly after being transferred to the federal penitentiary in Prince Albert, he met his untimely demise. He was found dead by the guards in the exercise compound. The coroner's report concluded that he died of natural causes. If there was any foul play, it was denied by both guards and prison authorities. Notwithstanding the official line, there was a rumor that he had been struck on the head by another inmate.

Although Tanya was relieved that she wouldn't have to go through the trial, Blain's death constantly haunted her. "Did I lead him along?" she wondered. "Am I somehow to blame for his death?"

CHAPTER
8

A week following the fight, Tom's ribs were still sore, but he returned to work anyway. Before the farmers could get into the fields with their binders though, sixteen inches of heavy wet snow flattened the crops. Most of the farmers just turned their cattle out into the crops to graze. Because of the early snow, Tom's job at the Blakely's was cut short. Through Jed, he got a job in a sawmill some thirty miles back in the foothills.

In late November, Tanya wrote Tom a letter.

Dear Tom,

I got your address from your mother. Thank you for fighting for me. I'm so glad that you got there when you did. You will never know how scared I was. I'm still having nightmares about being attacked. It's made me feel really mixed up. Mom and Dad have been helping me. They talk to me a lot. It would be nice if all men were kind like Dad or you. I hope to be able to see you again in the spring. When our picture about the attack was in the paper, I cut it out. Well, that's all I can think of for now.

Yours truly,

Tanya Osmond.

PS: Would it be O.K. if I told my school chums that you are my friend?

When Tom got the letter, he read it several times. He recalled his dad saying that helping others out was what life was all about. It felt good to have helped Tanya out of a real bind.

A few days later, Tom wrote Tanya a reply.

Dear Tanya,

It was nice to hear from you. I get pretty lonely out here. I hope you will soon get over your scare. I was glad to be able to help you out and save you from that animal. He was a real loser.

  You may think I'm a bit daft, but I'm sure I heard my dad's voice coaching me throughout the fight. You see, Dad was the Amateur Boxing Champ of Alberta before he lost his legs. I was glad that I was able to give Ruben a damn good licking. From what I've heard, the poor bastard died in jail. I'll come and visit you and your folks when I get out of the bush in the spring. Well, I'll sign off for now. I'd be proud to be your friend.

Yours truly,

Tom

Tanya kept Tom's letter by her bedside table and nearly wore it out re-reading it. When she thought of him as a handsome, strong young man, she got a warm feeling, but if she envisioned him kissing and hugging her, she became mixed up and fearful again.

When the sawmill shut down for the Christmas break, Tom and his mom drove to Red Deer to spend Christmas with their kinfolk. After the holidays, Tom returned to the bush. Because Ema's finances were tight, she stayed on and found work, cooking in a hotel café.

Ema's folks were certainly glad to have their daughter living with them. Shortly after Christmas, she met Ron Klassen, a widower who attended her mom's church. He was a mechanic who ran a small garage in partnership with his uncle. Ron lost his wife to cancer two years before. One thing led to another and before long they were going out together.

Tom was still working in the bush when he got a letter from his mother telling him about Ron. Even though it was over a year since his dad's death, he felt angry and betrayed that his mother would find a replacement for him so soon. He tried to accept that they cared for each other, but it still hurt that another man was replacing his dad.

Time helped lessen the sting though and by the time Tom returned home for the spring break-up, he was getting more comfortable with the idea of his mom's new relationship.

"I guess as long as they're both happy, that's all that counts," he thought. "Just as long as he's not a loser."

Tom was only out of the bush a couple of days when his mom and her boyfriend arrived to spend Easter at the farm. Tom tried to keep an open mind, but observed that Ron ran off at the mouth some. With Tom having the same volatile nature as his dad, Ema recognized that kid gloves would be needed to help keep things amicable between the two gentlemen.

Saturday, while they were eating dinner, Ema turned to Tom. "Ron and I are going to Easter service tomorrow. We were wondering if you'd care to join us."

"Thanks for asking, Mom," Tom replied, without making eye contact. "I just wouldn't be able to handle that."

Ema recognized that it was a sensitive issue for Tom and backed right off, but not so Ron. As a deacon of his church in Red Deer, he tended to be a zealot when it came to putting his religious views across to others. He took this as a golden opportunity to wax eloquent on the real reason for Easter and launched right into a sermon.

Tom put up with it for a bit before boldly interjecting, "Look here Ron, get off my case. If you don't understand why I'd feel uncomfortable being with the two of you in church, ask my mom." He got up and went outside for a breather.

"Honestly, Ron, you're so insensitive at times," Ema started, as soon as Tom was out of earshot. "Tom's still very tender over the loss of his dad. What he was trying to tell us is it would hurt him to have to sit with us in church. They were really close, very much alike for that matter. So please Ron, for his sake and mine, try to be a bit more careful and above all else, no more sermons."

Up until Sunday evening, Ron was careful to watch his tongue, and no other contentious issues arose. After supper, Ema began nervously. "Tom, we should talk about what we're going to do with the farm and if you can, do your best to keep a cool head. Ron and I will be getting married this summer so I'll be staying on in Red Deer. Do you want to keep on farming, or should we think of selling out? I'm not about to make any decision without your input. What are your thoughts?"

Tom was thunderstruck. He couldn't believe that his mother would even contemplate selling the farm.

Ron took Tom's silence as an opportunity for his input. "If you ask me, Tom, selling the farm is the way to go. You'll never be able to make much of a living off two quarters of poor bush soil. Just remember how hard you guys worked, trying to scratch a living off this land. Your mom says you're mechanically inclined. You could apprentice in my garage. All you'd have to do is work hard and you could make a go of it."

When Ema glanced in Tom's direction she knew by his flushed face that all hell was about to break loose.

Struggling to keep control, Tom looked daggers through Ron and replied acidly. "Why the hell don't you butt out and let Mom and I discuss this without giving your two-bits-worth?"

Turning to his mom, Tom continued. "I'm so shocked I don't know what to say. Level with me Mom, there must be some reason for you wanting to sell the land. Does it have bad memories for you? Do you need the money?" Tom took a deep breath. "For starters, I think we should seed all the land we worked up last summer. After that, I don't know if I like the idea of staying on by myself. I'm going to have to think it all over some. What about renting it out in the future rather than selling it? What do you want?"

"Well Tom, if you decide you want to stay on the land and farm, we won't be selling it. I'll take time off my job this spring to help you with seeding. Now, about me needing money. Well, Ron and I do have some plans. Ron's uncle, Frank, is getting up in years, and wants out of the business. If we were to sell the land, we'd be able to buy him out. Please remember, the idea of buying out Ron's uncle with the land money is as much my idea as Ron's and as I said, once we're married we'll be staying in the city. I guess the bottom line is I won't be forcing you off the land."

Tom was completely floored. It seemed so preposterous that his mom would be party to selling what they as a family struggled so long for, to buy into Ron's garage. He felt certain that Ron was trying to influence his mom to advance his own business interests.

Tom pounded the table with his fist. Ron was taken aback and refused to make eye contact with him. Tom kept glaring at his future step-father and was about to tear a large chunk out of him when he noticed the pleading look in his mother's eyes.

"Oh hell, what's the use?" he muttered. Without another word, Tom headed out the door, got into his car and drove out to the cemetery. As he sat on his dad's headstone, there were tears of frustration in his eyes.

"It's just not fair for them to sell the land, Dad," he blurted out.

Tom sat for a long time trying desperately to sift through his thoughts. Suddenly, despite the stillness of the evening, he felt a warm breath of wind.

"Tom, I'm here with you. I know selling the farm doesn't seem fair to you."

"Dad!" Tom exclaimed, "I can hear you, but I can't see you."

"Some day you'll see me, Tom. Your mother's relationship with Ron has you all wrought up too, but try to accept that they need each other. I can feel your pain as you think of losing the land. Remember, Son, caring for yourself and treating others as you would yourself is what life is all about. Always remember that, Tom. Whenever there's a crisis, I'll always be with you. You may not hear me or even sense my presence, but I'll be by your side. I have faith in you. Now I must go."

"Well what about them selling the land?" Tom cried out.

There was no response. As Tom glanced around he noticed it was now twilight. Again, despite the air being still and cool, Tom felt another warm puff of wind.

When Tom got back to his car he sat for a while, trying to assimilate his dad's visit and the talk with his mom and Ron. He thought back on all the struggles and joys he and his folks had shared in farming the land. 'Remember, Son, caring for yourself and treating others as you would yourself, is what it's all about,' kept repeating itself in his mind like a stuck record.

"Even if we hold on to the farm, it will be a lonely existence for me, with both Mom and Dad gone," he mused. "Mom is counting on the money from the sale of the farm to buy out Ron's uncle. She said it was her idea too."

It hurt an awful lot, but Tom finally concluded that it would be best to go along with his mom's and Ron's wish. At peace with himself, he headed home.

As soon as Tom left, Ema and Ron re-hashed the plan of selling the land in light of Tom's reaction. Ron was out in the driveway standing by his car when Tom pulled into the yard. Tom stopped and rolled down the window.

"I'm going to butt out for a bit and let your mother and you discuss things. I just want you to know that selling the land to buy my uncle out was originally my idea. Your mom said she'd be in favor of the plan, as long as you agreed."

"Thanks Ron," Tom replied in a conciliatory tone. "It will make it easier if just the two of us can talk things over."

"O.K. Tom, I'll be back in an hour or so."

"Been to your dad's grave?" Ema asked, as Tom stepped inside.

Tom nodded and his mom continued. "While you were gone, I did a lot of thinking. I don't know if you realize this, Tom, but the farm has been awfully hard on me. The first few years were alright, but then your dad's health started to slip. I got so tired of the struggle and came to resent the farm with a passion. Still, after seeing your reaction, it dawned on me just how much the land means to you. You're like your dad. He loved the farm, even though he suffered a lot trying to keep it going. While you were gone I had a long talk with Ron. We both saw that the thought of losing the farm was too much for you to bear. I just told Ron that the plan to sell the land is off."

"Mom," Tom interrupted. "Things can't remain as they have been. You and Ron are counting on the money from the sale of the land to help buy out Ron's uncle. I honestly don't fancy farming the land all by myself." Tom paused a moment to regain his composure.

"When Dad died, I promised to look out for you. I wouldn't be doing that if I insisted on keeping the land. Really, it's legally yours anyway. I have one condition though. The partner's share that is bought out with the land money is to remain in your name. The sale and buying Ron's uncle out must be done through a lawyer. I just want to protect you and I'm sure Dad would want that too."

Ema's eyes were misty as she whispered, "Thank you so much Son. You'll never know what this means to me. Remember, our home in Red Deer will always be your home too. If you ever need help I'm only a phone call away. As for this spring, I'd be happy to help you with the seeding. Even though I care for Ron a lot, I miss my two warriors so much. No one ever pushed you or your dad around, both of you so hot-headed, but at the same time, so kind and fair."

Tom looked away. It had been a rough day for both mother and son.

True to her word, Ema took a three week leave from her job to assist Tom with the seeding. By the end of her leave, the wheat and barley were seeded and all but thirty acres of the oats.

Early Saturday morning, before Ema left for Red Deer, she and Tom placed a few notices around the community, advertising their land for sale. If there was no local interest in the land, Ema would put an ad in the Red Deer paper.

Shortly after Ema left, Tom phoned Jed and made arrangements to buy enough oats to finish seeding. When he arrived to pick up the seed, he found Tanya at home alone. Jed just finished seeding and he, Betty and the twins were in Milden, shopping. Tom was amazed at how Tanya had filled out. She had beautiful features, long blond hair and hauntingly wild green eyes to compliment her trim figure. "Man, does she ever have it," Tom thought.

Tanya couldn't remember Tom being that handsome. He stood a shade under five foot eleven, had short black hair, a ruddy complexion and the dreamiest hazel eyes she'd ever seen. It took them three quarters of an hour to pail the oats into the wagon box. Once they were done, Tanya invited Tom in for tea. Conversation didn't come that easy as they were both shy.

Betty, Jed and the twins returned just as Tanya and Tom finished their tea. It didn't take much persuading to get Tom to stay for dinner. He told them about trying to sell the land, his mom's new boyfriend and their plans to get married in the summer.

"Just remember this," Jed said. "If you ever need a place to stay, think of this as your second home."

"Thanks for your kind offer. I'll keep it in mind."

Two weeks after the seeding was completed, the Parker's neighbour, Boris Yamshak, bought the land. In their sale agreement, Tom got to keep the crop. As Boris had no intention of using the house, he told Tom he could stay there as long as he wanted.

Ron and Ema were married on the fifteenth of July. Tom attended their wedding, and as he suspected, had a rough time. An era was at an end.

The buyout of Ron's uncle was transacted according to Tom's wishes. Initially Ron was quite upset with the stipulation that the share of the business that Ema bought out was to remain in her name. He believed that men were to be the heads of their households and wives were to be obedient and submissive to their husbands. Ema remained firm though and in the end, he grudgingly agreed to the conditions. The responsibility for the day-to-day operation of the garage remained in Ron's hands, with Ema becoming the silent partner.

Ema wanted Tom to keep the proceeds from the crop and all the equipment. He accepted the farm equipment, but insisted on giving his mom a half share of the crop. Once harvest was under way, Tom made a work exchange arrangement with his neighbours. He stooked for them and helped with the threshing in exchange for help harvesting his crop.

After harvest, Tom spent a few days getting the building site ready for the new owner. As he cleaned up the yard he felt raw inside. Everything he touched brought back memories of his childhood.

On Sunday afternoon, Tom drove over to Jed's and Betty's place to see if he could store his farm equipment there. Jed said he had lots of room and offered to assist Tom in ferrying it over. It didn't take much persuasion from Betty to get Tom to stay for supper.

When Tanya heard that Tom was coming over, she dressed up in a new outfit. Her folks were relieved that she was finally coming out of her shell.

It would be nice if every girl had their own knight in shining armor. Tanya thought she had hers. Since seeing Tom in the spring, she spent many an hour daydreaming about him. As she fantasized about her handsome hero, she wondered if there was a chance that they would get together some day.

She heard tales of his phenomenal strength. A fellow who worked with him at the sawmill told her dad he saw Tom lift over six hundred pounds off the floor. He swore that Tom was stronger than any two men he knew.

Being young, Tanya was a bit awkward and Tom would often catch her staring at him. Whenever they made eye contact, she would blush and quickly turn away. Tanya's attention pleased Tom to no end.

"She's still too young," he mused, "but give her another three or four years and then watch out!"

They just finished supper when Lars McGilverey and his wife Sibyl dropped by for a visit. Lars was a stocky, powerful man, good natured and chuck-full of malarky. The only one in the community he couldn't arm wrestle was Jed. They had a go at it years before that ended in a draw. He was forever challenging the younger fellows to arm wrestle him, but seeing he was so good, few of the locals ever accepted his challenge.

After monopolizing the conversation for over an hour with his tall tales, Lars turned to Tom with a twinkle in his eye.

"You're certainly a husky young pup. How about an arm wrestle? There hasn't been a man in these parts who could take me for the last twenty years. No sir, not one man."

"You don't say," Tom replied with a smile. "As they say, every dog has his day."

"Oh, this sounds good. Good, good, good! Let's see how this young one lasts with a real man. O.K. Betty, if you could clean off the corner of the table, we'll flip the tablecloth back. I must teach this young lad some respect for his elders."

"Now the King's rules apply. Feet must stay flat on the floor, left hands locked under the table. Jed will referee. He'll keep our right arms steady, then say 'go' as he takes his hands away."

"Whatever you say," Tom said, smirking. "Whatever you say."

"Oh I like this," added Lars, "A sucker with real spirit!"

Tanya's heart was racing wildly. She desperately wanted Tom to win!

With a grin on his face, Tom threw a five-dollar bill on the table.

"Hot damn!" Lars blurted out and threw his own five dollars on Tom's.

Had Lars known of Tom's phenomenal strength, he could have saved himself five dollars. Tom weight lifted since he was ten and had been training hard, pushing iron at the mill for the last eight months. At two hundred ten pounds, he could dead lift an incredible six hundred and ten pounds and bench press three hundred and fifty.

They locked their hands. Jed called out "Go!" as he took his hands away. Lars was used to a quick flip and bore down with all his might, his ruddy face contorted in effort.

Very slowly, Tom spoke. "Any time you're ready, I am."

There was a loud "rap!" as Lars' knuckles hit the table.

Lars, for all his bravado and BS, was a good sport. "You took me fair and square," he called out. "What the hell have you got in those bloody arms of yours? Take off your shirt, Tom. I've got to see those arms."

Tom was reticent, but Jed interjected, "Go ahead Tom, take off your shirt."

Tom pulled his shirt off and flexed his arms a little. The muscles in his chest and arms were huge, and stood out like thick ropes.

"You're built just like a damn gorilla!" Lars cried out.

Tanya drank in Tom's massive chest and bulging arms. She was so happy and relieved he won that she wanted to go over and hug him! For all intents and purposes, Tanya was completely under Tom's spell.

After Lars and his wife left, Tom shared some of the pain he was going through. "Having to sell the land really hurts, but in the long run, I guess it's best." Tom bit his lip. "Best for Mom and Ron anyway. It seems that everything that's close to me has been taken away."

Betty placed her hand on Tom's shoulder. "There's a lot of hurt in this world, Tom. Jed lost his first wife and baby daughter many years ago. I was abandoned by my first husband before Tanya was born and Tanya is still haunted by her attack. We're honored that you feel comfortable enough with us to share your pain. It does us all good to talk about our hurts."

As Tom was leaving, Jed shook his hand and Betty gave him a hug. Tanya felt a bit uncomfortable, as she didn't know quite how to say goodbye. Finally she reached out her hand awkwardly. When Tom grasped her hand with both of his, the feeling was electrifying. Then he gave her a man-sized hug. Tanya felt warm for hours afterwards. Her face was still beaming as she climbed into bed with Beth.

"Do you think Tom likes you?" Beth began.

"I don't know," Tanya replied, her eyes aglow. "It sure would be nice if he did. As long as I live, I'll never forget what it felt like being held in those powerful arms."

Tanya wasn't the only one to feel the hug for hours afterwards. As Tom drifted off to sleep, he wondered what the future held. Would a cute young girl with blond hair, beautiful green eyes and a tantalizing figure be sharing it with him?

CHAPTER
9

Within a few days, Tom and Jed began the job of moving Tom's farm machinery over to the Osmond place.

"What are your long range plans?" Jed asked Tom one evening while they were eating supper.

"Well, I don't really have any. For now, I'll be going back to the sawmill for the winter."

"Have you ever thought of getting yourself some homestead land?"

"Well I guess my dad homesteaded our land about twenty-five years ago."

"There's the Bill Rosser place for sale a mile and a half to the west of us. For the last twenty-five years or so, Bill's helped me with seeding and harvest. Of late his heart has been acting up and he wasn't able to help much this year. When he was here the other day he mentioned he wanted to sell out and move to town. He used to run a few head of cattle, but three years ago he got rid of them. The fifty acres that was under cultivation is starting to grow back to small poplar and willow. I imagine you'd pretty well have to re-break it. There's one quarter of deeded land and two quarters of homestead land that a person could assign from him. He wants sixty-five hundred for the whole lot."

"Sounds pretty interesting," Tom said eagerly. "Tell me more."

"About the only building worth mentioning is the house. It's small, but well built. Sixty-five hundred sounds like quite a lot, but on one quarter of the homestead land, there's about eighty to ninety acres of beautiful lodgepole pine. It's thick as the hair on a dog's back and just about the right size for railroad ties."

"I'm not ready to settle down just yet, but maybe I should look into it. I've managed to save three thousand dollars. If it looks like a good deal, I suppose I could go to the bank and see if I could borrow the other thirty-five hundred."

"Let's go look at it tomorrow, Tom. If it's to your liking, Betty and I could always help you out for the balance. As far as I'm concerned, it's just too good a deal to pass up, if one factors in the value of all that timber."

After they finished talking business, Jed took out his old guitar and they all sang together. As they were singing, Jed noticed Tom eyeing his guitar.

"Play any?"

"Oh a little," Tom replied.

Jed handed him his old six stringer. Tom strummed a few chords and then turned to Tanya. "Come sing with me. Do you know 'Mockingbird Hill'?"

Tanya nodded and sat next to Tom on the couch. After a false start or two, they finally got on track. With Tanya singing soprano and Tom harmonizing, their voices blended beautifully. They sang a couple more songs before Tom handed the guitar back to Jed.

Tanya's face was flushed and she was almost floating as she climbed into bed with Beth.

"Boy, Tanya, you two sing beautifully together. You must like him a lot."

"Yes I do. He sure is nice."

As she lay in bed, Tanya thought again about the hug Tom gave her and wondered wistfully if there was any chance that he would wait for her to grow up. "Sure wish I was older," she whispered to herself.

Tom bedded down on the front room couch, his mind awhirl with thoughts of getting some farm land again and setting up a sawmill. He also thought about the girl who sat by his side and harmonized so beautifully with him. Even though she wasn't quite fourteen, he felt very attracted to her. As he drifted off to sleep, he was thinking the same thoughts that Tanya was. "I sure wish she was a few years older."

Early the next morning, Jed saddled up Darkie and King and he and Tom made a detailed inspection of Bill Rosser's farm on horseback. With the exception of the pine grove, the tree cover was predominantly black poplar and willow, a sign of good soil. The soil on the pine land was lighter, but the pine stand was dense. By Jed's estimate, it contained from one and a half to two million board feet of lumber. Jed thought it would probably reach maturity in about five years.

After inspecting Bill's land, Jed and Tom stopped in for coffee with him.

"I'd sure like to sell out and get moved into town before winter sets in. Are you guys at all interested in it?"

"I like the look of the land," Tom replied. "I'm definitely interested, but I'll need a couple of days to think out all the angles and see if I can arrange the financing."

When they got home, after unsaddling the horses, Jed took out a can of snuff and gave each horse a healthy pinch under their bottom lip.

"What on earth are you doing?" Tom asked.

"Just a trick I picked up from an old horseman. You see, horses love the taste of the stuff. Once you get them onto it, you never have to use a pail of oats to catch them. Just wrap your knuckles on the snuff box and they'll come running."

After supper, Tom returned to his old farm and spent the evening and most of the next day mulling over the deal. When he worked it out on paper, it appeared viable. He decided to go for it if he could arrange the financing. Tom realized that Jed and Betty would help him out with a loan, but was determined to see if he could manage the transaction on his own. He remembered what his dad said about borrowing from friends. "If you want to keep them as friends, don't do it."

As soon as the bank was open the next day, Tom dropped in to see the manager. Victor Grimm was a dour, rigid old gentleman. The locals used to say that it was grim to have to deal with Grimm.

After hearing Tom out, the manager began. "Before we talk about a loan, let me say that it's quite commendable that a lad of your age has saved three thousand dollars. It's also positive that you have a fair line of farm equipment. Our bank, however, is usually reticent to lend money on bush land. With the exception of the fifty acres Bill used to farm, that's what you would be buying. Remember, buying bush land or taking over on a homestead that is in bush is just the start of your expenses. You will need many more dollars to clear the land and bring it under cultivation. After clearing the land, it would be at least two years before you could generate any income to start paying off your loan."

"I realize that the timber has potential, depending on the price of lumber and railroad ties. Here again though, you must first invest a great amount of money in logging and sawmill equipment."

"How old are you, Son?"

"I'll be eighteen in January."

"I am aware that your mother sold your farm and invested the proceeds in your step-father's business. Considering your age and our policy on lending money on homestead land, I would only consider a loan if your folks co-signed for you. Of course, this would mean that they'd be tying up their assets to back your loan."

"Thanks for your time," Tom said as he got to his feet. "I'd like to take a bit of time to think things over."

As he walked to his car he muttered to himself. "The last thing in the world I'm going to do is involve Mom or Ron in my dealings. All I'd need is for him to start lecturing me on my business affairs. He's not the kind of guy I'd want to be beholden to."

Later in the morning, Tom met his school chum Joe Bonner in the pool room. Over a game of snooker, Tom told Joe about Bill Rosser's land being for sale and his visit to the bank.

"You must be out of your mind to want to farm!" Joe exclaimed, "Especially taking on bush land. I'm going to join the Army as soon as I'm eighteen and see the rest of the world. Yes sir, the minute I'm eighteen, I'm down to the recruiting office to enlist. Anyway, seeing we're at war, if we don't enlist, we'll be conscripted. If a guy volunteers, he stands a lot better chance of doing what he wants to do. What do you think Tom?"

"I see where you're coming from, Joe. If I remember rightly, I'm three weeks older than you. It mightn't be a bad idea if we joined up together. I'll think it over."

There was a lot on Tom's mind that evening. Should he try for the Rosser land? Should he head back to the sawmill for the winter? Should he join up with Joe? One thing he knew for certain. He wouldn't be approaching his mom or Ron for financial backing.

"No way, just no damned way. Sure wish I could talk it over with Dad."

The next day Tom was back at the Osmond's, feeling down that the banker wouldn't agree to a loan. He thought it best to level with Jed, seeing he'd gone to so much effort to show him the land.

"Couldn't come up with the extra thirty-five hundred, Jed," Tom said glumly. "The bank manager figures I'm too young. He doesn't seem to like the idea of homesteading either."

"Look Tom, I could have told you what that old buzzard would say. I remember all my go-rounds with the banks when

I started farming. The irony with banks is that the bastards won't lend you one damn cent when you desperately need it, but just get into the position where you don't need their money and they'll fall all over themselves trying to get you to borrow. Why bother with them? Like I told you before, Betty and I can help you out."

"But, I just don't feel right borrowing from friends."

"Nonsense!" Betty interjected. "As we've been saying, it's too good a deal to pass up. Jed and I talked it over last night. If it would make you feel any better, we'll put the land in all of our names for the time being. You can buy us out over the years as you get the money. I can tell you one thing for sure, we owe you an awful lot more than the thirty-five hundred you're short."

After a bit more pressure from both Jed and Betty, Tom finally agreed to accept their help as long as the title was held jointly. After dinner Jed and Tom dropped in on Bill to tell him they would buy his land. He was all smiles.

"You don't know the load this takes off my mind. I was dreading the thought of having to stay here for another winter."

The next afternoon, they took Bill into town and drew up the paperwork. Once the transaction was finalized, they all returned to the Osmonds' for supper.

"Bill doesn't have a decent water supply, or the phone and the last half mile of road can hardly be called a road," Jed said, as they were eating. "It's more of a trail and is just about impassable in spring and after heavy rains. Seeing the house is still in relatively good repair, Betty and I would like to make you an offer, Tom. If you'd like, we could move the house into our yard as soon as the ground freezes. The house is built on skids and I'm sure if we hooked on to it with a couple of tractors, we'd have no problem moving it. What do you think?"

"I appreciate the offer, Jed, and it makes good sense. I don't know if you realize how good I feel having land again. I've felt so empty since we sold our farm."

Tom wanted to tell them about the possibility of enlisting in the Armed Forces when he turned eighteen, but needed to think the whole thing through a bit more. "I'll have plenty of time to get my thinking straight on that while I'm working in the bush."

Tom and Jed moved Bill into Milden the next day. As Tanya left for school, she crossed her fingers that Tom would still be there when she got home.

When she returned from school, she felt letdown. Her dad's pickup was at home, but Tom's car wasn't there.

"Tom left, eh?" Tanya asked her dad.

"Tell me if I'm wrong," Jed quipped, "but Tom must mean quite a lot to you."

"Yeah, he is kind of nice," Tanya said, turning beet red.

"Well, I guess you're in luck. Tom is going to spend the night with us. We just finished moving Bill to town. Tom had a few errands to attend to in town, but he should be back soon."

"I'd better go help Mom with supper," Tanya said, breathing a sigh of relief.

When Tom arrived he helped Jed with the evening chores while Betty and Tanya prepared supper.

After supper, Jed asked Tom if he remembered to lock Bill's door.

Tom shook his head. "No, I didn't. I guess it wouldn't be too bad an idea, seeing it will be some time before we can move it. I'll go back and lock it now."

"Want to go for a ride?" Tom asked, looking over at Tanya.

"Yes, sure. I'll finish the dishes when we get back," she said turning to her mom.

Half way to Bill's place Tanya felt something warm on her hand. When she glanced down, her heart began racing wildly. Tom slid his hand under hers, intertwining their fingers. Tanya was thrilled. She tried to think of something appropriate to say, but not one inspiring thought came to her mind.

Each time Tom shifted gears, he'd let go of Tanya's hand, but once the shift was made, he'd find it again. As they pulled back into the yard, Tanya leaned over to Tom and whispered, "Thanks Tom."

"Thank you too, Tanya," Tom replied.

Betty noticed the glow in her daughter's eyes and her flushed cheeks when she stepped into the house. She knew that some powerful chemistry was going on. She was happy that Tom was the one who was bringing her daughter out of her shell. She trusted him.

As Tanya and Beth lay in bed that night, Beth turned to her sister.

"You sure seem happy tonight. I'll bet it's because of Tom."

"Yes it is and I'll tell you a secret about what happened when Tom and I went to Bill's place, but you must promise not to tell anyone."

"I promise," replied Beth eagerly.

"Well, Tom held hands with me," Tanya whispered.

"Was it exciting?"

"Yes, I thought my heart would explode. My hand still feels warm."

After breakfast Tom drove Tanya and the twins to school. Once Beth and Ben left the car, Tom said, "Mom's asked me to spend Christmas with her and Ron. I'll stop in to see you and your folks after the holidays, before heading back to the bush."

As Tanya was getting out of the car Tom reached over and held her hand for a moment.

At noon Tom contacted his foreman and got Joe Bonner a job at the mill. In the afternoon, Tom and Joe left for the sawmill.

One of the native fellows in the bush camp brought along several pairs of Indian moccasins to sell to his co-workers as Christmas gifts. Tom bought a pair for Tanya's present. They were elaborately decorated with beads, with a band of white weasel fur around the top. Tom included the two five dollar bills from the arm wrestling contest with Tanya's gift. He attached a note to the parcel instructed Betty to use the money to buy gifts for the twins.

The gifts for Tanya and the twins arrived by mail a week before Christmas. Tanya's eyes were aglow when she opened her package from Tom. Her Christmas card read: To my special friend, Sincerely Tom. She cried out with joy when she saw the moccasins. Despite being slightly too large, her gift was very precious to her.

As they lay in bed that evening, Tanya turned to Beth. "I'm so happy I could cry. Tom's gift is the best present I've ever gotten."

Just before Christmas, Jed and Lars hooked on to Tom's house with their two tractors and moved it into Jed's and Betty's yard.

Tom spent an enjoyable Christmas with his mom and step-dad. It meant a great deal to his mom that Tom accompanied them to church. Despite some negative feelings he still harbored towards Ron, Tom did his level best to find common ground. For now, they had called a truce.

Tom stopped off at the Osmonds and spent the night with them before heading back to the bush. He and Tanya were very happy to see each other. She'd stayed up many a night, knitting on Tom's gift, a pair of socks and a matching toque. Tom was as thrilled to get Tanya's gift as she was to get his.

"I'm planning on joining the Army later this winter when I turn eighteen," Tom began, while helping Jed with the evening chores. "I've wanted to tell you guys for some time now."

"Well, what about us farming together?" Jed asked in a disappointed tone. "Have you given that any thought?"

"Yes I have. You and Betty treat me like a son. I can't tell you how much that means to me. Still, I'd like to see the world. I'm young and I'd kind of like to do my own thing."

Tom stopped a moment to gather his thoughts, then continued somewhat clumsily. "You see Jed, I've noticed that Tanya's kind of got eyes for me. To be perfectly honest with you, I really like her too, but I'm sort of scared of what might happen if we were living so close together, for now anyway. Give another three or four years and there will be a big difference in her and for that matter in me too. I just wouldn't want to do anything to screw things up."

"Damn it anyway Tom," Jed said, after pausing a bit. "I must have been born blind. At times I guess I'm not too bright. Betty's been mentioning just what you've said, but it didn't sink into the old block. I appreciate your honesty and your concern for Tanya more than you'll ever know. Usually guys your age are just hot to trot and every girl is fair game. It's obvious that you care a great deal for her. It's most honorable of you."

After supper, Tom wanted another look at Bill's old house. Tanya lit a lantern and accompanied him. Once inside, Tom took her hand as they walked from room to room. It was not all that clean, but it had potential.

As they were checking the house out, Tom said. "I'm planning on enlisting in the Army, come spring. I thought you'd want to know."

Tanya was stunned. "Well what about you living in our yard and us being together?"

"You see, Tanya, we've got to remember, World War Two doesn't look like it will be over all that soon. If I volunteer, I'll have some choice in what I do and where I go. If I wait till I'm conscripted, those choices will be the Army's. We can write to each other."

"I'd like that very much, but it makes me so sad that you'll be going just when we're getting to know each other."

"It makes me sad too, but there's another reason. You see Tanya, we're both still pretty young and you're so pretty and all. To tell you the truth, I'm kind of hooked on you. At any rate," Tom continued, turning red, "I was thinking with the way we feel for each other and us being so young, it would be pretty easy for us to kind of get carried away."

"I guess it would be hard for us. Still, the thought of you going to war makes me so scared. I'm so afraid that something might happen to you."

"We'll just have to make the best of it," Tom concluded as they headed back to the house.

In January, Tanya and Tom sent each other birthday cards. Tom's card was very precious to Tanya and she kept it on her bedside table beside his first letter.

A week later, a Chinook blew in and the temperature climbed to fifty degrees Fahrenheit. Tanya was a girl with a mission. From Friday afternoon till Sunday morning, she cleaned and scrubbed the inside of Bill's old house. It was a labour of love, as it was awfully dirty. Tanya even used some of her mom's old curtains to hang in the windows.

In mid-February, Tom and Joe drove into Red Deer to the recruiting centre and signed up. They both passed their medicals and were told to return to work until their call-up.

Tom dropped Joe off at his folks' place, then stopped in Milden to get Tanya a Valentine. He wondered what sort of message to write on the card. Even though they weren't really going steady, they still thought a lot of each other. Finally he wrote in pencil:

"To Tanya, I think of you always."

Tom read the message over several times, but it didn't seem quite warm enough for his liking. He corrected it to read:

"To my Tanya, I think of you always."

Tom was only at their place ten minutes when Tanya beckoned for him to come with her.

"I have a small surprise for you."

She led Tom over to Bill's house. When Tom stepped inside, he whistled and exclaimed. "Holy mackerel! Who did all this?"

"I did," Tanya replied, her face turning red.

"Can I pay you for your work?" Tom asked, as they walked from room to room.

Tanya looked directly into Tom's eyes. "You already did by saving me from Ruben."

"Yeah, I know, but still."

"That's alright," Tanya interjected. "I'm so happy to be able to do it for you."

Tom reached into his pocket, brought out the Valentine card and handed it to Tanya. As she read the card, her eyes were glowing and her heart felt ready to burst.

"I guess I'll be heading out in another three weeks or so, whenever my call-up comes. I'll write you as often as I can and I won't go out with any other girls."

Tanya was deeply touched. First the valentine, then Tom's commitment to her.

"I'd like that very much," she finally replied.

Tom took Tanya in his arms and held her close. He brushed his face against her hair and whispered in her ear, "I guess it's best that we go see your folks now."

"This weekend is the happiest time in my life," Tanya said to her mom on Saturday evening when they were making supper. "I just wish Tom didn't have to join the Army."

"Some time back Tom talked to your dad about you and him. He told Dad he has such an attraction for you that living in the same yard before you both are older might cause problems."

"Yes, I know," replied Tanya, her face turning scarlet. "Tom told me all of that too, when he stopped in after Christmas."

"There's no question in your dad's or my mind that Tom's a very responsible young man. His concern for your welfare is remarkable for a fellow of his age. I know the separation will be hard for both of you, but he's a young man worth waiting for."

Tanya nodded. "It's funny to be so happy and yet at the same time so sad that Tom's going to be leaving."

On March fifteenth, Tom and Joe got their notice from the Army to report to Edmonton for basic training. They would spend three months in training before being assigned to their first posting. On Friday they quit their jobs and came out to Milden. Tom dropped Joe off at his folk's place and headed out to Osmonds'.

The weekend passed all too quickly for Tanya and Tom. They went for a couple of walks and on Sunday afternoon Tom took Tanya for a ride over to his old farm. They agreed to correspond by letter as often as they could. If all went well Tom would be back in Milden some time in early June. The recruiting centre told him that he would get a one week leave after basic training before going to his first posting.

On Monday morning, all the Parkers accompanied Tom to the train station in Milden. Tom bade them all goodbye, saving his last hug for Tanya. Then he was up the steps of the coach and the train pulled out.

CHAPTER
10

Army life was quite an eye opener for Tom. He had no problems with the rigorous physical training, as he was in top physical condition, but the military discipline chaffed his free spirit. He made up his mind the only way to handle it was not to let it get to him. While he was in training, an incident occurred that nearly got him court-martialed.

Sergeant DeFoe instructed them in the basics of hand-to-hand combat. DeFoe was a good boxer and fair in the martial arts. For minor misdemeanors, he had the young recruits do the customary push-ups or rounds on the track, but for more serious infractions, he'd make the soldiers put on the boxing gloves and go two rounds with him in the ring. Usually he wouldn't be too brutal with them, just give them a good pummeling. He did this in the name of training.

Tom's falling out with Defoe came the day they were practicing tactics for disarming an attacker. Tom was paired up with a very small, slight fellow. Defoe was not pleased with Tom for not vigorously attacking his partner. Tom just didn't have the stomach for roughing up someone so much smaller that himself.

After several attempts to get Tom to use more gusto in disarming his partner, Defoe's temper flared.

"I've had it with you, Parker!" he shouted. "You need a lesson on showing more gusto in this hand-to-hand conflict. I've seen eighty-year old ladies more aggressive than you. Once you're in active combat your life may well depend on what you learn here. Put on the gloves with me. Maybe working you over a bit will make you more aggressive."

While they were tying on his boxing gloves, Tom was feeling very uneasy. He witnessed other sparring matches where Defoe roughed up some privates fairly well. He decided the best way out of the mess was to just spar with Defoe without giving or taking too much punishment.

As he walked to the centre of the ring to meet Defoe, Tom was muttering under his breath, "What an ignorant ass."

Instead of starting to box, Defoe kept braying away. "Try to stay with me, if you can," he said sarcastically. "For God's sake, though, try to show us that you're a bit of a man. Did your old man not teach you anything, or was he gutless too?"

"Leave my dad out of this," Tom roared, catching Defoe square in the mouth with a bone-rattling left hook. Defoe wasn't ready and had no guard up. The suddenness and power of the blow stunned him. The Sergeant attempted to box with Tom, but his legs were pretty rubbery.

Just before the end of the first round, Defoe's guard dropped and Tom landed a brutal right to his jaw. Defoe went down and was unconscious for some time.

They held Tom in detention until an inquiry could be staged. Striking a Sergeant, let alone knocking one out cold, was a serious offence in the military. When it became known at the inquiry that DeFoe often used sparring matches as a form of discipline and that he challenged Tom to go two rounds with him, the threat of a court-martial blew over. DeFoe was instructed to use an alternative form of discipline. Tom's moment of glory was short-lived. DeFoe confined him to barracks for two weeks and rode him relentlessly for the rest of the time he was in basic training.

Although it was a lonely existence for Tom, Tanya's letters and the odd phone call helped a great deal. The realization that he would see her in June was also a great comfort to him.

Once Jed completed the seeding, he started working on the Rosser land. Tom returned from basic training on a Sunday in the middle of June. Jed had just finished the breaking. Jed and Tom worked hard at floating, disking and root harrowing the fifty acres of re-growth. On Friday evening, Jed called a moratorium on work in the root patch, as Tom would be leaving Monday morning for his new posting.

The last few days Tom and Tanya spent together sped by all too quickly. They recognized that it could be up to a year and a half before Tom would be back again. He would be posted to the Army Service Corps in the east, but that could change and he could be shipped overseas to the battle arena on short notice.

On Saturday evening, Tom and Tanya went to a movie in Milden. As they sat holding hands, Tanya whispered in Tom's ear, "I'm the luckiest girl in the world to have you for my boyfriend. Why do we have to be separated by the war?"

On Sunday morning, Tom drove to Red Deer to bid farewell to his mom and Ron. Ema was proud of her son, but so concerned for his safety. She already lost one man due to complications of injuries from the First World War. She did not want to lose another one to the Second World War.

As they parted, Tom held his mom in his arms. "Please Tom," Ema pleaded, "take care. We all want to see you back here hale and hearty."

The next few years would prove hard for Ema. Without fail, she prayed daily for her son's safe return.

Monday morning, the whole Osmond family accompanied Tom to the railroad station. Seeing the train hadn't arrived, Tom and Tanya went for a short walk. Hand in hand they strolled, both lost in thought, each dreading the separation just a few minutes away.

"I know it's going to be hard for you not to go out with other guys when I'm gone," Tom finally said, breaking the spell. "You're so damned good-looking that I'm sure you'll have to beat them off with a stick. If you do date, I'll understand. All I ask is for you to give me a chance when I get back and above all, don't do anything foolish, if you know what I mean. As for me, if I say I won't go out with other girls, that's what it will be. In keeping my word, I'm like my dad. He used to say, 'Once you've given your word, that's it. No excuses. No alibis.'"

"Well Tom, I promise that I'll remain true to you too," Tanya relied, after a long pause. "Anyway, I can't imagine any boys who can hold a candle to you."

Tanya stopped and looked directly into Tom's eyes.

"I feel so good when we're together. You'll never know how much I've prayed that you'd wait for me. You've made me the happiest girl in the world."

With the train ready to pull out, Tom hugged them all good-bye, including Jed. As he held Tanya close, she was crying and there were tears in Tom's eyes.

"Be brave now. I'll write often." He kissed her on the lips and whispered, "I love you, Tanya." Then he was up the steps and the train started to move.

Tanya cried most of the way home.

"I know how it hurts, but I'm sure Tom will come back to you," Betty said. "He's a very special young man and if he's the right one for you, you'll wait for him too. All we can do now is pray for his safety."

Writing her final exams helped keep Tanya's mind off her loneliness. Three days after finishing them, Tanya got her first letter from Tom. The moment she started reading it, she felt warm all over. Tom would be working in the Army Motor Service Corps, driving truck and handling freight destined for the overseas war effort. She re-read his letter many times.

While Tanya's letters tended to go on and on, Tom's were much more succinct. He was a romantic by nature and not at all backward about putting words to his private feelings. Tanya would occasionally blush at how forthright he was. Through their letters they were courting by mail and getting to know each other better.

During basic training, Tom and Tanya were just over a hundred miles apart. Now they were separated by three thousand miles and would probably have to wait eighteen months before Tom would get his leave. Corresponding by letter made her feel much closer to him. Tanya felt special that young as she was, Tom wanted her as his girl.

Jed and Tanya were soon back working on the re-growth. In addition to working down the breaking, there was also the haying and harvesting to do. Besides operating the equipment, Tanya spent many long days and weeks picking rocks and roots by hand. Betty and Jed were amazed at the difference one year made in their daughter. She'd changed from a girl into a young women.

A week before school was to start, the work on the re-growth was finally completed and the last root pile burned.

"Damn it girl, you've sure worked your rump off this summer," Jed quipped, as Tanya and he surveyed their accomplishment.

Tanya smiled. "I did it for Tom." Quietly she added, "I did it for us."

In September, Tanya and her grade ten classmates began attending the centralized high school in Milden. As there were no school buses operating in the region, the rural high school kids boarded out in town, usually returning to their homes for the weekends and holidays. Tanya found a place with Edith Marsh, an elderly widow the family knew well. Mrs. Marsh was a kind, motherly lady and the two hit it off immediately. Tanya helped the old lady with the household chores in return for free room and board. It would prove a good and lasting arrangement for both of them.

High school was quite a challenge for Tanya, contending with a new school, new classmates, new teachers and new courses. Having some of her old classmates attending school with her eased the transition some. Mrs. Marsh's company and Tom's letters also helped her through the first difficult months. Mom and Dad were only a phone call away.

To the boys in high school, Tanya was a real knockout, but she made it known that she had a boyfriend in the Service. Boys being boys though, this in itself didn't dissuade them all that much. Although it was flattering to have the boys trying to make time with her, it was a constant challenge balancing being friendly without being too familiar.

When it froze up that fall, Jed hired a contractor to cut and pile another fifty acres of bush on Tom's land. Tanya was delighted with the plan to bring some more of Tom's land under cultivation and insisted that it be kept a secret from him until he came home on leave.

After the crop was seeded the following spring, Jed burned the brush piles and began breaking the land with his tractor and a one bottom breaking plow. It was a far cry from breaking the re-growth that he had done the previous spring. Because the tree cover was relatively heavy the stumps were fairly large and Jed would be fortunate to break three acres a day.

Once school was out for the year, Tanya rolled up her sleeves as she had done the previous year and worked right alongside her dad and mom. This summer, the twins helped out. It was amazing how industrious twelve-year-olds could be when their labour was rewarded with some hard cash. It was again a labour of love for Tanya and she scoffed at the idea of accepting pay for her work. They finally finished the last root picking in mid-October.

It was now over a year since Tom left and Tanya was desperately hoping that he'd soon get his leave. She was just four months shy of sixteen and for all intents and purposes, her social life was non-existent. She occasionally visited with the girls in her class and always attended the school dances, but whenever a boy asked her out, she declined.

Tanya's closest friend, Harriet, did nothing to help her through these trying days. In fact, the counsel she gave only added to Tanya's problems.

"Life's too short, Tanya. Are you going to put your life on hold for the next three or four years or however long this dumb war lasts? Why don't you start dating some? Tom is on an adventure, probably having the time of his life. How do you know for sure that he's being faithful to you? He's probably kicking up his heels with the girls down east."

"That's not so," Tanya retorted. "He tells me in his letters that he loves me and is faithful to me. He's just as lonely as I am, maybe more so. I'll admit there have been a few boys wanting me to go out with them, but I'm not about to two-time Tom."

"Well Tanya, it's up to you, but life's passing you by. With your good looks, you could have half a dozen boys dating you."

Despite her resolve to remain faithful, Tanya couldn't help but look on in envy at the other young couples on dates. Whenever Tanya had moments of doubt about the wisdom of remaining true to a boyfriend she hadn't seen in over a year, she'd recall how it felt being in Tom's arms and how totally unimpressive the boys in school were, compared to him.

Things came to a head at the school Halloween dance. Tanya went to the dance by herself and danced several dances with Derrick, a grade eleven student. Tanya found the attention he was paying her quite flattering.

As they danced the last dance together, Tanya said, "I've really enjoyed myself tonight."

"I've enjoyed myself too, Tanya. There's going to be a party a couple of miles out of town at Reg's place. How about coming with me?"

"Sure, that sounds like fun," Tanya replied without thinking. The second the words were out of her mouth, though, she was having second thoughts.

"Would Tom understand? It's really not a date. Still, maybe I've betrayed his trust. Why do I always have to feel so guilty?"

She had given her word to Derrick though, and uncomfortable as it made her feel, she felt obligated to go along.

Tanya was uneasy when she found out that Reg's folks were away for the weekend, but despite her initial misgivings, was soon enjoying herself. They had a record player and did some dancing. As she danced she noticed that a few of the boys were getting drunk. Although not a teetotaler, it bothered Tanya seeing her classmates getting pie-eyed. Tanya finally accepted a bottle of beer, but left half of it, as it was not to her liking. It alarmed her that Derrick was drinking heavily. At one-thirty she asked him to take her home. He wasn't at all enthralled with the idea of leaving the party so soon, but Tanya prevailed. She offered to drive, but Derrick maintained he could manage.

Although not completely inebriated, Derrick was feeling no pain. He tried to put his arm around Tanya, but she pushed him away. Tanya was now anything but comfortable. She was even more concerned when Derrick turned off into a dead-end driveway about half a mile from town.

"Nothing to worry about," he said. "I just really need to talk to someone. I promise to behave myself."

Derrick had always treated Tanya with respect, so despite having some misgivings, she said she'd hear him out.

"I'm in an awful lot of crap with my folks, especially Dad. Nothing I do measures up for him. Just last night, the old idiot told me I might as well get a job, seeing my marks are so poor. He's no hot shot himself and if it wasn't for Mom working part-time, we'd starve. I don't know. I've been thinking of quitting school, but I don't have any money and if I did quit and got a job, he'd start bitching that I was ruining my life. No matter what I do, I just can't seem to win. You got any ideas?"

"It sounds like you're in a tight bind. I guess you'll just have to do whatever it takes not to get them too upset. Somehow you've got to try to get along with them and make the best of it."

Suddenly, without warning, Derrick was across the seat and had his arms around her. Before Tanya could push him away, he began kissing her madly.

"I need you Tanya, I need you so much," he blurted out.

Tanya untangled herself from Derrick and pushed him back to his side of the car.

"I'm not at all impressed with you," she snapped. "Take me home this instant!"

"What's the hurry?" Derrick asked seductively. "Why can't we have a little fun? I kind of think you like me some."

Derrick slid over towards her again. In the dim glow of the dash lights, Tanya saw that he was holding a condom out to her, while his other hand was groping for her leg.

"Damn you!" she screamed, shoving him back again and yarding her door open. "Just you wait till I tell my dad! He'll eat you alive and Tom will make mincemeat out of you when he comes home on leave!"

Tanya was absolutely furious and started walking back to town.

"Please Tanya," Derrick pleaded as he ran after her. "Give me another chance. I'm sorry for what I did. I should have had more brains. You know I'd have never tried this if I hadn't been drinking. Please, Tanya, let me drive you home. I've made a real ass of myself."

Tanya finally stopped walking.

"O.K., Derrick, but it's straight home."

"I'll do anything Tanya, just don't tell your dad or Tom," Derrick begged, as he drove Tanya to Mrs. Marsh's place. "They're sure not the type of guys I want to tangle with. I'm in enough trouble with my folks now without them beating on me."

"I'm not blaming you for everything, Derrick. It was partly my fault. Maybe I was sending you the wrong message. Tom's been gone now for close to fifteen months and I do get awfully lonely. I like you, but I love Tom. I probably shouldn't have gone to the party with you. I don't think we should tell anyone at school about this, do you?"

"Yea, that might be best."

"I won't tell Dad either. He'd only blow a fuse. I'll mention it to Tom in my letter, but I'll tell him that I'm partly to blame. I'm sorry I led you along."

"I'd like to apologize too. I acted like a fool."

It was a most subdued young man that bade Tanya goodnight and headed for home.

Tanya cried herself to sleep. She was more upset with herself than with Derrick.

When Tom got her next letter, he was nearly beside himself when he read the opening lines.

"Dearest Tom, I love you so, but I'm afraid I've betrayed your trust and been unfaithful to you."

Tom scanned the letter in a panic. He breathed a sigh of relief when he discovered that Tanya's definition of being unfaithful was not the same as his. After getting over his initial scare, he reflected on what a lucky guy he was to have such a loyal girlfriend. Their love had been tried, but remained true.

These were also trying days for Tom. Joe Bonner was in the Motor Corps with him and was constantly after Tom to kick up his heels like he was.

"Man oh man, Tom, if I had your strength, your size and your looks, I'd have a harem."

Although Tom went to base dances, he comported himself carefully and always figuratively saved the last dance for Tanya.

It would be the second Christmas Tom was away from his loved ones. The care packages from his mom, Tanya and

Betty helped a great deal, but there was still that longing in his heart to be home.

He would again be spending Christmas with the Chaplain and his wife. Shortly after Tom arrived at the base, Chaplain Burke looked him up and introduced himself.

"I try to make the acquaintance of all new soldiers arriving at the base. I see you're from Milden, Alberta, Tom. Where in Alberta would that be?"

"It's sort of mid-western, up against the foothills, about seventy miles north west of Red Deer."

"I recognize Parker is a common name, but would there be any chance you'd know of a Bill Parker who lost both legs in World War I? If I recall correctly, he came from west central Alberta. He mentioned something about being an Amateur Boxing Champ."

"Good grief!" Tom exclaimed, completely flabbergasted, "you're talking about my dad!"

"Sometimes the world is small. Bill always stuck out in my mind. I met him when I was doing Chaplin duty in the First World War. At the time, he was having a hard time accepting his injury. I always wondered how he made out. Is your dad still alive?"

"Dad passed away close to four years ago. It was hard going for him without legs but he managed to farm for twenty years. His heart finally gave out."

"Tell me Tom, was your dad a bitter man?"

"I can honestly say I never heard him complain about the loss of his legs. He was always looking for the bright side of things. Mom and I were pretty down when we realized how bad his heart was, but Dad remained positive to the end. He said he was just thankful for all the good things that God brought his way."

"You'll never know how happy that makes me feel," the Chaplin continued, tears slipping down his cheeks. "It makes me realize how rewarding my work can be. It's good to know that God used me to help a despondent young man become a positive person and live a productive life."

A close friendship developed between Tom and Chaplin Burke. The Chaplin and his wife would often have Tom over for Sunday supper.

Just after Christmas, Tom got notice that he would be sent overseas in the last week of February transporting supplies to the front lines. He would be getting a two week leave before being sent to his new posting.

To phone rural western Alberta from the Maritimes was not all that easy a task during the war years, seeing you had to contend with rural party lines. Nine chances out of ten, the lines would be either busy or out of order. To by-pass busy times, Tom tried to phone after midnight on weekends. Despite the lateness of the hour, it was common for some of the neighbours to rubber in on incoming calls. This time, when he finally got through to Tanya, he heard a rash of clicks. By the end of the phone call, half of the neighbourhood knew that he would be arriving at Milden on Saturday.

CHAPTER
11

Tom managed to leave the base one day ahead of schedule and arrived in Milden on Friday afternoon. As the weather was decent, he left his bags at the station and walked to the high school. Tom was familiar with the layout of the school from Tanya's letters. He found her classroom and knocked on the door. It was three twenty-five, just five minutes before the end of the school day.

Mrs. McNaught, Tanya's English teacher, answered the door and stepped out into the hall.

"I wonder if I could see my girlfriend, Tanya Osmond?" Tom asked.

"Well, well. You must be Tom Parker. Tanya has told everyone that you're coming home on leave. I knew your folks. Your dad would be so proud to see you in uniform."

All the class had their eyes glued on the door as Mrs. McNaught stepped back into the room.

"Tanya, a handsome young serviceman is here to see you."

Tanya leapt out of her desk, raced for the door and jumped into Tom's arms. Their long wait was over! They were still hugging when the buzzer rang.

Hand in hand, they walked to Mrs. Marsh's place. They just couldn't stop talking and when they paused to catch their breath, they'd do a bit more hugging and kissing.

"So this is the young man who keeps all the letters coming," Mrs. Marsh said, after Tanya introduced her to Tom. "Doesn't he look handsome in his uniform, Tanya?" Turning to Tom, she added, "Tanya's such a responsible, hard working young lady. I honestly don't know what I'd do without her help."

Mrs. Marsh would not hear of Tom and Tanya leaving without having lunch. "This will be my homecoming celebration for Tom," she said. Tanya and Tom couldn't turn that offer down.

While Tanya was helping Mrs. Marsh with the lunch, Tom phoned the Bonners to make arrangements with Fred to pick up his car.

"I had your car running last fall," Fred said. "It's not too cold, so I'll go out and try to start it now. If it won't go, I'll come with my car and take you and Tanya to her folks' place."

Tom, Tanya and Mrs. Marsh finished lunch just as Fred arrived with Tom's car.

"That son of ours sure doesn't know how to write," Fred said as they were driving back to his place. "Have you heard what Joe's up to, Tom? We haven't heard from him in over six months."

"We're still stationed together. I was talking to him a few days ago. He's supposed to be getting his leave some time in

March. The Base Doctor told him that he probably wouldn't be shipped overseas because he's got asthma. I'm going to be sent to the battle zone as soon as I return from my leave."

Once they dropped Fred off, Tom and Tanya headed out to the farm. "Would you like to have a look at your land?" Tanya asked when they reached the old Bill Rosser road. "We had a Chinook last week and the road should be bare."

"We can give it a try."

When they got to the old yard site, Tom exclaimed, "Good Lord, what have you guys done now? I can see that you've cropped the re-growth your dad and I worked on, but you've cleared another chunk of bush and brought it under cultivation!"

"Well, Dad and I finished the re-growth a year and a half ago. Dad seeded it last spring and got a good crop of oats. Last winter he cleared another fifty acres. He broke it in June and we brought it under cultivation last summer. I wanted to keep it as a surprise for you."

"Man, I can hardly believe this. How will I ever be able to pay you guys back?"

"Well you can start right now," said Tanya as she sprang into Tom's arms. "I love you Tom. Remember, we didn't do all this just for you, we did it for us."

"Are you sort of saying you're planning on us getting hitched?" Tom asked with a smile.

"Yes, I guess so," Tanya replied, turning scarlet.

"I love you so much it would take an army and then some to keep me from marrying you," Tom said, holding Tanya tight.

Despite the cool breeze, their embrace was generating a lot of heat. The fact that Tom's hands were doing a bit of exploratory work certainly wasn't helping matters any.

"We'd better leave before we get carried away," Tanya whispered.

Betty, Jed and the twins were surprised when Tom's car pulled into their yard. They spent a joyful evening getting caught up on their respective lives. Jed brought out a bottle of sherry and they all drank to their good fortune. In fact, Jed and Tom had quite a few drinks to their good fortune.

Lars and Sybil McGilvary, the Crawfords and the Blakeleys dropped over later in the evening to join in Tom's homecoming celebration. Lars played a good fiddle, while Sibyl accompanied him on the guitar. Lars and Mel had the presence of mind to bring along some more liquid refreshments, in case Jed's cache ran out. Sure enough, before the evening was over, their supplies of spirits were needed. They played, sang and danced till two a.m. Tanya and Tom sang together again. Throughout the evening Tanya and Tom were never far apart. If they weren't holding hands or stealing a kiss, there was a hand on the arm, or around the shoulder. At two-thirty, everyone turned in for the night, or what was left of it.

By nine-thirty the next morning, Jed and Tom were out doing the chores, not feeling anywhere near as frisky as the night before. By the time they were finished, Betty and Tanya had breakfast made. The twins, showing more wisdom than their elders, slept in.

Over breakfast, Tom broached the subject of the improvements made on his land. "I still owe you guys three thousand on the purchase price. Now with all the improvements you've made, I'll be in a real bind finding the money to pay you off."

"Look here Tom," Jed responded. "I don't want to hear another word about it. The money I got from your crop last year, I took off what you owe us. As for the improvements, we can straighten out on that after this damned war is over. After all, you're fighting for this country. This is the least we can do for you. Now that's the end of this discussion. Period, Period, Period."

Tom smiled. "Well, thanks everyone, but I will pay you all back some day, somehow."

After breakfast, Tom phoned his mom and Ron and made arrangements to visit them and the grandparents in the afternoon.

"After I finish high school, I plan to go to normal school and into teaching," Tanya said to Tom once they were on the road. "Hopefully by then the war will be over and you'll be home."

"I hope so too," Tom replied, pulling Tanya close. "Seeing we'll be getting married when I get out of the Service, what do you think about us getting engaged now?"

"Well, Mom and I have been talking about that. She wonders if getting engaged now might be unwise, since we're going to be separated for so long. Much and all as I'd love to wear your engagement ring, I kind of think she's right."

"Maybe so, but if we don't get engaged now, at least we should exchange rings."

They went to a jewelry store in Red Deer to buy their rings. Tanya's gold ring had the initials T&T engraved inside a heart, while Tom's ring was sterling silver with identical engraving. Tanya put Tom's ring on a silver chain and wore it as a necklace while Tom wore Tanya's ring on his little finger.

Tom and his mom were overjoyed to see each other again. It was nowhere near as boisterous an evening as the previous one, since Ron was a teetotaler and only approved of hymns for music.

From his mom's letters, Tom knew that occasionally there was static between Ron and her. Being unsure of himself, Ron took Ema's memories of Bill as a threat to his manhood and was forever trying to paint Bill as a loser.

Because Tom stood up to him when the farm was to being sold, Ron also felt him a threat. Notwithstanding the tension between them, the evening passed without a problem.

At eleven p.m., Tom and Tanya drove the grandparents home. Like Ema, they were very taken with Tom's choice of a girlfriend. After a homecoming celebration drink, Tanya and Tom excused themselves.

Since the weather was still fairly mild, Tom and Tanya decided to park and talk a bit. It wasn't long before their necking had the windows steamed up. Tom was sitting with his back against the passenger door when suddenly, the door was yanked open. Tom fell out of the car backwards and landed in a heap on the ground. A young city policeman on his beat noticed the parked vehicle and was checking it out for illegal drinking and conveyance.

Tom scrambled to his feet, buttoning up his shirt with some difficulty. Meanwhile Tanya was trying to right herself in as dignified a manner as possible.

"Just checking for liquor," the officer said.

After shining his flashlight about the inside of the car, he continued. "Everything seems in order. Home on leave I suppose?"

"Yes sir."

"Well, have a good evening and carry on, or whatever."

"Thanks," Tom said sheepishly.

Still smiling, the officer strode off on his beat.

Tom and Tanya decided that they'd had enough embarrassment for one night. As the lights were out when they got to Tom's folks' place, they kissed good night and went to their respective bedrooms.

The fall from the car and the officer's visit did little to dampen Tom's earthy appetite. As for Tanya, she wasn't having all that easy a time falling asleep either. Being a determined sort, Tom felt his mission was to sneak into Tanya's bedroom without waking up Ron or his mom. As he crept stealthily along the hall, he felt certain the folks were lying awake, just waiting for the floor to creak.

Tanya held her breath as she heard Tom approach and tiptoe up to her bed.

Tanya's bed posed the next challenge. It had an old style, open steel coil spring base and even the thought of turning over made it creak. Using a great deal of patience, Tom finally crawled under the covers without waking the whole household, or so he thought. Tanya was uptight about being in bed with Tom, especially while they were guests at Tom's folks' place. With Tom embracing her though, her reticence soon began to fade and within a few minutes, they where back at where they had left off before being interrupted by the police officer.

Tom slipped Tanya's pajamas top off and began caressing her breasts. Tanya was becoming aroused and her breathing was getting quite heavy. Although she felt very stimulated, Tanya was still having qualms about them being so intimate. To add to her uneasiness, she was starting to have flashbacks of Ruben's attack. As Tom's hand crept down to her stomach, she panicked and grabbed his arm to keep him from going any further.

"Please Tom," she cried, "I'm just so frightened. I can see Ruben attacking me again."

"That lowbred son of a bitch! How long is he going to haunt us?"

"I don't know, but please go a little slower. It's especially bad here in your mom's house. I just need a little more time to work things through."

"Looks like we don't have a choice," Tom said, after collecting himself. "I'll just have to try to reign in a bit. I guess I'm rushing things and you're right, this is the wrong place."

"Thank you for being so understanding," Tanya said, as she hugged Tom. "It shows how much you love me."

Tom crept back to his room, suffering some from being over- stimulated.

At the breakfast table Tom and Tanya were under the impression that the older folk were oblivious to their nocturnal visit, but Ron and Ema had been awake during the rendezvous. Ema had her hands full keeping Ron from apprehending Tom when he heard him sneaking into Tanya's room.

Out of deference to his mom, Tom and Tanya accompanied the folks to church. Tom was not at all impressed with the young minister. Pastor Jones seemed intent on brow-beating the congregation and flailed away at them with complete abandon in a forty-five minute harangue. Tom thought of leaving half-way through the sermon, but knew that would upset his mom.

Ron was very disturbed with Ema for not allowing him to intercept Tom the previous night and for forbidding him from challenging him in the morning. As a church deacon, he maintained it was his Christian duty to keep his home a holy place. It deeply disturbed him that two unmarried people engaged in carnal relations in his house.

Pastor Jones was single and often invited out for meals by members of the congregation. After informing the pastor about Tom being in Tanya's room the previous evening, Ron invited the pastor home for dinner.

Ema was most annoyed with Ron for inviting the pastor home for their last meal with Tom before he was posted overseas. It was, however, too late to change things, so she decided to make the best of it.

Tanya was helping Ema prepare lunch in the kitchen while Ron was left with the impossible task of entertaining Tom and Pastor Jones in the living room.

After making some small talk, Pastor Jones zeroed in on Tom. "It has been brought to my attention by Deacon Ron that you and your young lady friend were engaged in sexual activity in her bedroom last night."

He reached for his Bible with the intention of reading the appropriate passage on the sin of fornication, but did not complete his mission.

Tom was taken aback, but only for a moment. He leapt from his chair, plucked Pastor Jones's Bible from his hand and laid it on the table.

"I want to tell you something, you pathetic excuse for a man," Tom roared, hovering above him. "If I didn't care for my mom a great deal, I'd throw you right through the door. If either you or Ron ever again mention what you think Tanya and I did in the privacy of her room, I'll make you both hard to catch. For your information, Tanya and I were not screwing in her room last night and if we were, it certainly wouldn't be any of your business."

Pastor Jones was very shaken and made no reply.

Ron remained riveted to his seat. He was not at all accustomed to seeing such a show of anger. Ema warned him about pushing Tom too far, but he really hadn't expected this.

Tanya and Ema heard the commotion and came running into the front room.

"Please, Tom," implored Ema, "what's going on?"

"This lame husband of yours told Pastor Jones that Tanya and I were screwing in her room last night. Well we weren't. Jones started to give me a hard time about it and I'm afraid I lost my cool. I guess you heard the rest of it."

"Did you tell Pastor Jones that?" Ema hissed at Ron.

"Yes I did," Ron replied hesitantly, not taking his eyes off the floor. "As the spiritual head of this household, it's my duty to use whatever means I can to keep this house free of sin."

"And just who made you judge?" Ema cried. "You call yourself a Christian, then you go out of your way to be hurtful to Tom and Tanya. As I told you last night, what Tom and Tanya do in private is none of our business. And you, Pastor Jones, as a single man you should know better than to give counsel on these matters. I'm just so upset with both of you. Come on Tanya and Tom, we'll have lunch in the hotel."

"I'm sorry for upsetting you, Mom," Tom began once they were in the car. "I just couldn't take any crap from those two. Yes, Tanya and I were together in her room last night, but that's none of their business. I'm fighting to save this country just like Dad did and those two gutless wonders try to lecture me."

"I'm the one who's sorry," Ema replied, on the verge of tears. "I've tried my level best to make your visit enjoyable. At times like this, I wonder why I married that man. He acted like a real rectum. You're a threat to him, Tom. I'm just so ashamed and disappointed. I wanted so much for you and Ron to get along better."

"Don't be ashamed," Tanya said. "It certainly wasn't your fault. You can't blame yourself for what Ron and Pastor Jones did. Tom and I know you've tried your level best. Please try not to feel bad about it."

"Tanya, I see that you too are a peacemaker," Ema quietly responded. "I always had to be one with Tom's dad and for that matter, with Tom too. I miss them so much Tanya, so much. I guess you'll have to take over from me and see that my boy doesn't get himself into too much trouble."

When Ema, Tom and Tanya returned after lunch, Ron and Pastor Jones were gone. Ema desperately wanted Ron there with her to bid Tom farewell.

With Tom being posted to the fighting zone, she was very concerned for his safety. As she hugged him goodbye, Ema was crying. "Take care, Son," she whispered. "I'll be praying for you every day. Remember Tom, I lost your dad because of the war. Please be extra careful."

"I've had it with you!" Ema shouted at Ron when he got home. "The way you treat my son! You didn't even have the decency to be here to wish him goodbye. I'm right up to the neck with you, Ron. One more time and I'm gone. Then you can go live with your Pastor Jones. Just remember this, if I leave, I'm gone for good!"

It would be an understatement to say that Ron was contrite and on his best behavior for quite some time.

The week of Tom's leave went by quickly. Tom drove Tanya to school in the morning, spent the day visiting old friends, then he drove home with Tanya when school was out.

On Saturday, they spent the day by themselves driving around the countryside and ended up at Tom's old home place. Tom carried in some wood, and within minutes, had a roaring fire going. In an hour's time, the temperature went from ten degrees to eighty degrees Fahrenheit.

Tom found an old kettle, melted some snow and brewed up a pot of tea. By the light of the old gas lamp, Tanya and Tom sat at the kitchen table reminiscing about when they met.

"You'll never know how many nights I lay awake, hoping against hope that you would wait for me," Tanya said. "Now we're together. You were so kind not putting pressure on me at your folks' place the other night."

Tom took Tanya by the hand and led her into his old bedroom. He lit a coal-oil lamp and put it on the dresser.

"When I was fourteen or fifteen, I used to lay in this bed, trying to imagine what it would be like having a beautiful, sexy girl by my side," Tom said, holding Tanya close. "Now my dreams have come true."

Whether it was the heat of the house, or the heat of the moment, Tom and Tanya were soon undressed. As they began exploring the wonders of each other's naked bodies it wasn't long before they were into some mighty heavy petting.

As they lay contentedly in each other's arms, Tom whispered. "It's hard for me to believe that tonight is just the first night in a lifetime of loving you."

Tanya cried softly in Tom's arms. She was so much in love, so grateful that Tom waited for her.

The lights of a vehicle coming up the driveway sent them scrambling for their clothes. They managed to get dressed before the knock came at the door.

It was Boris Yamshack. "How are you doing Tom? Home on leave I suppose. I saw the lights and thought I should come over and check things out."

Tom introduced him to Tanya and while she made a pot of coffee, Boris brought Tom up-to-date on all the local happenings. As Boris got up to leave, he again extended his invitation for Tom to stay in the house anytime he was around.

Once Boris left, Tanya and Tom returned to the bedroom. The house had cooled down enough for them to get under the covers. After first checking out the bedding for mice, they undressed and got into bed.

Suddenly Tanya blurted out, "Please, Tom, we'd better stop."

"Why do we always have to stop just when we're getting warmed up?" Tom sighed. "I guess you're right, though. We both agreed not to go all the way."

"I think we're both too hot-blooded to carry on like this without losing control," Tanya added. "Maybe we shouldn't tempt ourselves anymore."

They dressed and soon were on their way back to Tanya's folks' place.

"Thanks again for not putting pressure on me," Tanya said as they were driving along. "It wouldn't have taken much more and I'd have said, 'let's go for it.'"

Tom smiled. "You know, there are times I wish I was a bit more of a rotter."

They spent Sunday quietly with Tanya's family. Everyone was preoccupied with the thought of Tom leaving. Tanya and Tom felt glum as they realized that this would be their last day together, perhaps until the war ended. They both tried desperately to be cheerful, but it wasn't easy.

On Monday morning, all awoke early. Tom had not slept well. Having finished the chores, they sat down for what was to be their last meal together for a long time. Although everyone tried desperately to be upbeat, any bits of cheer were at best short-lived.

With breakfast over, they all climbed into Tom's car and headed for the station in Milden. Tanya secretly hoped that the car would break down, forcing Tom to miss the train, but no such luck. As on their last parting, Tom and Tanya had time to go for a short walk before the train arrived.

"You've made me the happiest girl in the world," Tanya said to Tom, as they walked, hand in hand. "I'll never forget the wonderful times we shared, especially the time in your bedroom on the old farm. I'm just dreading the thought of you going."

"Try to be positive, dear. I'll write as soon as I get to my new posting."

The train was about ready to pull out when they returned to the platform. Tom hugged them all goodbye, saving his last farewell hug for his Tanya. As he held her close and kissed her, Tanya was sobbing. There were also tears in Tom's eyes. Tanya didn't want to let go of him. Finally the conductor tapped Tom on the shoulder and he was up the coach steps. Slowly the train pulled out.

Long after every one else returned to the car, Tanya stood on the station platform, tears slipping down her cheeks. "Will I ever see my precious Tom again?" she whispered. "Please, God, keep him safe."

CHAPTER
12

As they pulled away from the station, Tanya was crying uncontrollably. "Please, Mom, I can't go back to school like this. Can I come home with you for a bit?"

"Of course you can, dear," Betty replied, putting her arm around her. "We'll drive you in to school tomorrow."

Tanya did her best to bear down with her school work, but she was fighting a losing battle as her despondency wouldn't lift. Finally, three weeks after Tom left, things came to a head. When she couldn't control her crying in class one morning, the school phoned her folks, and her dad came in to pick her up.

"You're feeling pretty rough, eh?" Jed said, pulling Tanya close. "Is it Tom's leaving for the war zone that's still upsetting you, or is there something else?"

"I don't think so, Dad," Tanya sobbed. "It's just that I'm so worried and lonely for Tom. I'm really trying to hold up, but I can't seem to manage."

As they drove home, Jed continued. "It hurts Mom and me to see you so upset. I've got a few thoughts that might help you some. It seems to me that you're falling all to pieces while Tom is risking his life to keep this country free. He needs all your support, but you're coming apart at the seams. I don't think that's really fair to him, do you?"

"I guess not, but now that Tom is near the front lines and involved with the actual fighting, I'm terrified that something awful will happen to him. God only knows how hard I'm trying to keep up with my school work."

"You've heard me talk about coming to Alberta and how bitter I was over the death of my first wife and baby daughter. I was well on my way to becoming a sour old codger controlled by anger and then I started to reach out to help your mom. The more I helped your mom, the less bitter I felt. If I hadn't reached out to help her, I'd still be in my little shack, all by myself, being right peed off with my lot in life and feeling powerfully sorry for myself."

Tanya stopped crying and began gathering her thoughts, as her dad went on.

"Other than the pain of your separation, you're a fortunate young woman. Make a list of the things you can be grateful for and then a list of the things that are negative for you. On the positive list, start with: I am a beautiful, kind, young woman. I can vouch that you're both. Right now you're reaching out to help Mrs. Marsh. Start reaching out again in your letters to Tom. The encouragement you give him will not only help him, but will be healing for you too."

"Thanks Dad, I needed that," Tanya whispered, as she slid across the seat and gave him a kiss on the cheek.

That evening, Tanya made a list of things to be grateful for and then a list of negative things. To her astonishment, she discovered that the positives far overshadowed the negatives. It was a turning point for her and while she still had her not-so-good days, she was beginning to get control of her life again.......

Tom was now stationed near the battle zone, trucking everything from soup to ammunition to the front lines. The convoys were not in imminent danger of planned attack, but there was always the possibility of an enemy aircraft slipping through the lines and strafing or bombing them. There was also the added danger that when near their drop off, a stray artillery round could take them out.

Tom still tried to write Tanya every three weeks or so. Now his letters were opened before they were mailed for security reasons. The soldiers might inadvertently mention classified information in their letters and there was always the chance that the mail could fall into enemy hands.

Tom's letters were censored at Tanya's end, albeit for different reasons. When she read Tom's letters to the family, there were large sections she had to delete. Tom had a natural bend for writing poetry and would often end his letter with a couple of stanzas of an erotic love poem. Tanya often blushed at the explicit, forthright language he used and it made her long to be his wife. The twins, being curious, asked Tanya to read the unabridged versions of Tom's letters, but she drew the line there. She managed to find a safe hiding place for the letters and despite Ben's rigorous searches, he never found them.

Once school was out, Tanya decided to stay at home and work on her own project, rather than look for summer work.

The old Bill Rosser house hadn't been finished on the outside and was in bad need of siding. As well, the inside needed to be wallpapered. Jed used some of the money from Tom's crop to cover the cost of the materials and was there for technical advice when Tanya needed it.

With Ben's assistance, the work began. It took two and a half weeks to complete the siding and another week to give it two coats of paint. At times, Tanya worked alone, as Ben would be helping his dad with haying. It was her project and she was not above telling her dad to butt out whenever he tried to oversee the job too much. The wallpapering and interior painting was a real test of brotherly-sisterly forbearance. Notwithstanding their disagreements and occasional fights, Tanya and Ben finished by mid-August. Tanya felt proud of their accomplishments. As with the land clearing, it was her gift of love to Tom and she again declined any wages.

Grade eleven seemed to last at least a hundred years for Tanya. As Mrs. Marsh was failing, Tanya was doing almost all of the housework. Although still mentally alert, physical activity was becoming difficult for the old lady. Tanya didn't mind the extra responsibilities, since being busy helped keep her mind off being lonely. Just before school let out for the year, Mrs. Marsh's daughter, Mona, met Betty and Tanya at her mom's place.

"Mom and I have been talking about what's going to happen come fall," Mona began. "If you'd stay with her for your grade twelve year, Tanya, Mom would be willing to pay you twenty dollars a month in addition to free room and board. Mom looks on you as a daughter and it would make her very happy if she could spend at least one more year here in her home."

Tanya was very pleased with the new arrangement. Mrs. Marsh was like her second mother and she wouldn't have to worry about getting a new place to stay.

Through one of their teachers, Tanya and Harriet found summer employment in Banff at one of the large hotels. The money wasn't all that glorious, but the scenery was. They did a fair amount of biking and hiking after work and on their days off.

Harriet marveled at how faithfully Tanya wrote on Tom's letter every evening. Fidelity was not a priority for her. Despite having a steady boyfriend back in Milden, she was soon dating one of the fellows who worked in the hotel. Harriet introduced Tanya to a young busboy named Minus and suggested they double date. Tanya declined. She knew what Harriet was up to. If she could convince her to two-time Tom, Harriet would feel more comfortable with her own lack of commitment!

Minus tried hard to shine up to Tanya and although the attention was flattering, Tanya was determined not to make the same mistake she made with Derrick. Minus had to settle for a platonic friendship.

In September, Tanya again moved in with Mrs. Marsh. It was now eighteen months since Tom had left. She felt she couldn't bear the loneliness much longer. Every time she saw another couple holding hands or kissing, her heart died a little. Although she prayed daily for Tom's welfare, she constantly worried for his safety, as he was now exclusively hauling ammunition to the front lines.

The evening of October twenty-third, Tanya's world shattered. She just started her homework when there was a knock at the door. Strangely, her heart began racing wildly in fear. She opened the door. It was her mom and dad. A quick glance at their somber faces confirmed her worst fears.

With panic gripping her stomach, she blurted out, "There's news from the Army, isn't there?"

Her dad nodded gravely.

"Its bad news isn't it?" she cried. "Oh please God, don't let it be Tom."

"I'm afraid it is," Jed replied, placing his hand on Tanya's shoulder.

"Oh my God, I can't take this," she sobbed. She went to her mother and collapsed into her arms.

Betty held her distraught daughter and they sobbed uncontrollably.

The horrible scene was all too familiar during the war years. A loved one would not be returning.

The telegram from the Army read: Regret to inform you: Tom Parker missing in action: Presumed dead.

Jed alone offered a glimmer of hope. "The telegram didn't say, killed in action, only missing in action, presumed dead." His wishful thinking fell on deaf ears.

Mrs. Marsh phoned for her daughter to come for her and Tanya and her folks left for home.

"Why would God do this to Tom?" Tanya sobbed hysterically. "Why would He allow Tom to save me from Ruben and let us come together, if he was going to allow him to be killed? I'm just so mad at God!"

Tanya sobbed all evening, at times lashing out at God, at times trying to come to grips with the painful realization that her beloved Tom was no more. Her mom and dad tried desperately to comfort her, but their efforts didn't seem to help. As Tanya lay in bed she tried to pray, but the words stuck in her throat. Finally she cried herself to sleep.

Shortly after falling asleep, Tanya had a vivid dream. She saw a convoy of trucks winding along a dirt road heading for the front lines. She knew Tom was driving the lead truck and that the trucks were loaded with ammunition. A light rain was falling and she could see puddles on the road. Tanya saw Tom's truck round a corner and almost collide with a small boy and a few cows crossing the road. To her horror she saw the truck swerve into the ditch and start bounding out of control. Tom leapt from the truck, hit the ground, rolled a few times and came to rest under a thicket. Tanya heard the earth-shattering explosion as Tom's truck flipped high into the air and landed upside down on a huge boulder. She woke with a start and cried out to her folks.

Jed was instantly awake and ran into Tanya's room with Betty right on his heels. Tanya was standing by her bed wide-eyed and breathing heavily.

"Mom, Dad, its amazing! I just had this wonderful dream. Tom is still alive. I saw his truck swerve into the ditch, hit a large boulder and explode, but I saw him jump from the vehicle before it blew up. I know he's hurt, but he's still alive. I just know that, Mom and Dad. Don't ask me how I know, but I just feel it so strongly!"

Neither Betty nor Jed knew what to say, much less what to do. They all had a cup of cocoa and again turned in for the night. As Tanya lay in her bed, tears of relief were glistening in her eyes.

"Dear Lord, thank you so much for saving my Tom. He's hurt bad, but I know you'll help him. I'm sorry for being mad at you. Thank you for the dream." She continued praying for Tom's well-being until she drifted off to sleep........

At day break Tom and the other drivers in the convoy had left base camp with loads of artillery ammunition. It had been drizzling all night and the roads were getting slippery. Tom was driving in the lead position. Some two hundred yards separated the trucks. As the number two truck rounded a sharp corner he saw a huge fireball and heard an earth shattering explosion. The truck drivers couldn't see Tom's truck ahead so stopped to investigate. They walked right by Tom, but the thicket was so thick they couldn't see him. Tom was loaded with three tons of ammunition and all they found was a large smoldering crater, close to thirty feet in diameter and a few scattered pieces of the truck. Assuming that Tom died in the explosion, they radioed base camp and continued on their way.

By the time a medic unit arrived, steady rain was falling. They did an extensive search, but like the truck drivers, walked past the briar thicket and concentrated on the site of the explosion. Other than the few truck parts, all they found was two coins. Feeling sure the coins were in Tom's pocket, they were positive he had been killed. The search was called off and they headed back to base camp.

The medical officer made out his report and the telegram "Missing in action," was sent.

If it hadn't been for Tom's excellent physical condition, the injuries from his forced jump could have been fatal. Tom lay unconscious under the briar thicket until midnight. As the night wore on, he began floating in and out of consciousness.

Then he heard a voice he knew so well. "I'm here with you, Son."

"Dad, is that you?" Tom whispered, fighting hard to remain conscious.

"Yes it is and I'm watching over you. I'm proud of you for taking the ditch to save the youngster. You're badly hurt, but you'll make it. Your Tanya received the telegram that you're missing in action. I've already been to her in a dream to give her hope. She knows you're alive. I must go now."

"Thanks for looking in on her, Dad. I know that will comfort her." Tom tried to open his eyes, but again lapsed back into darkness.

As day was breaking, Tom regained consciousness. He was suffering a lot of pain in his chest and knee. His memory was hazy and his head felt like it would explode. It took him several minutes to drag himself out from the depression under the thicket and up the muddy slope to the road. He had a long wait before an officer and a radioman came by in a jeep.

They got Tom on board and returned to the field hospital. After examining his injuries, the doctor made out his report and sent another telegram correcting the telegram sent the previous day.

At breakfast, Tanya was the most cheerful of the lot. "I just know Tom will come back to me, I just know it. Before I fell asleep, this very strange feeling of warmth and peace come over me. I'm sure God was telling me that all will be well with Tom."

Although Betty and Jed were hoping desperately that Tanya was right, they feared that her dream may have been caused by wishful thinking.

They were finishing breakfast when the phone rang. Tanya leapt to her feet and grabbed the receiver. It was the station agent in Milden with a telegram for Jed, from the Army.

"Would you please read it to me?" she asked eagerly.

"I'm sorry, but I'm not allowed to read it to anyone except Jed."

Jed took the phone from Tanya's hand. "It's O.K., Larry, go ahead and read it to my daughter."

Tanya listened, her heart racing, as the station agent started reading the telegram.

"Further to telegram sent you two p.m. October twenty-third: Be advised: Tom Parker reported missing in action, presumed dead, has been located: Is now hospitalized in serious but stable condition."

Tanya gave a cry of joy and between sobs of relief, whispered, "Thank you God. Thank you for saving my Tom."

After a week in the field hospital. Tom was sent on a flight back to England. Because of his head injuries, he was checked out by a neurologist and an ophthalmologist in a large military hospital near London.

"We will have your knee operated on when an operating room becomes available," the neurologist stated. "Your broken ribs, though painful, will heal up in about a month's time. The injuries that are causing your double vision though, are more serious and have us somewhat concerned. We'll be doing some extensive testing today. Out of curiosity, Tom, do you play any musical instruments?"

"I play the guitar a little. I'm not all that good, but I get by. Why do you ask?"

"Just part of our testing. Have you tried to play since your injury?"

"No sir. I haven't had a guitar in my hands for about eighteen months."

After lunch, the doctor surprised Tom by handing him a guitar.

"I don't know if this guitar is in tune, but could you play me a tune?"

Tom took the guitar, spent a few minutes tuning it, then tried playing a song requiring a bit of finger picking. To his astonishment and dismay, he couldn't coordinate his hands. He struggled for several minutes before handing the guitar back to the doctor.

"Damn it," he said in frustration, "it just won't work any more. You probably don't believe I ever played a guitar."

"Yes I do and I have another test for you." He handed Tom a long dress tie. "Put this around your neck as if you had a dress shirt on and tie the knot for me."

"No problem," Tom said confidently. "What will it be, a Windsor or a four-in-hand knot?"

"Whatever."

Tom flipped the tie around his neck and started on a Windsor knot. Again, to his horror, he discovered he couldn't do it. As with the guitar, he struggled for several minutes before handing the tie back to the doctor in frustration.

"Just what in hell is going on?"

"It's an indication that you're suffering loss of fine motor coordination. I'm not surprised considering the crack you got on your head. Your loss of fine motor coordination, your headaches and your memory loss are all symptomatic of a head injury. All these problems should correct themselves in four to six months. I wish we could be as optimistic about your double vision. The injury that often causes double vision is a severe blow to the back of the head. I have discussed your condition with the ophthalmologist who checked you over yesterday. He feels that because of the complexity of your injury, an operation would not help you any. He said that as yet, they don't have the expertise to treat your condition. In his opinion your double vision will remain static. I see that you have already discovered, by holding your head down and cocked to the left, you have a small field of focused vision. I imagine this will help you for driving a vehicle and operating equipment. Unfortunately, you will always have to read and write with one eye."

"We will be recommending you be given a medical discharge because of your sight problem. The Army will assess you for a pension when you return to Canada. We'll be keeping you here until your headaches show signs of subsiding."

After they operated on Tom's knee, he spent three weeks in a rehabilitation centre. His knee finally healed to the point where he could walk with a cane and his headaches were becoming infrequent and much less severe. Adjusting to his double vision was very frustrating, but he was slowly learning to cope with his loss.

Tom often recalled his dad's words before he died. Like his dad he vowed to be thankful for his good fortune, rather than being bitter and resentful for what was taken from him.

Towards the end of November, Tom returned to Canada for his pension assessment and discharge from the army. He was able to walk without a cane, albeit with a bit of a limp. Finally on December fourteenth, Tom boarded the train for his return trip to Milden, back to his Tanya, family and friends. As the miles slipped by, uppermost in his mind was how Tanya would react to his crossed eyes. "Will she be able to handle it?" he pondered. "Will she still love me?"

CHAPTER
13

Tom's train pulled into Milden in the early evening. Tanya, her family and a large contingent of friends and relatives were there to greet him. As Tom stepped off the train, Tanya rushed into his arms. Their long wait was over!

Everyone gathered at the Osmonds' for Tom's homecoming celebration. Ron, Ema and the group from Red Deer would spend the night rather than returning to Red Deer after dark. Ron was in a conciliatory mood, apologizing to both Tom and Tanya for his antics with Pastor Jones. Out of deference to Ron, no one drank too much. By twelve-thirty the party ended and everyone headed to their respective homes and beds.

With the party finally over, Tanya said to Tom. "Let's go to your house. I put some coal on the fire before we left to pick you up, so it should be nice and warm by now."

"I hope my crossed eyes don't bother you too much," Tom began once they were outside. "I'm still having some difficulty trying to adjust to them."

"Crossed or not crossed, they're the most beautiful eyes in the world," Tanya whispered, as she held Tom close.

"Whenever I look into your eyes, I'll remember you sacrificed your good eyesight to save a life."

As they neared the house, Tom exclaimed, "Good God, Tanya, you've got the old house all spruced up!" By lantern light, Tanya led Tom around the house. As he held her in his arms, he said, "I imagine, like with the breaking, there's no way you'll accept payment for all this hard work."

"I don't know about that," Tanya replied with a smile. "Maybe you can pay me back a bit tonight."

Once in the house, Tanya lit a lamp and took Tom on a tour, ending up in the bedroom.

"I have a little something for you," Tom said.

He reached into his shirt pocket and brought out a small velvet box and handed it to Tanya. With trembling hands, she opened it. There was her engagement ring, a solitary diamond mounted on a white gold band! Again Tanya was in Tom's arms, hugging and kissing him and crying for joy.

There in the dim lamplight, they lay close together, their hands rediscovering each other. Tanya need not have worried that her past would again haunt her. As her passion grew, she found herself an eager, participant in their lovemaking. Fully spent, they snuggled close together, savoring the moment, so in love. Still basking in their newly discovered closeness, they lay in each others arms for some time.

Finally Tanya broke the spell. "I really should be going now. I'd love to spend the night with you, but I guess we'll just have to be patient for a bit longer."

In the morning, rather than relighting the fire and waiting for the house to get warm, Tom slipped over to the folks' house and woke Tanya up. While she began making breakfast, he started on the chores. Jed awoke to the smell of fresh biscuits. He was quite sheepish when he discovered that Tom was already out in the barn and joined him in short order. By nine-thirty, they all sat down for breakfast.

Before they began to eat, Tanya showed off her engagement ring. Everyone was happy for them and a fair amount of hugging ensued.

Beth was ecstatic. "I can hardly wait to get back to school to tell my chums. All my friends will be so excited! You guys sure are lucky."

It was a wonderful Christmas for Tom and Tanya. They shopped together for the first time and attended a number of school Christmas concerts. There would always be a few servicemen home on leave, or on early discharge like Tom. They would be recognized, acknowledged by the emcee and given a round of applause.

Christmas Day was spent with Tanya's folks. Throughout the day, neighbours dropped in for a visit, some Christmas goodies and oft times some Christmas cheer. In the afternoon, Tanya noticed that Tom was not in the house so she threw on her coat and went over to his place. He was sitting by the stove looking off into space.

As she came up beside him she could see tears in his eyes. "What's the trouble, dear?" she asked putting her hand on his shoulder. "Is there anything I can do to help?"

"I'll be alright. I needed to be by myself for a few minutes to remember my army buddies that won't be coming home. I was only a hair's breadth from being one of them. Then, as I told you the other day, I'm having a rough time coping with my double vision. Once in awhile I have to get away from everyone, feel a bit sorry for myself and try to recharge my batteries. Don't mention it to anyone else. It will only put a damper on things."

"Do you want me to leave you for a bit?"

"No, I think I'm O.K. now. We'd best go back to the house before they think we're up to something."

Late in the afternoon of the twenty-sixth, Tanya and Tom drove to Red Deer to visit Tom's mom and Ron. The trip took longer than expected as Tom was having great difficulty learning to drive with his double vision. Ema was overjoyed that Tanya would be her future daughter-in-law. Ron and Tom again did their best to be amicable with each other.

During the holidays, Tom found a fill-in job for the rest of the winter in a town east of Milden, sorting and delivering mail to the rural post offices in the area.

When the job at the post office ended, Tom joined forces with Jed putting the crops in. Over the years, Jed relied on extra help at seeding and harvest, but few of his hired men possessed much ambition or drive. Tom, like Jed, was full of energy. They often vied with each other to see who could be out to the field first in the mornings, or work latest at night.

Tanya and Tom set their wedding date for the first week-end in July, one week after Tanya finished her grade twelve exams.

When they met the local Baptist minister in his church study to discuss their wedding plans, Pastor Brock was in a real quandary. One of the church deacons told him that Tom and Tanya were sleeping together.

After exchanging pleasantries, the pastor said, "I'm pleased you've come to our church to discuss your wedding plans. Prior to your wedding we'd like you to attend church sponsored pre-marital counseling sessions. I feel awkward in broaching this, but you should be aware of our church policy on marrying divorced people and couples who have been living together. We will marry them, but not in the sanctuary."

A lengthy, uncomfortable silence ensued.

Sensing the pastor was reticent to get into the nitty-gritty of their relationship, Tom barged right in. "Does this have something to do with Tanya and I sleeping together the weekend we were in Calgary?"

Bob nodded gravely.

"Well, we have slept together a few times, but really, whose business is that other than Tanya's and mine?"

"It is not my intention to be offensive. I'm now relying on your own words, Tom that you and Tanya slept together rather than the local gossip. You're right. This is your choice, your own business. Notwithstanding this, try to appreciate that if our church allowed you to be married in the sanctuary we feel we'd be condoning pre- marital sex, which in biblical terms is fornication."

Tanya gripped Tom's hand firmly, hoping against hope that there wouldn't be another donnybrook like there had been with Pastor Jones in Red Deer. She could tell that the volcano was starting to bubble.

"Now just a minute, Bob," Tom interjected, fighting for control. "Are you saying that the few times Tanya and I had sex is sinful?"

"That is correct," Bob replied quietly. "That is both my view and the church's view."

"Hold it a bit," Tom shot back. "Years back I remember mom and dad having a whale of an argument about some neighbours who were living common law. Dad said that nowhere in the Bible are we told what makes a marriage vow or even a marriage ceremony. From what dad read, the parents would come up with some sort of a dowry and the girl would go to the father's house and become his son's wife. He said that they might have a feast or the like, but that we aren't told much more. The way Tanya and I figure it, her accepting my engagement ring and our promise to love and be faithful to each other as long as we live, is the same thing as a wedding ceremony in God's eyes. It tells the world that we are going to spend the rest of our life together."

Bob was deep in thought and did not reply, so Tom continued.

"Tanya is the only woman I ever slept with. I had lots of chances to sow my wild oats while in the Armed Forces, but I said no and remained true to my Tanya."

"As for me," Tanya began in a shaky voice, "there were lots of boys wanting to go out with me, but I remained true to Tom. We both think that for the sake of our kids, our folks and ourselves, a church marriage is the way to go. That's why we're here."

"Tanya and I don't expect you or the church to accept everything we believe in," Tom continued. "All we ask is for you to show us some kindness and not force your beliefs down our throats. And just so you know, Bob, Tanya and I didn't go all the way until we were engaged."

"I'd like to apologize to both of you if my remarks caused offence," Pastor Brock replied, after a long pause. "Your dad's views and your comments do raise a number of questions, Tom. I must be honest and tell you I don't have easy answers for them. You are right. There is no standard form of marriage vow laid out for us in the Bible. I think we all agree though, that whatever form the wedding took, it was a statement to the community and God that these two individuals were now man and wife and would remain so till death. I'm sure the three of us agree that an exchange of vows in God's sanctuary in front of a group of witnesses is the right way to go."

"I've known both of you since you were youngsters and without question, you are upright people. I recognize you probably would have married much sooner if Tanya had been through school when you got your discharge, Tom. After listening to both of you, I have decided in this instance not to be your judge. With God judging all our actions, I will marry you in the church."

"Thank you Pastor Brock," Tanya said, relief in her voice. "This means a lot to Tom and me."

Bob smiled. "Thank you for coming to see me. We'll set up some counseling sessions and I might add, Tanya, I'm looking forward to them. You both have some real depth. I think we've all grown some today."

CHAPTER
14

Once seeding was completed, Ema joined forces with Betty and the wedding preparations began in earnest. It was extremely hard for Tanya to keep her mind on her school work with her wedding just around the corner. With departmental exams to write though, she had to concentrate on her studies.

Like most brides, she deliberated long and hard about her choice of a wedding dress. After spending several Saturday afternoons visiting bridal shops in Red Deer with Tom and trying on four or five dresses, she turned to him. "I just can't make up my mind, dear. What do you think?"

"Whatever turns you on, as long as it doesn't look like a sack!" Tom wisecracked.

Harriet's mother was a seamstress and came to Tanya's rescue. She helped Tanya pick out a style and two weeks later, the dress was finished.

When Tom saw Tanya in her wedding gown, he gave a low whistle and couldn't stop smiling. Finally, he found his voice. "Good God, girl, you're beautiful! Just looking at you gives me weak knees! You'd only look more beautiful if you weren't wearing anything!"

Beth was right in the midst of the wedding plans, while Ben did his best to keep himself as far removed from the action as possible. Beth was thrilled to be the maid of honor while Ben was not at all thrilled to be the best man. A week before the wedding, Ben was saved by the bell. Joe Bonner got a leave for the first two weeks in July. He would be the best man. Ben would be the other groomsman, Harriet the other bridesmaid.

As they were eating breakfast, the day before the wedding, Tanya turned to Tom and Ben. "You guys should wash and decorate the wedding cars this morning and then there are some bad ruts in the church parking lot that need to be leveled off. We want to get every thing finished before the wedding rehearsal. It's at eight tonight."

"Ben and I will look after that later this afternoon," Tom replied. "Bob Ross will be here in a half hour with his cat. That last field you guys cleared has a bad water problem at the west end. There's been ten acres of crop under water since that last heavy rain. We're going to ditch it down to the creek. Ben and I will have to be with him to do some chain saw work."

"Couldn't you pick some other day to do that?" Tanya said, near tears. "Remember, it's your wedding too."

"I'm sorry, but Ross is very busy. I asked him if we could come a few day's earlier, but this is the only time he had open. If we don't get that water off there, the crop will die. I just finished telling you we'll get at your work this afternoon."

Tanya burst into tears and ran to her room. "I just don't see why it's all that important to play around with a cat on the day before your wedding," she sobbed.

"It will all turn out O.K.," Betty said holding her distraught daughter close. "I'm sure they'll get the cars looked after this afternoon."

"I'm not counting on it. As soon as Beth and I have the church cleaned up, we'll start on the cars ourselves. 'We'll look after your work later this afternoon.' Isn't he getting married too?"

Later in the morning, as they took a breather from their work, Ben turned to Tom. "Tanya sure is uptight about the wedding. You into all this big wedding stuff?"

"Not at all, not at all, but what's a man to do? That's what the women want, so a guy just has to go along with them."

"Not for me," Ben shot back. "No damn way. If I ever get married, it's straight to the Justice of the Peace. No big hairy deal for me, no sir."

"Bets?" retorted Tom. "When your day comes you'll have no more say in it then than I have now, or for that matter than your dad did, some twenty years ago."

"You're on," Ben replied enthusiastically. "How much?"

"Whatever."

"Fifty bucks?"

"Fifty bucks it is. If you're smart, you'll start saving your money now."

Tom was making the last pass with his tractor and float, leveling the parking lot, when Betty and Ema pulled up to the church for the wedding rehearsal. "It looks like Tom is running a bit behind schedule," Betty said to Ema with a smile. "It's just as well Tanya and Beth looked after the cars. Some guys have a hard time getting into the wedding spirit."

"I felt sorry for Tanya this morning," Ema replied. "I sometimes wonder about Tom's strong drive. He's like his dad, strong willed to the point of being bullheaded. Maybe Bill and I put too much pressure on him as he was growing up. It was awful hard on Tom with Bill being a cripple. Tom had to become a man while he was still a boy."

"Jed and I love and admire Tom very much. A strong personality he has, without question, but at the same time, we see his kindness."

"Yes, he's a wonderful son. Still, for Tanya's sake, the sheer force of his character concerns me some. I was married twenty years to his father. At times it was like being harnessed to a wind storm. Tom is even more intense than his dad. I just hope Tanya won't be intimidated by his strength, but then, maybe I worry too much. That's what mothers do though. I hope it works out as well for them as it did for Bill and me."

"You're right about mothers worrying over their children," Betty went on. "Sometimes I wish Tanya was more sure of herself. Maybe it's the memory of her attack that still affects her. I know what that's like. I was abused by my first husband."

The wedding day dawned clear and warm. Ten minutes before the ceremony was to start, there were more people outside the small Baptist church than inside. The organ, the pulpit and the pews were carried out to the south side of the church and the wedding proceeded.

"Thank you Betty and Jed for my beautiful Tanya," Tom said as he began his speech at the reception. "A giant thank you to Mom for raising me and to my dad for showing me how to become a man. Thank you Pastor Brock for marrying us and giving us counsel. Thanks to all the friends and family for pitching in to make this a special day for us. A big thank you to all the guests who've traveled far, especially Tanya's grandmother Grace, who is eighty-nine and traveled all the way from Tennessee."

"I'd also like to thank all the guys who've given their lives fighting for the rest of us," Tom continued after pausing to gather his thoughts. "I guess that includes my dad, because he died of complications from injuries in World War I." With tears in his eyes, he raised his glass: "To my beautiful Tanya, to my fallen buddies and to my old man."

Ben could not blame Tanya too much for shedding a few tears.

The rest of the reception and dance went without incident. Tom was so proud of his bride! Whenever she danced with others, he waited eagerly for the music to stop so he could get back with her.

There was some talk of stealing the bride, but the reputation of both the groom and the groom's father-in-law put a damper on that old tradition. "I've seen both Jed and Tom in action," Joe said. "If I had ten good men willing to have their heads split open, we could give it a try. All things considered though, I think we'd be wise to let it pass."

Tanya and Tom spent their honeymoon in Banff. Tanya preferred lazing around, but Tom soon became restless and started hounding Tanya to do some hiking.

"How will I ever get you to relax?" Tanya wheezed, out of breath, after a three mile hike up a steep trail.

"There will be plenty of time for that when we're old fogies," Tom replied with a smile.

One evening, after a session of intense love making, Tanya whispered. "I'm certainly not complaining, but don't you ever get tired of making love? If we keep this pace up, we'll both wear out."

"I wouldn't worry too much about it, dear." Tom replied softly, as he held her close. "I promise to slack off a little bit in thirty or forty years."

Tanya enrolled in Normal School in Red Deer as soon as they returned from their honeymoon. Once she completed the six week teacher training course, she received her temporary teaching certificate. In September, she started teaching in the old Stella School where she, Ben and Beth took their elementary and junior high school. Tanya was now teaching some of her former classmates.

Tom and Jed worked together haying and harvesting. Tom was still learning to adjust to his double vision. His knee had pretty well healed, but if he pushed it too hard, it would live up to its name "trick knee" and buckle on him.

Once fall work was completed, Tom, Tanya, Jed and Betty began scheming on ways to make their farming operation more viable. They decided to bring their four hundred fifty acres of bush land under cultivation and then begin logging the pine timber.

Fred Bonner had a lot of experience running heavy construction machinery and helped them to locate all the equipment.

While Tom was eager to get into the venture, Jed was somewhat unnerved by it all. He was quite relieved when Tom assured him that he would operate the caterpillar tractor. It was all scary business for a couple of greenhorns. One in his fifties, not even knowing how to start a Cat, let alone run one, the other with poor eyesight and limited experience running heavy equipment.

In mid-November, Tom and Tanya went to the bank to get financing for the venture. The manager gave them a ten thousand dollar line of credit to buy the land clearing and logging equipment. Having Jed and Betty for partners in the venture helped as they were well-established and had a good track record with the bank.

By Christmas, all the equipment was purchased and they were ready to start clearing land. Once the equipment was ready to roll, keeping Ben in school became a Herculean task. Being close to sixteen, he felt that running a Cat would be far more profitable and a whole lot more interesting than sitting in a classroom. Betty finally gave up trying to keep him motivated about his studies.

Seeing that Ben viewed the Cat operation as a man-thing, Tom and Jed talked with him privately. "You've heard me go on about the importance of a good education," Jed began. "No one can force you to stay motivated about your studies though, so Tom and I are prepared to make you a deal. If you stay in school till June without bitching and bear down on your school work, Tom will let you run the Cat piling on weekends. Come fall, if you still haven't come to your senses about the value of an education, I won't push too hard to force you back to school. Remember, Ben, this is to be kept from your mother and Tanya."

The women were amazed at Ben's change in attitude. He no longer chaffed at the bit to quit school and his marks were coming up.

Jed was very apprehensive about operating the Cat cutting brush. He finally gave in to pressure from Tom and Ben and climbed onto the D-7 Caterpillar for his maiden voyage. Just a couple of hundred yards into the forest primeval was enough. Pure fright lightened his complexion several shades.

"I'm ready to meet my maker, but wouldn't mind a few more years of grace," he said at the supper table. "Clearing land is a young man's job."

After Jed's attempt at clearing, it took several days of artful persuasion to convince him to try piling. A brief stint of twenty minutes was sufficient. Jed brought the Cat back to the fuel trailer more convinced than ever that a wise man, especially a wise old man, should pursue less challenging work.

Although pretty green at running heavy equipment, Tom did the brush cutting. Ben was an eager apprentice on weekends. In addition to teaching Ben to pile brush, Fred piled some at night and helped with the mechanical problems.

By mid-April all the brush was cut and piled. The brush rows weren't perfectly straight, but considering the crew's experience, they all thought it a pretty fair job.

Tom was feeling so elated with their success at clearing that he started lobbying Tanya and the folks to do some custom work. His plan was vetoed three to one. Ben was on side with Tom, but his vote didn't count seeing he had no money invested.

Tanya was very relieved to see the brush cutter go. "You'll never know what a tough winter I've put in, worrying over you operating the Cat," she said to Tom one day. "It's such a dangerous job, especially for someone with double vision and little or no depth perception. It would make my life a lot easier if you weren't such a risk taker."

"I know, but that's how I'm made. Sometimes taking risks is the only way you can get ahead."

"I wish you weren't so bull headed," Tanya sighed, "but I don't imagine harping away at you will make you change."

With money from the sale of the brush cutter, Tom and Jed bought a breaking plow and a root harrow. Once the crop was in, they were at the second stage of the work, breaking and root harrowing. They soon learned the sad reality that cutting and piling the bush was only the tip of the iceberg and were forced to split the work into two years.

Despite strong lobbying from both his parents, Ben could not be talked into returning to school in September. "I'm disappointed that you're not going back to school," Jed said to Ben when they were alone. "I'll live up to my part of the bargain though and not force you."

Although upset that Ben wouldn't take anymore schooling, Betty finally accepted his decision.

As they were lying in bed one night, Betty said, "you know Jed, if I didn't know you better, I'd say that you and Ben made some sort of a father-son deal to allow him to quit school."

Jed sucked in his breath. He was glad Betty couldn't see his face.

As soon as the ground froze, Tom and Ben started working in the timber berth felling trees and skidding them to the landings with Jed's old team, Darkie and King. Tom dozed out a mill yard close to where Bill Rosser's old house used to be and using the Cat, skidded the logs from the landings into the mill yard and stock-piled them.

They were back in the root patch once seeding was completed. Jed and Tom hired several of Ben's friends to help with the root picking. Jed swore that every time you worked the soil, a new crop of roots germinated and grew. Finally, as the ground was freezing, they finished for the year. There would always be roots coming to the surface every time the land was worked. It would be years before the land would be completely free of roots.

As the last root pile was burning, Jed made a vow. "Tom, if you ever try to con me into clearing any more land, I'll not only disown you as a son-in-law, but I'll work you over with a big stick. Just remember, Tanya, Betty and I did your first one hundred acres while you were away in the Armed Forces."

"Well, we can be proud that we got it all licked," Tom replied with a smile. With tongue in cheek he added. "It's really a shame to quit now though, just when we've got it down to a science."

Once the breaking plow and root harrow were sold, Tom and Jed bought an old sawmill. By late January, the sawmill was set up in the mill yard and they began sawing rail road ties. Tom and Ben operated the mill and did the logging. Betty took over the major share of the cattle chores during the winter months, allowing Jed time to give a hand with the sawmill operation.

After seeding was completed the following spring, Jed found Darkie dead in the barnyard. Knowing Tanya's fondness for King, he gave the old fellow to her. Tom would use him a bit skidding logs.

When they began logging the next winter King was right in his glory. Tom would hook him to a log, tap him on his behind and say, "the landing, King." The old fellow would head off to the landing by himself. Ben would unhook the log, hang up the single tree on the harness and King would head back for another load. Like Jed, Tom always gave King his weekly chew of snuff.

* * * * * * * * * * * * * *

After a couple of years of farming with his dad and logging with Tom, Ben decided to move on. The excitement over the farming and sawmill ventures faded as the allure of the oil patch began beckoning him.

"Somewhere in the future I'd like to come back to the farm, but for now, the oil patch is where the money is."

With Ben gone, Tanya was none too happy with how things were turning out. Although her dad was helping with the sawing, Tom was doing all the logging by himself. She was now constantly worrying for his safety. When she mentioned this to Tom, her concerns seemed to fall on deaf ears. She pondered how unfeeling Tom appeared to be. "At times I think he's more married to his work than he is to me."

That spring, after seeding was finished, Tanya talked to Tom about taking an extended holiday. Although they always spent a week in Banff or Jasper during the summer school break, her dream holiday was a Caribbean cruise.

"We've earned an exotic holiday, especially you. Just remember all those years you worked on the farm helping your folks. I can't think of anyone who deserves a break more. Wouldn't it be wonderful, lying on some tropical beach, drinking in the sun with not a worry in the world? I'm sure we could manage, if we planned for it. What do you say dear?"

"Let's back up a bit, Tanya," Tom replied curtly. "I wouldn't mind taking an extended holiday either, but with our finances as they are, we'd have to borrow a pile of money to pull it off. That would be plain stupid. Our priority right now should be to pay off our old debts, rather than make new ones."

Tanya was disappointed with Tom's position, but knew that arguing about it would only make him more determined. "I was right," she thought. "He is more married to the farm than he is to me."

CHAPTER
15

Tanya taught for four years before she and Tom decided to start a family. No sooner was she pregnant than Tom started talking about them building a new house on their own land.

"We need our independence," Tom began one day. "You're too close to your mom, from what I can see. With us starting a family that could cause problems. It would also help to be nearer to the sawmill."

"The sawmill aside, I don't know why you're all knotted up about me being close to mom. I see nothing wrong with Mom and me being good friends."

"I think the world of your folks, but you're far too dependent on them. When we have a problem, rather than talk to me about it, you go straight to them. You married me, not your mom."

"Yes I admit I sometimes do that, but it's not because I don't want to talk to you. It's just that every time we have one of those talks you back me into a corner. When you get your mind made up, there's no way you'll ever slack off."

"Is that so," Tom retorted sarcastically. "Someone around here has to do some planning. When I ask for your input, you say you don't know, that planning isn't your thing. So I go ahead and make plans, then I'm a bully for backing you into a corner. I just can't win."

The next afternoon Tanya went over to her mom's place and briefed her on Tom's idea of them moving.

"Much and all as I enjoy having you living in the yard, I'm afraid I have to agree with Tom. If you always come to your dad and me for guidance, you're marriage won't be as strong as it could be. Is Tom not approachable?"

"I love Tom dearly. For the most part we get along well. It's just that he's so strong and stubborn. When I try to discuss things with him, he overpowers me. He loves to debate. I hate it. Most of the time, I find it easier not to challenge him. It's much less of a hassle."

"You two need to work on communicating. Moving to your land might help out in that area," Betty concluded.

Tom cut enough lumber for the new house in the winter and once the crop was in, they began building. There was still some finishing to do inside, but Tom and Tanya were able to move in before freeze-up.

Tanya taught until Christmas, then quit to have the baby. In spite of her initial misgivings about moving, Tanya was happy in her new home, on their own land. In their new location, Tanya had much easier access to Tom. Even when he was logging, she could still hear the Cat. Tom installed a phone line to the mill yard. When she needed to contact him, a loud buzzer and a flashing light would go off at the sawmill.

Tanya's pregnancy proceeded smoothly. She was very excited about having a baby. Tom was also delighted that he'd soon be a father and was becoming over-protective. He constantly prevailed on Tanya not to exert herself too much.

Tanya finally had enough. "For God's sake Tom, will you lay off trying to coddle me?" she said with a twinkle in her eye. "I'm not as fragile as you think. Women have babies every day, you know."

On March sixth, Tom and Jed were sawing ties when the phone buzzer went off. Tom hit the throttle on the mill and ran for the house.

"No need to get excited," Tanya said, meeting Tom at the door. "This is just my second contraction and they're still fairly far apart."

They shut the mill down and Tom and Tanya headed for the hospital in Milden. Tom stayed with Tanya in the labour room all afternoon. Finally at eleven-thirty p.m., with the contractions becoming more intense, the nurse moved Tanya into the delivery room and contacted Dr. Reed.

Dr. Reed just emigrated from England and was not accustomed to, or in favor of having fathers in the delivery room.

When Tom broached the subject with him, the doctor curtly replied, "The delivery room is no place for fathers. I just don't allow it."

"Well, Doctor, I don't want to cause a scene," Tom shot back, "but Tanya wants me in there with her, and that, Sir, is exactly where I'm going to be. End of discussion."

When Dr. Reed glanced at the father-to-be, he saw a big, most determined man. Reed was not at all accustomed to such disregard for a doctor's authority. After a moment or two of reflection though, he realized that he didn't have much choice in the matter.

Tom kept well out of the way, standing at the head of the bed, holding Tanya's hand. Tanya remained as collected as the labour pains allowed her to. At twenty to one, with a loud cry, a baby boy was born. There were tears of joy and relief spilling down Tanya's cheeks, while the tough old man at the head of the bed rubbed his eyes so no one could see his tears.

Within five days, mother and baby were back home, doing well. Tanya was a natural mother, easily bonding with her baby. Tom's chest size increased at least two inches with the birth of his son. In honor of Tom's and Tanya's fathers, they named the boy Billy Jed Parker. Tanya breastfed the baby, keeping him in a wicker basket on her side of the bed. At night when the baby got hungry, Tanya would just lift him out of his basket, feed him and then put him back, all without getting out of bed.

"Good grief, Tanya," Tom said one day, with a wry smile. "The way you play and talk to Billy makes me wonder if you had any dolls as a youngster!"

"I sure did," Tanya retorted. "I just can't get enough of the little guy."

When they were by themselves, Tom enjoyed sitting with Tanya as she nursed the baby. Although not possessing the same intense parenting instinct as Tanya, Tom spent a lot of time holding and playing with his boy.

Tanya was enjoying her new role as a mother and full time home-maker. In addition to housekeeping, she was now able to help Tom out with some of his work. A few months after Billy's birth Tanya and Tom started attending church on a regular basis. Tanya would help in the nursery and occasionally Tom and she would sing in the morning services.

When Billy was fourteen months old, Tanya became pregnant again. Her second pregnancy progressed without a hitch. Tanya belonged to that lucky group of expectant mothers who never experienced morning sickness. As with her previous pregnancy, Tom was always after her to take it easier.......

Tanya was now seven months pregnant and unable to help much with the farm chores or sawmill. Tom was spending the day building a logging road at the far end of the timber birth. In the morning he drove his truck out to the far landing, three quarters of a mile from the house. He dozed over all the trees on the new road right of way and was starting to windrow them.

Tom didn't see it coming. A frozen tree exploded and a shattered piece flew back hitting him in the face. He saw an explosion of stars, then felt excruciating pain. Instinctively he slammed the clutch ahead. Stupefied, he sat there, blood squirting from each nostril with every heart beat. Tom was trying desperately to hold on.

"I'm hurt bad! God, I know it's bad. Got to get help. Got to get back to the truck." Fighting panic, Tom shifted the D7 into third, lowered the blade and started back to the landing. Before he had gone a hundred feet his eyes were swelling shut.

"Damn it, I can't see" he muttered as he threw the clutch ahead. "Now what? Don't panic, don't panic. "You got to stay calm. You got to, for Tanya's and Billy's sake. You'll just have to try to stay warm and wait till someone comes for you."

Tom told Tanya he'd be back in the mill yard by three, but by three-thirty he still hadn't come. She went to the door to listen for the sound of the Cat. Suddenly her heart froze. She could hear the faint sound of the motor revving up for a few seconds, then idling down. This was the method they used in the bush to signal an emergency.

"Oh Dear God," Tanya cried, "Tom must be hurt! I've got to get help to him, but how? What can I do? That man of mine! Why is he so bullheaded, working in the bush by himself with his poor eyes?"

Tanya phoned her folks, but they were out. In desperation, she then phoned a couple of neighbour ladies, but their husbands were gone with their vehicles.

"Come as soon as you can," Tanya told them frantically. "I'm going to try to get to Tom with the horse and stone boat."

Tanya bundled Billy into his winter clothes and headed for the stable. It was a warm day and King was sleeping on the south side of the building. Tanya got King into the barn and with a great deal of difficulty got him harnessed. She hitched King to the stone boat and threw on a bale. She sat on the bale with Billy sitting in between her legs. He was overjoyed to be going for a ride.

When Tanya got to the far landing she could hear the Cat idling some distance further in the bush.

"Oh dear Lord," she cried. "The motor isn't revving up and down any more. Tom must be badly hurt."

Tanya called out several times, but got no response.

"Dear God help us," she sobbed and headed towards the sound of the Cat.

Because of the rough terrain, she nearly upset the stone boat a couple of times. Finally, when she was thirty feet from the Cat, she saw Tom slumped over in the seat, his face covered in blood.

"Tom, are you alright?" she screamed.

Tom sat up, idled the Cat down some more and turned in Tanya's direction.

"Yeah, I got clobbered pretty good, but I'll make it," he shouted. "A big frozen chunk of log flew back and hit me in the face. It's really smarting, but the bleeding's nearly stopped. My eyes are swollen shut so I can't see. Thank goodness my head is made of solid bone."

"Your face is a bloody mess," Tanya cried, "and I don't see the slightest thing humorous about it. Billy and I came on the stone boat with King. How in the world are we going to get you out of here anyway?"

"No sense panicking. We can send King home. Just unhook him, hang up the traces, fold up his lines and he'll find his way back. I'll use you for my eyes. I'll run the cat and steer, you tell me where to go. When we get to the truck you can drive us to the house, then we'll get help from the folks or the neighbours."

"I hope you realize I don't like this one little bit! Why are you such a risk taker? If you were in your right mind you wouldn't be working at such a dangerous job. Once I get you out of here I'm taking you straight to the hospital."

With trepidation Tanya sent King on his way and then she and Billy got on the Cat. With Tanya co-piloting, they were soon back at the landing. A few minutes later they were at the house.

Once in the hospital, the Doctor gave Tom a thorough examination, sutured up the cuts in his face and set his broken nose. He couldn't find any sign of concussion, but chided him for working at such a dangerous job with poor eye sight. "We'll be keeping you under observation for a few days. You bled quite a bit. We have no way of determining how much damage has been done and I'm a bit concerned you might start hemorrhaging again."

At 2 a.m. Tom started to bleed profusely. The medical staff in Milden were unable to control the bleeding, so he was rushed to the Red Deer hospital by ambulance. The hospital phoned Tanya. By the time she got to the hospital in Red Deer, Tom's surgery had been completed and he was in the recovery room.

When Tanya met the surgeon, he assured her that although Tom had lost a lot of blood he'd be O.K. "We'll be giving him several transfusions over the next while. Some of the blood vessels in your husband's face were severely damaged. We had to go in under his cheeks and staple many of them off. Everything is under control now, though, but it will take him quite a while to regain his strength. We'll be keeping him here for a few days."

Tanya spent two days with Tom before returning home. When she stopped to pick up Billy, she was feeling very down. "What can I do with that man of mine?" she lamented to her mom. "He's so damned bullheaded. When I visited him in the hospital I tried to convince him that because of his poor eyesight he should stay out of the bush. I might as well have saved my breath. I feel so helpless. It seems he doesn't pay the slightest heed to my feelings. All I got from him was the promise he'd be more careful."

"I know you feel helpless dear. They say the only thing harder than living with a man with too much drive, is living with one without any drive."

Tanya was feeling under the weather so didn't go back to visit Tom again until he was ready for discharge. When she and Jed picked him up they were shocked how weak Tom was and how much weight he'd lost. Tanya desperately hoped that Tom would come to his senses and realize that he couldn't work alone in the bush any more. He laid around for three weeks to build up his strength, but was soon raring to go again. To keep Tanya from going into orbit, he agreed to take a break from the logging until after the baby was born.

With Tanya in the late stages of her pregnancy, Tom was spending most of his time in the mill yard. On February second, a Chinook blew itself out over-night, the temperature dropped to minus fifteen degrees Fahrenheit and a winter storm was blowing in from the Northwest. Tom was working by himself in the mill yard when Tanya's first contraction came.

"I don't like this," Tom said when he got to the house. "With the weather going to pot, we'd better pull freight. The hospital's the place where you should be."

By the time Tanya's folks arrived to look after Billy, a full fledged blizzard was under way.

"Damn it, this weather sure brings back bad memories for Mom and me," Jed said. "There was drifting like this when Tanya was born."

While Betty helped Tanya get ready, Jed and Tom loaded fifteen railroad ties into the back of Tom's pickup for extra traction. The going wasn't bad until they got to the north-south stretch some four miles out of Milden. Here the snow drifts were completely across the road and getting fairly deep.

When Tom would see a drift coming, he'd cry out, "brace yourself, dear, we're going to hit the drift full bore."

The extra weight of the railroad ties gave them enough momentum to bull their way through, and they arrived at the hospital without any problems. Tom phoned back to tell the folks that they arrived and that he'd stay with Tanya until she delivered.

Doctor Bruce was far more liberal in his outlook than Doctor Reed had been. He even encouraged fathers to be present with their wives for the delivery, if they were comfortable with the arrangement.

As with Billy's birth, Tom stayed at Tanya's side, holding her hand. The delivery went smoothly and at eleven p.m., a baby girl was born. They named their baby girl Grace Elizabeth after Tanya's grandmother.

"A boy and a girl," Tom boasted. "What more could we ask for? Our family is complete, or is it?" he questioned, smiling slyly.

"I think two is just fine," Tanya responded firmly. "If you want anymore you can have them yourself."

Tanya was busier than ever with two children to attend to. She spent so much time playing with them that her housework sometimes suffered.

At times Tanya wondered about Tom's interaction with the kids. "I know he loves them," she mused, "but I wish he'd spend more time with them. He's so fixated on getting ahead."

That spring when they were seeding on Tom's and Tanya's land, old King seemed agitated. As they worked the field adjacent to the pasture, King would follow them back and forth, from one end of the pasture to the other. It was almost as if he wanted to be back in the thick of things. Tom and Jed felt sorry for the old fellow and always gave him his snuff treat.

The last day of seeding, King didn't make an appearance. Tanya saw him lying out in the pasture. She got the kids in the car and drove out to check on him. There was a large pool of blood at his rear and he didn't seem to have the strength to get up.

When Tanya stopped Tom at the end of the field, she was in tears. He shut the tractor off and headed back with her and the kids to check King out.

"I'm afraid the old boy's about had it," Tom said, after looking King over. "The only thing we can do now is put him out of his misery."

"Please, couldn't we call the vet?" Tanya pleaded. "There must be something they could do for him. At any rate, don't do anything till Dad gets here. Where is he anyway?"

"He slipped over to his place to get a couple bags of seed. Maybe it would be best if you and the kids went home. It looks like we'll have to shoot the poor old fellow."

"No way," Tanya retorted. "King has been my pet for years. Whatever happens to him, I want to be there."

"Alright, I can't deny you that, but you should take the kids to your folks' place. You can drop me off at home so I can pick up my rifle."

"Please, Tom, don't do anything till I get back," Tanya implored.

Tom was back standing beside King when Tanya and Jed got to the pasture.

"It doesn't look too good," Jed said gravely, after checking King over. "I'm afraid the old guy's close to the end. His breathing's getting very shallow. I hate the thought of it, but the only merciful thing to do now is to put him out of his pain. That's all a vet would do."

Tanya wept silently as she squatted by King and offered him his last sugar cubes. As she petted his soft nose she whispered, "I love you King, happy journey."

"You'd best not look, Tanya," Tom said quietly, as he stepped forward with the gun in his hand.

Tanya made no response. She was in her dad's arms sobbing uncontrollably. Tears were also slipping down Jed's cheeks.

"I'm sorry old boy," Tom continued with a lump in his throat, but first, how about a last pinch of snuff?"

The sound of Tom tapping the snuff box with his knuckles revived King. With a mighty groan, he tried to lurch to his feet. He was up on his front feet and trying desperately to get his back feet under him. Suddenly, he collapsed like he'd been struck by lightning. The poor old fellow died trying to get his last chew.

In the silence that ensued, Tom took out his jack knife and cut two locks of hair from King's mane. He silently handed one to Tanya, the other to Jed. The horse era had come to an end.

CHAPTER
16

The year Billy was four, Matthew Schwartz came to teach at Stella school. At twenty-nine, he'd tried his hand at several lines of work without finding his niche. Finally he took his normal school with the intent of giving teaching a try. This was his first school.

On a Thursday afternoon in late October, Matthew phoned Tanya. He introduced himself and asked Tanya if she could sub for him on Friday. A close family member passed away and he wanted to attend the funeral. Tanya said she'd be glad to fill in for him. After supper, she drove over to the teacherage and got his lesson plans for the next day.

Tanya's first impression of Matthew was favorable. He stood close to six feet, but was slight of build. Tanya thought him quite handsome with his dark brown hair and swarthy complexion. Although he didn't appear to be all that self-confident, he seemed genuinely concerned for the welfare of his students. After talking over the lesson plans for the next day, they continued chatting for another half hour.

Tanya didn't have any more contact with Matthew until late November, when they invited him for supper. Matthew and Tom hit it off immediately. Since both were raised on farms, they shared a lot of common interests and spent the evening swapping stories.

"I've begun a shop class for the grade eight and nine boys and it's working out well," Matthew said toward the end of his visit. "I sure wish there was some local woman who could teach the older girls home economics."

"Why don't you get Tanya to teach the girls?" Tom said.

"That's a great suggestion. What do you think, Tanya? Would you be at all interested? I know you'd do an excellent job, but maybe you need **some** time to think it over."

"Well, it certainly **would** be nice to get out of the house for a bit on a regular ba**sis**. I love teaching, but do you think the Superintendent **would go** for it?"

"If you'd like I **could check** with the School Division on Monday to see what **they say**. After I talk to them I'll give you a call."

Matthew phoned Tanya on Monday with the news that the School Division approved the plan. She would have two hours of teaching time each Friday afternoon to coincide with Matthew's shop class. Tanya would take her home economics class to the teacherage where there was a kitchen. The Superintendent said he'd be happy to have Tanya back teaching, even if only if for two hours a week.

The extra money was of secondary importance to getting out of the house and back to her first love, teaching. Billy and Grace looked forward to Friday afternoons nearly as much as Tanya did, as they would often end up at Grandma's and Grandpa's place.

"Matthew sure seems desperate to talk," Tanya said to Tom one evening. "Would you mind if I stayed for a while after school to chat with him?"

"Go for it. It sounds to me like the poor guy just needs some adult contact. The three and a half years I spent in the Army make me understand loneliness."

As the weeks passed, Tanya began to realize that in addition to being lonely, there were many unresolved issues in Matthew's life.

"My childhood certainly wasn't happy," Matthew said one afternoon. "Our family immigrated to Canada from Russia when I was one year old. Dad died when I was four and Mother remarried. My stepfather was a very domineering, cruel man. He used to beat us all, even my mother the odd time. Mother and we kids feared him. He didn't seem capable of showing love to any of us and was fixated on following his interpretation of the Bible to the letter of the law."

"I dated a girl a few times in high school, but when I brought her home to visit the folks, it ended in disaster. My stepfather grilled her on her religious beliefs and hammered away at her until she cried. I hated myself for not standing up to him, but I just couldn't seem to get up the courage. As you can imagine, that was the end of our dating."

"I can feel your pain, Matthew. Life can be rough at times. Getting back to the present, though, how are you enjoying teaching?"

"I'm in a real quandary," Matthew said in a disconsolate tone. "I thought teaching would be my thing, but I'm finding it heavy going. Maybe I'm not cut out to be a teacher. I'll give it to the end of the year, I guess."

As time passed, it appeared to Tanya that Matthew needed their talks just to get through the week. He seemed relieved to have finally found someone he felt comfortable in sharing his problems with.

Tanya summarized the gist of her and Matthew's conversations to Tom. She felt more comfortable if he knew what they talked about.

One day, Tanya asked Tom if he had any ideas that might help Matthew with his problems, especially his concern of finding the right vocation.

"Tell Matthew to quit feeling sorry for himself and stop blaming his upbringing for all his problems," he replied tersely. "Blaming the past isn't going to solve a damn thing. He's got to get off his butt and get on with life. For some people, figuring out what to do is hard, but crying the blues won't help any. Sure, he might bomb out a few times, but if he keeps at it, eventually he'll end up doing something he's not only good at, but something he really enjoys doing."

"I should have known better than to ask Tom," Tanya mused. "He's so cock sure of himself. He just doesn't understand anyone who suffers from low self-esteem. Why does he have to be so insensitive?"

"I too have my own personal problems," Tanya said to Matthew on one of their Friday after school chats. "I've been too busy to think about them for the last few years with raising the kids, but now that I'm helping you, my old feelings are starting to resurface. You see, I've always felt unsure of my spirituality and to be honest with you, I'm still not too confident of myself. Part of my problem is I grew up in Tom's shadow. God only knows how hard I've tried to get his help, but it just hasn't worked. He's so single-minded and argumentative. Whenever I tried having meaningful discussions with him, he'd back me into a corner and mow me down. After a few years I gave up trying."

"Perhaps I can assist you in that area," Matthew suggested eagerly. "I believe I'm fairly well-grounded in biblical truths. I'm sure I can help you with your spirituality."

As they focused more and more on each other's personal issues Tanya was telling Tom less and less of Matthew's and her conversations. Finally she stopped summarizing their talks altogether. This bothered her for a spell, but soon her uneasiness passed.

Initially Tanya thought of Matthew as just a needy friend. As the weeks passed by though, she found herself looking forward to their Friday afternoon sharing times a great deal and was becoming increasingly attracted to him.

Although at the beginning of their friendship, Matthew's feelings toward Tanya were platonic, as they interfaced more and more, that too was changing. Of late, even though he considered it sinful, he would often fantasize about being sexually involved with this kind beautiful lady.

While Matthew was away for the Christmas break, the teacherage burned down. Matthew lost a few items in the fire, but had taken most of his personal belongings with him. As Matthew needed a place to stay, Tom suggested that he board with them until the teacherage could be replaced.

Tom and Tanya enjoyed having Matthew around. He got along well with the kids, wasn't afraid to help out with the household chores and would occasionally babysit. While the three of them had some interesting talks, Matthew and Tanya waited until they were by themselves to do their real sharing.

Tanya was starting to look on Matthew as her spiritual mentor. In Matthew's view, the solution to Tanya's spiritual problems was closer adherence to biblical principles and prayer. To this end, they often prayed together when they were alone.

The physical component of their relationship began innocently enough. One afternoon when Tom had gone to the folks' place and Billy and Grace were having a nap, Matthew became quite emotional as he recounted some injustice from his childhood. Tanya wrapped her arms around Matthew and held him till he gained control again, then sat close to him and held his hand until he finished his story. In Tanya's mind the hugs and hand holding that ensued in the coming days were solely to support her distraught friend. To Matthew however, the new closeness was becoming quite titillating.

When they did their soul searching, Matthew's views on sexual matters often came to the fore. This made Tanya quite uncomfortable and had she not viewed him as trustworthy, she would have pushed the panic button.

"Did you and Tom engage in any premarital sex?" Matthew boldly asked one day.

"Well, we did have sex a few times, but we never lived together," Tanya replied hesitantly. "Why do you ask?"

"What you did was morally wrong." Matthew continued in a concerned voice. "It was sin. I haven't the slightest doubt that Tom pressured you."

"No, not really. Tom didn't use any pressure on me. We'd waited so long, seeing he was in the Army for just about four years. We were both eager. We were in love and knew we'd be getting married soon."

"Those excuses are hollow in God's eyes," Matthew said in a shocked voice. "If I were in your shoes, I'd be asking God for forgiveness."

One Friday afternoon, Tanya began discussing Tom's inadequacies with Matthew. "He's totally fixated on getting ahead. It seems that financial success is all he wants. He's even planning to buy out the folks in a few years. I've always longed to go on a Caribbean cruise. When I talked to Tom about us taking an extended holiday, he really tore into me. He said it was stupid to even think about a cruise while we were still in debt and that there would be plenty of time for cruises when we're old. At times, he gets me very upset."

"It must be difficult living with someone who is so self-centered. I admire you for putting up with him, but you have another problem that's even more critical. Tom's lack of discipline with the kids is ruining them. Not only does he not support you when you attempt to correct them, he prevents you from lifting a hand to them. The Bible tells us 'spare the rod and spoil the child.' Unless you start using some corporal discipline on Billy, you'll end up with a rebel on your hands."

One day while discussing Matthew's difficulty in finding a girlfriend, for the umpteenth time, Tanya said, "You've got to have faith in yourself. You're an attractive, kind fellow who should be out there beating the bushes, looking for the right girl to spend the rest of your life with."

As he lay in bed that evening, Matthew continued pondering Tanya's last comments. "I feel confident that God has led me to the right girl," he mused. "Her name is Tanya. There's no question in my mind that it's the Lord's doing that brought us together. I'm not sure how God will bring it all to pass, but I have a very strong feeling that eventually Tanya and I will be living together. Until I'm positive of Tanya's feelings towards me, though, I guess I'd better keep these thoughts to myself."

During the Easter break, Tom was at Tanya's folks' place all day, cleaning seed. Rather than concentrating on getting his report cards ready, Matthew chose to spend several hours each day with Tanya, sharing their joint concerns.

Another dynamic was now coming into play. Matthew's bedroom was right next to Tom's and Tanya's.

"I can't help but overhear you and Tom in your bedroom," Matthew remarked one day. "I'll lay odds that Tom is taking advantage of you with his insatiable sexual appetite."

"I'm shocked that you should say that," Tanya responded bluntly. "That's just not so."

Although she recognized that their relationship was becoming too close, Tanya did nothing to cool things down. Her lack of action was only adding fuel to the fire.

One evening, Tom was at the folks' place and Tanya didn't expect him back until ten-thirty. She put the kids to bed, read them their story and they were finally asleep. Instead of marking school papers, Matthew was lamenting to Tanya about his lonely existence.

"You don't know how much I envy you married couples. I feel so left out. I've tried to imagine how wonderful it would be to have someone to sleep with. Believe it or not, I've never seen a nude woman before. I'm sure a loser." Matthew bit his lip to keep control.

"You are not a loser," Tanya whispered, holding Matthew close. "You're a good man suffering from painful childhood memories. It does us good to share our pain."

Tanya brushing her lips against Matthew's cheek. Matthew reached up, cupped Tanya's face and they kissed passionately. "We'd better stop," Tanya finally said, pushing Matthew back. "I'm going to rest for a bit."

Tanya lay on her bed, desperately trying to gather her thoughts. "I wonder if Matthew and I should have kissed, but really he is suffering so much emotional pain. Is there anything else I can do to help him out of his despondency?"

Through the crack in the door, she saw Matthew bent over the table, marking papers. Her heart bled for him.

"I wonder. Would there be anything wrong in posing nude for Matthew?" she thought, her heart beating wildly. "I know he's completely trustworthy. I'd only be doing it to help him."

The thought of showing her naked body to a man other than her husband had her quite flushed. She quickly undressed, put on her bathrobe and went out into the living room. Tanya stopped in front of Matthew.

"I have a little gift for you," she whispered.

As Matthew looked up from his papers, Tanya untied her housecoat belt, shrugged her shoulders and let the robe slip to the floor.

Matthew stared in awe, his mouth dry. "Thank you so much Tanya," he finally gulped. "You don't know how much this means to me."

Tanya reached down, picked up her housecoat and headed to the bedroom without saying another word.

"Damn my upbringing anyway," Matthew muttered to himself. "It's wrong to make a pass at a married woman and adultery and divorce are sinful. Besides, I'm in Tom's house."

As Tanya dressed she was starting to feel guilty. "There's a lot I'll have to keep from Tom now. Really though, I did it strictly out of kindness to a very trustworthy, lonely man who is suffering a lot of emotional pain." Phrasing it in her mind was one thing, believing it in her heart quite another. The next few days were very hard for her, especially when she and Tom were intimate.

During the latter part of March, the School Division moved in a small house to replace the old teacherage. Once the wiring was completed and a few renovations made, Matthew moved in. He was relieved to be out of Tanya's and Tom's home. Although he knew he'd miss being close to Tanya, it was torture to lie in bed and listen to Tom making love to the woman he was sure would someday be his wife.

With spring seeding now in full swing, Tom would leave at seven a.m., returning at dark. When they were seeding on the folks' place, Tanya wouldn't see him all day. On Friday, Tanya and the kids just finished dinner when Tom pulled into the yard. "I came back to get some oil," he called out. "I might as well grab something to eat while I'm here."

"I wish you'd give me a little forewarning," Tanya countered curtly. "I have to teach this afternoon and the kids and I have already eaten. I guess I'll have to make you something from scratch."

"Never mind," Tom shot back sarcastically. "I haven't got time for you to start cooking. I'm in a hurry. We've got a crop to plant you know. I'll just grab something."

"Please, Tom, can't you wait a few minutes?" Tanya pleaded.

"Forget it," Tom said, as he put a couple of apples in a bag and headed for his truck.

Tanya was still steaming when she got to school. Once she finished her class, she immediately went over to the school and vented to Matthew.

"I'm some tore up with Tom! He's just so impatient and inconsiderate! The only thing on his mind is production!"

Later at the teacherage, as Tanya was making tea, her mind was mulling over the harsh words Tom and she exchanged at noon and the new closeness she now felt towards Matthew. Since posing nude for Matthew, their relationship was becoming more physical. When the opportunity afforded it, they were holding hands and doing some necking.

As Tanya sat sipping her tea, she noticed pain on Matthew's face. "Is anything the matter?" she asked. "You seem preoccupied."

"Just one of my painful childhood experiences coming back to haunt me. It would help me if I could tell you about it."

Tanya nodded. "Go ahead."

"This is kind of a sick story and I hope you won't think lowly of me. As I've told you many times, my step-father was a very cruel man. When I was about ten years old, there was a funeral in the community. My uncle and aunt stopped in at our place. They, my folks and the rest of the family all went to the church in the same car."

"My cousin Nelly was around my age and stayed behind with me. As soon as everyone left we went up to my parents bedroom and started play wrestling. Well, one thing led to another and before long, both of us were undressed and exploring each other's bodies."

"We were just a couple of curious kids. I'm positive neither one of us had any idea of what sex was all about. It was horrible. Suddenly the bedroom door burst open. It was my step-dad! We hadn't been watching the time and everyone had come home from the funeral. There Nellie and I were, naked and scared spitless."

"My step-dad roared at me, 'GET DRESSED AND GO TO YOUR ROOM.'"

"Nellie quickly dressed and Dad went downstairs with her. I was so fearful of the beating I knew I was going to get that I peed my pants."

"Then he was back in my room. He was wild with rage as he beat me with his heavy belt. 'You perverted little animal,' he screamed, 'I'm going to beat the devil right out of you.'"

"He beat me until I fainted. I remember my mother washing the blood off my back and legs and crying with me. I was so sick and marked up that I couldn't go to school for a week."

Matthew was shaking uncontrollably as he continued. "The hardest part for me wasn't the beating, though. It was the confessions I was forced to make. My stepfather made me apologize to Nellie's folks, but far worse, he marched me up to the front of our church on Sunday morning and made me ask forgiveness from the congregation for a sin of the flesh."

Matthew couldn't go on as a wave of emotion hit him. He pulled up his pant leg and showed Tanya a scar on his calf.

"I got this from that beating," he said, his voice breaking. "I had no one I could turn to other than my aunt Sandra, but she lived in the city. I'd usually spend a week with her during the summer holidays. She was aware that I was having problems with my stepfather and her support helped me a lot."

"The pieces are starting to fall into place," Tanya thought, tears glistening in her eyes. "Now I can understand Matthew's reticence to find a girlfriend. There must be something I can do to comfort him and help him out of his despondency."

Tanya got up, went over to Matthew, took him by the hand and led him into the bedroom, her heart ruling her actions. "Remember, Matthew, if I didn't totally trust you, I'd never be here with you. We must both be aware that we're playing with fire. We cannot go all the way."

"You know you can trust me. I'd never do anything to hurt you."

Tanya pulled Matthew close to her and they began hugging and kissing passionately. Slowly Tanya unbuttoned Matthew's shirt and helped him undress. As she lightly brushed her hand across his chest, she whispered softly, "Come, let's lie down on your bed."

Tanya undressed and lay down beside Matthew. He was ecstatic and soon they were engaged in some heavy petting. Matthew's fingers felt electrifying and Tanya was becoming quite aroused. Suddenly though, a wave of guilt swept over her and she started feeling cold and dirty. Her feelings of betrayal to her husband became so strong that her mind began shorting out. Although in emotional turmoil, she allowed Matthew to fondle her for a few minutes before reaching down and pushing his hand away.

"Stop," she whispered, "It's just not going to happen for me."

Matthew was breathing heavily, but stopped immediately. He had never been so turned on in all his life.

Tanya quickly dressed, then sitting on the bed, lightly ran her hand down Matthew's chest to his stomach. "It didn't work for me, but at least I can help you to relax."

Although Tanya's touch felt heavenly when they were lying on the bed, now, despite Tanya's fondling, Matthew too was being overpowered by feelings of guilt. It intensified until finally he blurted out, "It's not going to work for me either. Damn my upbringing anyway." Totally frustrated, he reached down and pushed Tanya's hand away.

Spiritually, Matthew felt dead. "It's all so complicated and screwed up," he groaned. He dressed and they went back into the living room.

They sat across from each other in shock. "How could I have started out trying so hard to help you and ended up lying naked with you in your bed?" Tanya finally blurted out. "Now what?"

"I don't know," Matthew replied in a daze. "I hate myself. I'm the one who is supposed to be your spiritual guide and

I allowed my sinful nature to take control. How will I ever live with myself? What a loser I am!"

"Matthew, We both have to do a whole lot of soul searching."

"I know,"

"I keep telling myself that I did this to help you out, but still, I feel so devastated that I've been untrue to Tom," Tanya cried.

When Tanya stopped for the kids, she could not look her mom in the eye. She had Billy and Grace in bed by the time Tom arrived home. He stepped into the house just as full of vim and vinegar as he always was. He'd picked Tanya a bouquet of wild crocuses on the way home to make up for being short with her at noon.

As he held her close, he whispered, "I'm sorry for being such an ass at noon. I promise to make it up to you tonight."

Tanya stiffened as she thought of them in bed together. Despite taking a long shower, she still felt unclean.

"I can't take a rain check," she thought as she was dressing. "How could I ever live with myself if I turned Tom down because of what Matthew and I did this afternoon?"

To make love to Tom that night was one of the hardest assignments she ever faced. It was difficult for the first time ever and Tanya finally was forced to disassociate her mind from her body.

"It feels like there's a thick cloud over my soul," she moaned. "Will I ever be able to get rid of this feeling of guilt?"

The more Tanya tried to ferret out her relationship with Matthew the more convoluted it became. "I'm glad that our sexual intimacy didn't really work out for either one of us," she mused. "At least Matthew and my consciences aren't seared that much. Even though I'm confused, one thing is very clear. We'll have to avoid any kind of sexual contact like this in the future."

By the time Matthew and she met again the next Friday afternoon, however, his outlook had undergone a complete turn-around. Instead of feeling guilty, he was now sure that the intimacy Tanya initiated was in God's overall plan. Tanya was not only perplexed with Matthew's view, but felt herself in a no-win situation. It was she who took the lead in both the necking and their sexual involvement. Although of the firm belief that further intimacy would be wrong, she capitulated.

Over the next three or four weeks, there were a few more necking sessions. Although Tanya could not bring herself to make any more sexual overtures toward Matthew, she did allow him to again do some heavy petting with her. Each attempt by Matthew was as frustrating for Tanya as their first episode.

Finally, during the fourth intimate encounter, Tanya blurted out, "Matthew, stop! It's not happening and I'm nearing emotional collapse. I've come to dread Friday afternoons with a passion because this is all you want to do. You can't be intimate with me anymore, or I'll have a nervous breakdown!"

Matthew was upset by Tanya's decision, but grudgingly accepted it.

Making love with Tom continued to be extremely difficult for Tanya. "The cloud of guilt, if anything, is thickening," she moaned. "I know that Tom's and my love is on a down-hill slide. When will all this insanity end?"

CHAPTER
17

The last few months of teaching went much better for Matthew, so with school out, he enrolled in summer school at the College in Red Deer to upgrade. His Aunt Sandra was spending the summer in the East, but before she left, he made arrangements to stay in her apartment.

The evening after the first day of summer school, was the lowest Matthew had felt in his life. Although he was stymied while living in Tanya's and Tom's home and even when he moved back to the teacherage, at least he'd been able to enjoy Tanya's company from time to time. Now he felt completely bereft.

"I know that Tanya loves me," he mused. "She's told me so. If she really loves me though, why has she cut off pretty well all physical contact with me? Is it possible she still loves Tom some? Just how long will Tanya and I have to wait before we can get married? Neither one of us believes in divorce, so how on earth will it all come about?"

After a few hours of deep thought and prayer, Matthew crawled into bed totally exhausted.

"BELIEVE IN ME AND IT WILL COME TO PASS," a voice boomed out. Matthew awoke from a heavy sleep with a start. "This is incredible," he whispered. "God has sent me a message about Tanya's and my relationship. It couldn't be clearer. I'm positive now its God's doing that brought Tanya and me together. Seeing that divorce is not acceptable to God, there's only one solution. In his wisdom and justice, God will have to remove Tom. God must do this in order to allow me my rightful place as Tanya's husband and Billy's and Grace's step-father. It may be harsh, but what other choice does God have?"

In the days to come, Matthew began praying earnestly that God would remove Tom so that Tanya and he could come together. Along with his prayers, he began an insidious scheme to discredit Tom, while at the same time building himself up. Until things solidified a bit more, Matthew thought it wise not to inform Tanya about God speaking to him, or his prayers for Tom's death.

In mid-July Tanya took Billy and Grace into Red Deer to see their great-grandparents. It also gave her the opportunity to visit Matthew. One evening she left the kids with her grandparents and dropped in on him.

As they sat on the couch, holding hands, Matthew asked, "Are you sure that Tom's always been true to you? A couple of weeks ago I talked to a guy who served with Tom in the Motor Corps. He told me Tom was a real womanizer, chasing anything that wore a skirt."

"I have a hard time believing that," Tanya replied, taking her hand away and cutting Matthew off in mid sentence. "I've talked to his buddy, Joe Bonner. He was stationed with Tom in the Motor Corps. Joe told me that Tom was no fun to be with, a real party pooper. He said Tom had no time for any girls other than me."

"I'll have to check on my source," Matthew quickly responded. "They may have taken Tom for someone else."

"Let's talk about your summer school courses, Matthew," Tanya interjected, changing the subject. "How are you making out?" After discussing his studies over a cup of tea, Tanya bid Matthew goodbye and headed back to her grandparents.

With summer school over, Matthew returned to teach at Stella School and Tanya continued her Home Economics class. Now firmly convinced that God would answer his prayers and allow Tanya and him to come together, Matthew stepped up his character assassination of Tom. Although he would occasionally come over for a meal, Matthew now felt quite uncomfortable in Tom's presence.

Shortly after school started, Matthew told Tanya an incident about Tom that greatly disturbed her.

"Did you ever ask Tom the details about his accident when the ammunition truck blew up?"

"Well, he told me a bit about it, but didn't go into the details. Why do you ask?"

"A week or so ago I was talking to a fellow at college by the name of Rob Hanks. When I told him about the teacherage burning down and spending the winter at your place, he asked if Tom was a big bruiser with crossed eyes. I said he was and told him about Tom's accident in the Armed Forces overseas."

"Rob shook his head. He said that had to be the Tom Parker he served with. According to him, he was driving in the convoy with Tom that day and was there when his accident happened."

"Rob said on the day of the accident, Tom was pretty drunk and ran his truck off the road. He said that Tom had a drinking problem and usually stashed a bottle somewhere in his truck. By Rob's account, there were no cows on the road. Tom just lost control of the truck and hit the ditch."

Tanya couldn't fathom this new version of the accident, as she still vividly remembered her vision. After praying about it for a few days she decided not to challenge Tom with Matthew's account.

"Did you know that Tom fleeced Bill Rosser when he bought his land?" Matthew asked Tanya one afternoon. "Bill told me so when I was visiting him the other day."

Tanya was again confused by Matthew's story, as she remembered some of the details of the transaction. After deliberating on Matthew's version of the incident, she again chose not to question Tom about it.

"The other day I had a phone call from my Aunt Sandra," Matthew began one Friday afternoon. "She told me that her husband Morris and Tom's dad were buddies from the First World War. When Morris was still alive they used to visit Tom and his folks. Sandra said that on one of their visits, when Tom was about ten, he exposed himself to her daughters and forced them to fondle him."

"There's another incident that's even scarier. You must know old Roy Jabs. Well, Roy told me he saw Tom go into the bush and expose himself to a group of young girls at last year's school picnic. I don't want to alarm you, but I feel it's important that you be aware of both incidents for the safety of the kids."

When Tanya heard the two stories, she was nearly paralyzed with fear for Billy and Grace. She was, however, reticent to discuss the incidents with Sandra or Roy Jabs. She feared Sandra might be very sensitive about it and as for Roy, she was intimidated by his forthright style and unsure how he would handle her inquiry.

Tanya indicated the quandary she was in to Matthew and asked for his advice.

"We must learn to leave all our concerns in God's hands," Matthew replied earnestly. "God will do as he sees fit in his own time frame. By your own account, Tom has a terrible temper. He might become violent if you confronted him with these stories."

"Tom has never turned his temper on me or the kids. He's occasionally lost his cool with me, but when he does, he always leaves until he simmers down. Still, I know he's been violent with others. I guess his temper is something I'd better be careful about."

Matthew's last attempt to discredit Tom hurt Tanya deeply.

"I hope you'll be able to handle this," Matthew began gravely one afternoon. "I've heard from a reliable person that Tom was unfaithful to you. He had a brief affair with Ann Clark, a teacher from Red Deer, when you were in the late stages of your pregnancy with Billy. Your friend, Mary Gunther is my source. Mary said Ann called it off for fear her husband would find out."

Tanya recalled that because of spotting in the last two months of her pregnancy with Billy, they didn't have sexual intercourse. She was perplexed though, because she remembered Tom and her still being sexually intimate during this period. Tanya was sorely tempted to ask Tom about the alleged affair, but after agonizing over it for a few days, decided to leave it in God's hands as Matthew advised.

Matthew's stories were casting doubts in Tanya's mind about Tom's character. She was finding it increasingly difficult to love and respect her husband in the light of Matthew's allegations.

Matthew, in the interim, was wrestling with his own problems.

"I'm sure that Tanya loves me, but why isn't God taking any action? All that I get now is the odd chance to hold hands with her."

After praying for several months for the Almighty to remove Tom, Matthew was becoming extremely impatient. As Tanya was about to leave the school yard one Friday afternoon in the fall, he told her about God's message that woke him up and his Aunt Sandra's and his prayers for Tom's removal.

Tanya sat in her car in a daze, unable to absorb what Matthew just said. Without responding she headed out the driveway. "What a maze it's all becoming," she muttered as she drove along. "To top things off, now Matthew and Sandra are praying for Tom's death."

At the supper table, everyone was upbeat except Tanya. The kids were still excited over spending the afternoon at Grandma's place while Tom went on and on about his winter logging plans, completely oblivious to Tanya's disconsolate mood.

Tanya was feeling very down that evening. Long after Tom and the kids were in bed, she sat in the front room knitting mitts for Billy and Grace. Over and over again she kept asking herself. "How did I get myself into such a mess?"

Finally Tanya headed to the bedroom and crawled into bed. With a heavy heart, she glanced over at Tom sleeping peacefully by her side. "Dear Lord," she began, tears slipping down her cheeks. "I'm so confused and sad about Matthew and Sandra praying for Tom's death. I don't know what to think, Lord. All I ask is for your will to be done. Please help me, Lord. I've no resolve left. I'm at the breaking point."

The next evening, in desperation, Tanya made a half-hearted attempt to talk to Tom about her relationship with Matthew. She failed to get through to him though. Not being perceptive, Tom simply couldn't grasp what she was trying to say and Tanya didn't have the courage to be more explicit.

With the passage of each day, the situation was becoming more complex for Tanya. Matthew's constant lobbying finally convinced her that she should boycott sexual encounters with Tom. After a week, the boycott was still holding, but Tanya was becoming worn down by Tom's persistence. She didn't know how much longer she could hold out.

"It's becoming really urgent," Matthew said to Tanya on Friday afternoon. "I'm at wits' end. I just can't understand God's inaction. It's imperative the children start getting better grounding in biblical beliefs. Both kids need a firm hand, especially Billy. He's becoming a rebel like his dad."

After his talk with Tanya, Matthew left for Red Deer to spend the weekend with Sandra. They talked and prayed for many hours about Tanya's and his relationship. Like her nephew, Sandra also had problems separating the real from the imaginary.

"I had a most interesting dream the other night," she said. "It was horrible. I saw a man working beside a huge pile of logs in a mill yard. Suddenly the pile shifted and the logs came down on him, crushing him to death. Then I found myself standing with some mourners at a graveside service. I overheard one of the mourners say, 'such a shame to leave a young wife with two small children.'"

"My dream changed again and I was at a wedding. I saw you standing at the front of the church waiting for your bride. I didn't notice who the bride was, but saw a small boy and girl sitting with an older person who may have been their grandmother."

"I'm sure God gave me these dreams to forewarn us that our prayers will soon be answered. The young man crushed by the logs and being buried must be Tom. The two small children sitting with their grandmother were no doubt Tanya's children, Billy and Grace."

Gruesome as the dream was, it reassured Matthew that God was soon to answer his and Sandra's prayers and remove Tom. He wondered what he could do as a show of faith that God would soon bring Tanya and him together. Then he remembered Tanya speaking longingly of a Caribbean cruise.

On Saturday afternoon, Matthew stopped at a travel agency and bought tickets for a Caribbean holiday for Matthew and Mary Schwartz. Mary was Tanya's middle name. He told the agent he'd get back in touch, as soon as he decided which cruise they'd take. There was a sizeable savings for paying for the cruise in advance, but Matthew still winced at the price of the tickets.

"Things are finally looking up for me," Matthew thought as he was walking back to the teacherage the next Friday afternoon. "As near as I know, Tanya's boycott on sex with Tom is still holding and Aunt Sandra's dream gives me renewed confidence that Tanya will soon be my wife."

When Matthew told Tanya of his Aunt Sandra's dream, he was surprised and perplexed when she replied in a flat voice, "Oh, isn't that interesting."

Finally Matthew handed Tanya the envelope with the cruise tickets.

"This is for us, Dear," he gushed. "It's my show of faith that God will soon answer our prayers. Please accept this gift as an expression of my love. I'm really excited about it. I know we'll both enjoy it."

"Matthew, you shouldn't have done this," Tanya said bluntly, after opening the envelope. "It's all very lovely and I do thank you for it, but remember, I'm still a married woman."

"I know, I know, but I'm sure we'll be together soon."

"Should we be praying for that?" Tanya questioned in a shocked voice. "Sandra's dreams are interesting, but are they proof that God is about to end Tom's life? Remember Matthew, despite the urgency you feel, is it right for us to try to force God's hand?"

Matthew looked glum, but chose not to argue the issue.

"While I'm thinking of it, Tom and I ended the freeze on sex a few days ago. There's only so much pressure a person can take and I started wondering if I was doing right, seeing I'm still his wife."

Trying to hold back his emotions, Matthew replied in a strained voice, "I won't hold that against you, dear. I know you tried your best. Still, I was expecting that you'd have been excited with the thought of going on a cruise with me, and at least a bit interested in Sandra's dream."

As he glanced over at Tanya, his desperation was fast returning. There she sat, so beautiful, so desirable, yet so unattainable.

"I'm confident Tom's only interested in you to satisfy his ravenous sexual appetite," he said in a voice full of venom. "Just how much more of this can I take! That animal forcing sex on you again."

"I just told you, I am his wife and besides, Tom didn't force himself on me. It was my decision."

"I don't believe that," Matthew interrupted. "He's the godless one and it's plain to me you're his innocent victim."

A vehicle wheeled up to the teacherage. It was Tom with Billy and Grace. When they stepped inside, both kids ran to their mom.

"Mommy, Mommy!," cried Grace. "Daddy killed two gooses with his gun."

"They're not gooses, they're grouses," corrected Billy. "And know what Mom? Dad pulled their heads off and they bleeded on the snow, and then you know what Mom? Dad let me touch them, and they were warm, and he let me carry one to the truck, and it wasn't even heavy for me."

"Tom, I've told you I don't want the kids hunting with you," Tanya said icily. "They're still too young and impressionable."

"Good God woman, I always hunted with Dad when I was Billy's age. I was going to drop them off with your mom, but I guess your folks must be in town. It's all part of life. They've got to learn about it sooner or later. At any rate, the kids enjoyed themselves."

"They're still too young," Tanya continued, growing even more testy. "Regardless of how you were raised, I don't want Billy and Grace to be taught to kill at their age."

"Have it your way," Tom bristled. "The minute Billy's six, though, he'll be hunting with his dad on a regular basis and that, Mrs. Parker, is that."

Tom brazenly reached over, took Tanya's cup and poured himself a cup of tea.

Tanya was seething. Although she was brought up in a home where they depended on hunting for a lot of their meat, because of Matthew's influence, she now believed that hunting was barbaric. Matthew said he only used his gun for target practice.

"Say, Matthew," Tom interjected in the lull that followed his and Tanya's spat. "Jed and I are heading up to the Ghost Meadows tomorrow to hunt. Why not join us? Our neighbour got an elk up there about a week ago."

"Well, I'm kind of busy. I have to mark some papers."

"Oh, come on, you need the break. Do you have a gun?"

"I have an old 2-70 Winchester."

"Good elk gun," Tom carried on. "So what do you say Matthew? Can I pick you up at seven?"

"Well I'm really..."

Tom interrupted him. "Hey, I'm not taking no for an answer. It will do you a world of good to have a break. You can use my license if you want to and I've got plenty of old tags. I've yet to see a game warden up there. So, I'll be here at seven."

"Really, I shouldn't."

"Baloney you shouldn't. It doesn't matter if we get anything or not. Just being out in the bush does a man a world of good."

Tom jumped to his feet and turned to Billy and Grace. "Come on you little twerps. Let's head for home. I'll show you how to take the insides out of the birds."

Tanya followed Tom in her car. In the angry frame of mind she was in, she thought it best not to stay behind and rant and rave to Matthew about her husband. The minute she got into the house she started in on Tom again.

"Honestly, at times you're so pig-headed! Why don't you listen to what people are trying to say? Matthew didn't really want to hunt with you. He's not into hunting."

"Well why the hell didn't he say so?" Tom snapped back.

"Maybe he would have, if you'd have given him a chance. You're so insensitive at times."

"For God's sake," Tom roared. "It's a shame we all can't be perfect like you. I was just trying to be kind to the guy. All he would have had to say was no."

Although very upset, Tanya bit her tongue. There was a dearth of conversation between her and Tom for the rest of the evening.

Back at the teacherage, Matthew was not feeling all that euphoric either. Just when he thought things were starting to come around for him, everything took a tailspin. To top it all off, now he was going hunting with his rival.

"Man, I wish he'd get out of the action," he muttered to himself. "It's all getting so perplexing, but I guess I'd best not rock the boat. I'd better get back to my marking and try to keep him out of my thoughts."

Despite all, the mental picture of Tom forcing sex on a helpless, naked Tanya kept flashing again and again in his mind.

"I hate that son-of-a-bitch. He's no better than a rapist," he muttered. "When will all this rot come to an end?"

Seven a.m. found Tom banging on Matthew's door. As Jed was feeling under the weather, it would be just the two of them. Matthew did his best not to show how upset and raw he was inside, while Tom, oblivious to all, carried on in his normal friendly manner. After driving down a few bush trails, they headed to Ghost Meadows. Tom stopped when they came to an old abandoned logging trail that intersected the main road.

"Let's walk in on this a bit. The trail goes in about two miles and ends at an old sawmill site."

Despite the re-growth on the old road, they managed without too much trouble. When they came to a knoll, Tom stopped.

"We'll try something here, Matthew. If you stay put, I'll go back about a quarter of a mile and make a big circle. I just might scare something out onto the road for you."

It took Tom about twenty-five minutes to make the circle. Seeing no signs of game or any fresh tracks in the snow, Tom headed back up the trail to where Matthew was. From there, they'd continue on towards the mill site.

While Matthew was waiting for Tom to make the circle, a new surge of rage gripped him as he visualized a distraught Tanya, pleading for Tom not to have sex with her." God help me!" he cried out. "I just can't take anymore. I'd like to kill that rotten bastard."

Then, as he glanced down the cut line, he saw Tom coming back towards him. Matthew leaned up against a deadfall, disengaged the safety on his gun and put the cross hairs of his scope on Tom's chest. His rifle had a two stage trigger on it. He squeezed the trigger through the first stage and was holding.

As Tom was climbing out of a creek bed that crossed the trail, an eerie overpowering feeling of danger swept over him. The next instant he was on the ground rolling back into the creek.

"Now what?" he blurted out. "What in the world is going on with me?"

When Tom wiggled up the creek bank on his elbows and peered through the re-growth with his binoculars, his heart froze! He could see Matthew, leaning up against a deadfall, looking towards him through his gun scope with his forefinger on the trigger.

"Damn it, that stupid idiot must have thought I was a moose or elk," Tom muttered.

Tom crawled back into the creek bed, headed into the bush some fifty feet and then walked parallel to the trail until he was adjacent Matthew.

"Man, you scared the living crap out of me," Tom shouted. "I was just coming up out of the creek a couple of hundred yards or so to the south when I saw you pointing your gun at me. I figured you took me for a moose or elk so I stayed in the bush."

"No, not really," Matthew replied in a shaky voice. "I just saw some movement and was checking it out with my scope."

"I hate to be a poor sport, but I might have to get you to drive me home. I must be getting the flu too. My stomach's doing a lot of churning."

Tom dropped Matthew off at the teacherage. Matthew spent the rest of the day and most of the night in mental agony. He was still enraged at Tom for forcing sex on Tanya, but in addition, he was now tortured with guilt for being so sorely tempted to kill his rival. Finally, in the wee hours of the morning, he could stand the emotional pain no longer. He got in his car, drove to Red Deer and poured out his heart to Sandra. Time and time again he asked her, "Would I have pulled the trigger, if Tom hadn't fallen back into the creek bed?"

CHAPTER
18

"Why did I fall back into the creek?" Tom mused, as he did the evening chores. "I'd swear I didn't see Matthew until I spotted him with the binoculars. If I didn't know better I'd say something pushed me, but how could that be? Did Matthew really see some movement on the line, or was he aiming the gun at me? Am I missing something?"

Tom's thoughts drifted to Tanya's and his relationship.

"Of late we're always quarrelling. Tanya seems to tolerate sex rather than being eager like she used to be. She dresses so bland and has such a sexless hair style now. I'm glad the boycott on sex is over, but what brought it on? Is it normal for some of the spark to fade as your marriage grows older? Is our relationship getting shaky?"

On the Friday that school was to be let out for the Christmas break, Tanya invited Matthew for supper. Tom and the kids dropped her off at the school after dinner and she would come home with Matthew.

All that afternoon Tom was preoccupied with Tanya's and his marital problems. Supper was on the table when

Tanya and Matthew pulled up in the driveway. "Strange," he muttered, as he watched them get out of the car. "Matthew has his right glove off, Tanya her left."

After supper was finished, Tanya put the kids to bed. As they sat chatting, Tom was still sifting through Tanya's and his problems.

Suddenly, something dawned on him. "Aren't those looks that Tanya and Matthew are exchanging more than just friendly glances?" After reflecting for a bit he said under his breath, "Not my Tanya, not a chance. She'd be the last person in the world to be unfaithful!"

When Tom was in the bathroom, he glanced in the direction of the kitchen table through the crack in the door. His heart nearly stopped. Had he just seen Tanya taking her hand off Matthew's shoulder?

"No it couldn't be. Your double vision is playing tricks on you. But wait a minute," he whispered, a sick feeling washed over him. "Matthew's right glove and Tanya's left glove were off when they stepped out of the car. Could they have been holding hands? They were doing some pretty heavy flirting last winter, even play fighting. Tanya said she did it to build up Matthew's self-esteem. Was there something more to it? No, rubbish! Tanya two-timing me? Never! Still, what if?"

Tom returned to the table feeling very unnerved.

Suddenly he leapt to his feet, a plan forming in his mind. "Damn, I think I left the key on in the tractor at the mill yard. The battery is none too good and it will be dead by morning if it's on overnight. I'd better go check it out."

Tom put on his coat and boots and headed for the door. There was an unrestricted view of the kitchen table through the front room window and just before stepping outside, he grabbed his binoculars from the porch cupboard. Instead of heading to the mill yard, he trotted to the machine shed, leaned up against the shed and focused the binoculars on the house. He could see Tanya and Matthew sitting across from each other at the kitchen table.

"Thomas, you've flipped right out," he said out loud. "You know this is stupid. You know you can trust Tanya."

Still, something made him keep watching.

Tanya got up, went to the stove and returned with the teapot. She finished pouring Matthew's tea and was setting the teapot down, when Tom's heart nearly stopped again. Before Tanya could take her hand off the teapot, Matthew reached out and rested his hand on hers. They sat there, holding hands and talking. Tanya looked in the direction of the front room window and pointed to it. Matthew too glanced toward the window and took his hand away.

"DIRTY ROTTEN SON OF A BITCH!" Tom roared. "What an idiot I've been for being such a dupe and not reading the signs before. Tanya two-timing me and that lowbred Matthew trying to steal my wife. I'll break every bone in his useless body!"

Tom raced for the house, but pulled up short just before he got there. "I must play this cool," he mumbled. "I've got to try to control my temper and think things out. A donnybrook that wakes up the kids is not the way to go. If I blow up in front of Tanya and Matthew it will put them onside, defending each other. Even though I'd love to hammer him senseless, I'd best deal with Tanya by herself when Matthew leaves. I'll straighten that bastard out later!"

Matthew was facing the door when Tom stepped inside. A feeling of horror enveloped him when he saw Tom set the binoculars back on the shelf. "Was he using the binoculars to spy on us? Did he see us holding hands?"

Tanya was very unnerved when Tom came to the table. She hadn't seen Tom with the binoculars, but was familiar with that look of controlled rage on his face. She thought of Matthew and her holding hands while Tom was out. Was he onto them? Fighting back panic, Tanya turned to Tom.

"Was the key on?" she asked, her voice trembling.

"Don't know," Tom replied bluntly. "Didn't go to the mill yard."

Tom sat down, poured himself a cup of tea and drank it down without stopping. Tanya felt sick. Both she and Matthew made nervous attempts at small talk, but it was futile.

Suddenly, Tom cut Matthew off in mid-sentence, changing the subject. "I'll never forget an incident that happened years ago when I worked in the bush. One of the fellows I worked with was Andy MacDonald. Andy was quite a character, a half-breed he was. One of the strongest men I've ever known. Built just like a bull. We used to wrestle. Man, what a tussle."

Tom was watching Matthew's face.

"He had a nice wife too. She had a bit of a problem with liquor though. Anyway, Andy took off for a few days and came home unexpectedly. I guess when he opened the door, he caught some young guy and his wife with most of their clothes off. Both of them were pretty drunk. Old MacDonald beat the supreme daylights out of the guy, then kicked his crotch until it was mush. From what I heard the doctors had to castrate the poor fellow. The last I heard, Andy and his Mrs. were living somewhere down on the Coal Branch."

Matthew would not look Tom in the eye. "That story was tailored for me. I'd best keep a low profile."

As he glanced over at Tom's huge chest and bulging arms, he shuddered.

In the silence that followed, Matthew was desperately trying to figure out his options. "Well folks," he began after a lengthy silence, "if you'll excuse me, I'll be going. I've got a bunch of school work I should finish before I leave for Christmas. Thanks for having me over for supper."

"Why do I always have to run from my problems?" Matthew thought as he was putting on his coat. "Why did I lie to them about the school work? Tanya has such a pleading look in her eyes. I wish I could stay and straighten out the mess, but I just can't handle it. Dear God, how will I ever live with myself if anything happens to Tanya?"

"Going to be home tomorrow?" Tom called out.

"I believe so," Matthew replied in a shaky voice.

"Good, I might look you up."

As Matthew's car pulled out of the driveway, Tanya turned to Tom, her voice breaking. "Is there anything wrong dear?"

"We'll talk about it later," Tom replied curtly and headed for the bedroom.

As Tanya washed up the tea cups she was praying earnestly, but feeling so hopelessly trapped.

"Why would Matthew promise to protect me and stay by my side, then slink away without one word of support when he sees trouble looming? He knows that Tom is cluing in about us. I could see fear in his eyes. What a mess I'm in!"

With trepidation, Tanya stepped into the bedroom. The light was out and Tom was already in bed, not a good sign. She crawled under the covers, feeling tense enough to break.

"We've got to talk," Tom began, his voice controlled. "Care to tell me what's going on between you and Matthew?"

"Just what do you mean, Tom?" Tanya asked, hesitantly, her heart beating wildly.

"Don't play innocent," Tom barked. "Try to explain all those warm glances you and Matthew share."

Tanya could hardly breathe. "I don't know what you're talking about," she finally blurted out.

"I'll tell you what I'm talking about," Tom snapped, "you lying, gutless bitch! When I went out tonight, it was a trap. You and that lowbred Matthew played right into it. I took the binoculars with me and instead of going to the mill yard, I went to the shed and looked back at the front room window. I saw you and Matthew holding hands."

The dam burst. "Oh God," Tanya cried out, "I can't take it any longer!" She leapt out of bed, turned on the light and began pacing the floor in abstract agony.

"It's all just driving me crazy. I tried to tell you about Matthew and me a couple of times, but I couldn't get through to you. Oh God, I've got to tell it all now," she sobbed, "I'm so terrified. Yes, there is something between Matthew and me. Yes, I love him."

It was now Tom's turn to jump out of bed. He rushed to the bathroom and threw up. When he returned, Tanya was still pacing, wringing her hands and crying.

"Just how long has this cheating been going on?" Tom roared.

"Maybe nine or ten months," Tanya cried.

"Do you still love me?"

"I certainly did," Tanya replied between sobs, "but I'm so confused now. I just don't know."

"Do you want a divorce?" Tom shouted.

There was no response from Tanya. Fighting to maintain control, Tom went on. "If you decide on a divorce, it will be you who wants it, not I. Still, if that's your decision, the kids stay with me. Just remember this Tanya, you can go if you have to, but I'll kill to keep the kids. If you want to screw up your life with that asshole, that's your decision. I care for our kids too much to allow them to be warped out of shape by that jerk. How the hell could he support you and the kids anyway?"

"Divorce is out of the question," Tanya finally whispered. "I couldn't stand the thought of losing my babies. I love them too much. Besides, Matthew and I don't believe in divorce."

"I've got to be honest and grant you this much, Tanya, you've been a good mother to our kids. If you don't get a divorce though, where in hell does this leave you and Matthew?"

"I don't know," sobbed Tanya. "I'm just so mixed up and scared."

"This is going to be the hardest question I've ever asked anyone in my life. You've lied to me for close to a year now, so for God's sake, will you have the decency to tell me the truth? Did you guys do any shagging? Before God, no BS. Give it to me straight."

"No, before God, Matthew didn't screw me. We were somewhat intimate four or five times, but didn't go all the way."

"Go on," Tom hollered, "go on."

"Well," Tanya said, trying desperately to pull herself together, "when Matthew stayed with us after the fire, we had more time to talk and share. You remember how desperately lonely he was and how I was trying to counsel him. Well later on, I started to share my problems with him. He felt he could help me out with spiritual matters. I just felt so bad for him. He had such a lonely life. One day, I told him I loved him."

Tom grimaced and groaned.

"At the time it wasn't physical or sexual love I felt for him. It was just that we had a lot in common and I felt so sorry for him."

It was impossible for Tanya to control herself and she wept bitterly. Still sobbing, she tried to continue.

"One day he was feeling very dejected. He said how lucky we couples were, that he was such a loser and that he'd never even seen a naked woman before. So"...... Tanya could not continue. Finally she blurted out, "so I undressed and posed nude for him. After that, we started to occasionally hold hands and a bit later on, started to do a bit of necking."

Tom roared like a wounded animal and drove his fist right through the wallboard.

Tanya was curled up in a tight ball on her side of the bed.

"Please," she pleaded, "Billy and Grace. Please Tom, for their sake."

"Carry on you little whore!" Tom growled.

Tanya was almost hysterical and it took her some time to gain control.

Finally she continued. "Well, on the first week he was back in the new teacherage, we talked as usual on Friday afternoon. You and I quarreled at noon when you came home for dinner and I had nothing prepared. Matthew was totally dejected again and told me a horrible story from his childhood. It moved me so much to see how that old memory was still affecting him, that I guess we did something we shouldn't have."

Tanya again had to stop to collect herself before she could continue.

"After he told me his story, we went into his bedroom. It was my idea, not Matthew's. We undressed, lay on the bed and held each other for a few minutes. After necking a bit, we got into some heavy petting. Seeing we were both feeling so guilty and hung up it didn't work for either of us, if you know what I mean."

Tom listened, his jaw clenched, vibrating with rage. "You lowbred, groveling slut!" he bellowed. "I opened my home to that insignificant prick. I trusted you both without questioning either of your motives. You betrayed that trust. I even encouraged you to show kindness to him. I made the horrible mistake of thinking you were strong, of thinking you were loyal, of thinking you were decent. My wife, the mother of our children, lying naked with Matthew on his bed, entertaining him. I don't care what you call it, you were still being sexually intimate with him."

"Please Tom," Tanya pleaded, "I can't take any more. I'm feeling sick. I've got to go to the bathroom."

By the time Tanya returned, Tom was again in control of himself. "Now listen and listen carefully. What you and Matthew did was morally wrong. You have broken the vows you made before God and before our friends, vows of being faithful to me until death. You have lived a lie to me, to our precious kids and to our folks."

"Tell me, what would Billy have thought if he woke up, came to his bedroom door and saw you standing naked in front of Matthew? You didn't even have the decency to go elsewhere when you did your striptease. What would you have done or said if some student barged into the teacherage and caught you and Matthew in the act?"

"How could you be so low? How could you hurt me so? Is this part of your new-found religion to rip the heart right out of the one who loves you, the one you promised to love till death? I've always been faithful to you. I risked my life fighting to save you. Is this how you show your gratitude?"

As he sobbed uncontrollably, Tom beat his fist against the wall until it was raw. "I've loved you so much, Tanya, and now you've betrayed me."

Tanya wept quietly by Tom's side. Finally she spoke. "I'm so sorry Tom, so confused. You indeed have been so good to me and I so rotten to you."

She tried to put her arm around him to comfort him.

"Get your filthy hand off me," he growled.

Tanya recoiled. There they lay, each on their own side of the bed, Tom so enraged, so broken hearted, Tanya feeling so wretched, so dirty, so confused, both of them crying.

Finally, after several minutes, Tanya spoke. "You asked me earlier, Tom, if I still loved you. I said I wasn't sure. I don't know if it's too late, but I can now say without the slightest shadow of doubt that I do love you. I've just seen the true depth of your love for both me and the kids, and how I've nearly ripped you apart. I can say without a qualm that I desperately want to stay with you and love you and our kids forever. If you can't live with me anymore though, I'll understand."

It took some time for Tom to gain control. Finally he whispered, "Stay."

"What about the why's of it all though? I can see you and Matthew befriending each other and trying to help each other with your problems. Even though it makes me wild, I can even see you guys becoming intimate, but there must have been something more, some other reason for Matthew staying interested in you. You say the intimacy didn't pan out for either of you, and that divorce was out of the question. Just what in blazes was there in it for Matthew?"

Tanya started to cry again. "There's much more, Tom, some of it's awful. You'll have to try to hold on to yourself."

"Go on," Tom urged, "go on."

"You see," Tanya sobbed, "I'm against divorce in most instances, but Matthew doesn't believe in it under any circumstance. He thought the only way for us to get together was for you to die. Matthew and his aunt have been praying for several months for God to take you away."

Tom lay in stunned silence, tears glistening in his eyes, his teeth clenched.

Tanya braced herself. "Matthew felt that since God brought us together, your death would be in God's plan. Actually, because you and I slept together a few times before we married, he figured that our marriage vows were void in God's eyes. He felt that our kids needed his corporal style of discipline. He was confident that God would act quickly. I guess that's why he kept so interested in me."

"And you, Tanya?" Tom asked, composing himself again. "This is another gut-wrenching question for me. Were you also praying for my death? How did you fit into all this insanity?"

Tanya could not answer Tom. She cried uncontrollably, at times nearing hysteria. Finally she continued. "Well, when Matthew first told me of his Aunt Sandra's and his prayers, I was heartbroken. I just hadn't thought about how Matthew's and my relationship would work out. I honestly just prayed for God's will to be done. Please don't hate me for that, but I was just so confused."

Again Tom fell silent. Finally he carried on. "That hurts, damn it. God, that hurts. I know I'm far from perfect, but if you decided that you didn't love me anymore and that you loved that creep, why didn't you just tell me it was all over and go live with him? It happens every day. I just can't believe it. Matthew and his aunt praying for my death because you guys didn't believe in divorce. I'm so hurt that I can't even be angry about it."

"You see, there are quite a number of things that Matthew told me about you that made me question your love, question your honesty, just plain question your character. I'll try to go through them for you now, but I'm still a bit scared of you and terrified that the stories he told me about you might be true. I know now that I should have checked them out, but Matthew advised me that the best thing I could do was leave everything in God's hands. I was relying on him as my spiritual coach. He told me if you found out about us, you'd become violent."

"Like I'm violent now," Tom interjected. "Didn't you ever stop to think that this was just a trick he used to keep you with him as long as possible?"

Tanya shook her head and cried. "I suppose so, I don't know. Anyway, the first story Matthew told me was that he'd heard from reliable sources that you'd been unfaithful to me while you were in the Armed Forces. His source told him that you were quite a womanizer."

"But why didn't you talk to me about it?"

"I don't know. I told him that Joe Bonner told me you were true to me, but then, later on, I even started to question Joe's word. I was fearful that maybe he was covering up for you."

"There must be more."

"Yes, a lot more. He told me that you lied about your accident while hauling ammunition. He said he'd talked to a fellow who was a truck driver in your convoy. By this guy's account, you weren't number one in the convoy and there weren't any cattle on the road. You were just drunk and drove into the ditch. According to Matthew's source, you had a serious drinking problem while you were posted overseas."

"That lying little bastard," Tom exploded. "His story is all garbage. I can prove my account, Matthew can't prove his. Why in the world didn't you check his story out? Is there more?"

"Yes there is. He said that when you were growing up, you were lazy, mean and disrespectful to your folks."

"Good God!" Tom roared, "Why on earth didn't you check that out with Mom?"

"Well, I have a letter from Matthew's aunt that backs up his claim. His Aunt Sandra apparently knew your folks when you were a youngster. I've never met her, but we have exchanged a few letters. In fact, Matthew got a lot of his information from her. I guess I should have asked your mom about Sandra's stories, but I felt awkward about it."

"You'll be checking it out now. We're going to phone Mom so you can get to the bottom of these lies."

"It's midnight," protested Tanya. "We don't want to wake your folks."

"You're damn right we do," Tom shouted.

Tanya reluctantly followed Tom to the phone. Finally he got his mom on the line.

"I'm sorry for phoning so late, but Tanya and I are having some serious problems. There is a bit of our family history I'd like you to fill Tanya in on. A Mrs. Sandra Schwartz and her nephew have been spreading some bull about me when I was a youngster. For God's sake Mom, give Tanya the truth. There's been far too much BS peddled up till now."

At first Tanya was hesitant, but finally started blurting out Sandra's story. Before she could finish, Ema interrupted her.

"Listen dear, your story is all a pile of rubbish and considering its source, I'm not at all surprised. Mrs. Schwartz, her husband Morris, Bill and I did visit a few times over the years. Bill and Morris were buddies in the First World War. I got so I couldn't abide her negative attitude and her tall tales, so we stopped inviting them out. Bill did visit Morris in Red Deer a few times after that, but Tom and I never went with him. Where she got the notion that Tom was hard to handle, I'll never know. It's all hogwash. Tom was such a help to Bill and I."

"Do you remember how old Tom was when you last visited them in Red Deer?"

"I think about six or seven. They had a couple of girls, a year or two younger than Tom. Tom was seven, maybe eight when she and I had words. That was the end of the contact Tom and I had with them."

Tom took the phone from Tanya. "Thanks Mom, I'm sure your comments will help Tanya a lot. Please keep us in mind. We're going through some pretty deep waters."

"Ron and I will be praying for you and the kids. Please stay in touch," Ema concluded.

Tanya sat on the edge of the bed in stunned silence. Finally she said, "I can't understand why Sandra would lie to me."

"Maybe you should ask her that. From what Mom told us, this isn't her first fabrication."

"I hate myself for being so weak and gullible," Tanya sobbed.

"Let's go to bed Tanya. We've both had enough for tonight. We'd better try to get some sleep. We'll talk more in the morning."

As Tanya lay in bed she felt like mush. In a desperate attempt to help resolve things, she tried to snuggle close to

Tom. He moved away from her and she quickly retreated to her side of the bed. Despite feeling totally devastated, Tanya finally fell into a troubled sleep.

Not so Tom. He had never felt so emotionally raw. As he glanced at his sleeping mate, part of him wanted to shake her till her teeth rattled, part of him wanted to comfort her and say, "I forgive you."

In the morning, neither Tanya nor Tom were all that hungry, but Tanya made breakfast for the kids. Her eyes filled with tears as she watched Billy and Grace eating their breakfast, so innocent and unaware of the horrendous things that were transpiring.

At 8 a.m. Tanya phoned her folks to see if they could look after the kids for the day. Ben and his girlfriend Gail were home for Christmas and just leaving to shop in Red Deer. They offered to take the kids with them.

After Ben and Gail picked up the kids, Tanya and Tom resumed where they'd left off the night before.

"Here," Tanya said, handing Tom a letter. "Matthew gave me this letter from his aunt a couple of months ago. Read the part I underlined."

"When Tom was about ten, he came with his folks for a visit," Tom read aloud. "My daughters were in tears after the Parkers left. They said when they were alone with Tom, he exposed himself and forced them to fondle him."

"There's something rotten here!" Tom exploded. "Like Mom said, the last time we visited them in Red Deer, I was about six or seven. I could sue those idiots for defamation of character!"

"That was scary enough for me, but Matthew's story of what Roy Jabs told him terrified me for Billy's and Grace's safety. According to Matthew, Roy witnessed you standing in the bush, exposing yourself to some young girls last year at the school picnic."

"Damn Matthew's rotten hide and damn yours for not having the guts to get to the bottom of it! If it were true, you'd have reason to fear for our kids' welfare. Good God woman, I just went into the bush to take a leak! Why in the world didn't you go to the police, or at least to your folks? I'm phoning Roy to get his side of it."

Roy was a local farmer in his early sixties and quite hard of hearing. Tom got right to the point, telling him Matthew's story.

"I said what?" Roy hollered into the phone.

Tom retold the incident.

"That's what I thought you said, but I just couldn't believe my ears. That lying bastard! I'll be straightening him out and real soon. Here's what happened. At the picnic, Matthew asked me if I had seen you. I said I thought you had gone into the bush to take a leak and without a bathroom, one was liable to get an eyeful. That was it. That's exactly what I said, no more and no less. That lying ass hole, I'll be taking a strip off his rump the first chance I get."

Because Roy was shouting, Tanya heard every word he said.

"I just can't imagine why Matthew would spin all those lies about you," Tanya said when Tom got off the phone.

"There's one more story that hurt me deeply. Matthew told me that you had a brief affair with a teacher from Red Deer when I was pregnant with Billy. Mary Gunther who teaches in Milden was his source."

"Like all the other lies that Matthew peddled about me, I suppose you checked this story out," Tom said sarcastically.

"I was terrified that it might be true. I knew Mary from my teaching days and she's a reputable person."

Again they headed to the phone. This time Tanya made the call. Mary became quite concerned when she recognized the gravity of the situation.

"Good Lord, Tanya, Matthew has his lines completely crossed again and it's certainly not the first time. I'll try to piece it all together for you. The last year you taught, the Fall Teachers' Convention was in Red Deer. Tom was with you at the dance at the end of the convention. If you'll remember, I introduced you and Tom to Ann Clark. As I recall, Tom asked her for a dance. I believe you were two or three months from your due date."

"Yes, it's coming back. She was rather dark with quite a full figure."

"That was her. Anyway, you and Tom left early. Later that evening, Ann had quite a shine on. She told me that Tom turned her on and that she wouldn't mind a fling with him."

"I guess I should take some responsibility for Matthew getting his story. A few weeks back, he was here in Milden for a workshop. Someone mentioned that Ann Clark was divorced. I replied, 'I'm not at all surprised' and recounted this incident. How Matthew took that to mean that Tom and she had an affair, I'll never know. As I've said before, Tanya, it's best to be careful what you tell Matthew."

Tom and Tanya returned to the couch. As Tanya was shaking uncontrollably, Tom got up, found a quilt and draped it over her shoulders.

"I've made such a fool of myself believing or half-believing all of those stories. I know you're enraged with Matthew and tore up with me. I feel so dirty. I honestly wouldn't blame you if you did beat me."

She glanced over at Tom, the man Matthew portrayed as being so evil, the man who would be physically violent with her if he ever found out. There he sat, tears streaming down his face.

"How could I ever beat the one I love so much?" Tom finally whispered.

Tanya reached over and wiped the tears from his cheeks. "I love you too, Tom. I hope someday that you'll be able to forgive me."

A big arm reached out and pulled Tanya close. "My heart feels pretty well chewed up, but I'll continue loving you till I die."

"Thank you Tom," Tanya whispered. "What an idiot I've been, allowing myself to be fooled into thinking you were some kind of a monster to be feared."

Tanya got up and made them a cup of tea. As they sat at the kitchen table, she went on. "Matthew felt so confident God was going to take your life that he bought us tickets for a Caribbean cruise. It was to be for our honeymoon," she sobbed. "He told me he did it as a show of faith."

"That's hard to take," Tom grimaced. "I was to die so you and that nitwit could have your cruise. Now isn't that an example of true Christian compassion! I'm hurting so bad it would be easy for me to go and rip Matthew's heart right out of his chest. That wouldn't be the answer though. I'm going to phone Mr. Schwartz right now and see what he has to say for himself."

For most of the night Matthew lay awake lambasting himself for not staying and defending Tanya. He answered the phone with trepidation.

"It's all over," Tom shouted. "Tanya has told me the whole story."

Tanya was close to the phone and blanched when she heard Matthew reply, "I'm sorry Tom, but I don't follow you."

"You know damned well what I mean. The whole bloody mess. Your sexual intimacy with Tanya. All those lies you invented about me and your prayers for my death so you could get at Tanya. Now, about my accident in the Service. Where did you get that bull from?"

"I was told about your accident from a fellow who said he drove in your convoy," Matthew said hesitantly.

"What a crock," Tom shot back. "I never served with a Rob Hanks when I was overseas. I can give you the names of all the drivers that day. Those lies about me being lazy and mean to my folks. Another pile of crap. Tanya has already checked it out with Mom. Your story about me exposing myself at the school picnic. Roy Jabs is some tore up with you over that tale. Tanya phoned Mary Gunther and got to the bottom of your BS about my phantom affair with Ann Clark. Now what about this bloody Caribbean cruise you booked for yourself and Tanya? She tells me it cost you a fortune."

"Well, I acknowledge that I bought two tickets for a cruise," Matthew said, his voice breaking. "The other ticket was not necessarily for Tanya though."

"My God!" Tanya gasped. "I've been betrayed."

"Tanya and I are going to meet with her folks this afternoon. We want you to come over to the Osmond place at seven-thirty this evening. We're hoping that we can straighten out this bloody mess."

"Why would Matthew lie about those cruise tickets?" Tanya said when Tom got off the phone. "I distinctly remember him saying, 'These are for us dear.' Time and time again he said he'd come to my aid if things got dicey and now, not a word of support for me. How could I have misread him so badly? How can I ever forgive myself? How can you or the folks ever forgive me?"

"I'm trying hard," Tom sighed, "but it may take some time."

"So far we've only talked of your foul up. I know I must take some responsibility. Where did I go wrong? There must have been some things I could have done differently."

"Really Tom, you've been a good husband and father," Tanya said hesitantly. "I'm certainly not going to assign blame to you for the trouble Matthew and I got ourselves into. There may have been a few things that might have contributed some, but really, I shouldn't be making excuses for myself."

"No Tanya, give it to me straight. Tell me what I did, or didn't do, that made you turn to him."

"Well, all right. You see, your strength at times makes you an island unto yourself. Sometimes you don't seem to need people. Your fierce independence, your self-confidence and your impatience at times make you a little hard to approach."

"I'd have to say you're on the money," Tom said after some thought. "I know I'm not the easiest guy to live with. I have the feeling you're holding back though. There must be more. Tell it like it is."

"Okay," Tanya responded after a long pause. "When we married, I didn't have too much self-confidence and was unsure of my own spirituality. I hoped you would help me grow into a more complete person. Your aggressive, argumentative style was the wrong approach for me. After several attempts to get your help, I gave up. I suppose I found in Matthew someone searching for his own identity as I was. He also claimed to be well-grounded in spiritual matters. Perhaps if you could have helped me grow, I wouldn't have turned to Matthew. Who knows? I would so welcome your help now, as I still have a long way to go."

"I see your point, I see your point," Tom replied, shaking his head. "I guess I'm not as sensitive as I could be. I take responsibility for my part. I'm going to make a real effort to smarten up a whole lot. Feel free to give me a good clip behind the ear if I don't."

"I know we're in for some rough times ahead as we work this all out," Tom went on. "Some of it we'll be able to do together, some of it we'll have to do on our own. As for me, I need to talk with another man. I sure wish Dad was still alive. If you can manage for a couple of hours, Tanya, I'm going to see Les Corbit."

"That's alright. I have a lot of thinking I need to do by myself."

After Tom left, Tanya sat at the kitchen table, trying to sort out the events of the last twenty-four hours. As the minutes slipped by, her feelings of guilt intensified. "I loath myself," she finally mumbled. "I can't think of one valid excuse for what Matthew and I did. It would serve me right if Tom left me."

Tanya was feeling very low as she headed into the bedroom to rest. She was about to lie down when she noticed a scrap of paper on her pillow.

"I wrote this poem yesterday afternoon, while I was waiting for supper to cook," she read aloud. "I'm not much of a poet, but I meant it then, and I mean it now. I'll be back in a couple of hours. Have faith that we'll make it through."

I risked my life to save you then

I'd gladly do it all again

My love for you is still so strong

And that, my Tanya's why I long

To spend my life here just with you

And always to our love be true.

Love, Tom

As tears streamed down Tanya's face she whispered, "I love you too, Tom."

CHAPTER
19

"Why did Tanya do this to me?" Tom mused as he drove the ten odd miles to Les Corbits place. "Why didn't I clue in last winter? How will it all work out?"

"Come on in," Les called out. "Pardon me for not coming to the door, but this arthritis kind of makes me slow on the draw."

"You're hurting pretty bad, eh?" Tom asked as he stepped inside.

"Yes, a fair bit, but God gives me the strength to bear it and the medications I take help some. It's been a few years since I've seen you. Beulah and I used to visit you and your folks quite often when you were still on the old farm. What brings you out?"

Tom couldn't hold back the pain and poured out his soul to Les. "It's so hard to take," he sobbed. "I was the evil one. I was to be slain by God so that Matthew could sleep with my Tanya and raise our kids."

When Tom finally finished, Les put a hand on his shoulder and prayed a humble prayer for him, Tanya, their family and then for Matthew.

"Let's get this straight, Tom. What Matthew and Tanya did was wrong. It was sin. God does not now, nor ever has, condoned such wrong doing. They were trying to bend God's rules in order to give credence to their actions. By what you say, they both had good motives to start with, but unfortunately, allowed themselves to become too close."

"No doubt you could have been more approachable and more helpful assisting your wife in spiritual matters. You're a very strong, independent type. For those of us who are strong, and I guess that includes me, it's hard to appreciate that others can't be as resolute as we are."

"I know how kind and supportive you were to your folks. It's a shame Tanya hadn't checked with me about your childhood. You, my friend, have been hard done by. You're hurting bad. What are your immediate plans?"

"Our marriage is going to stay together. I've had to swallow a lot of crap, but I do forgive Tanya, and that makes me feel a whole lot better."

"What about Tanya? How's she doing?"

"She's pretty well tore up, really devastated. She feels so bad that she's betrayed me and lived a lie to me and the family. She even offered to leave if I couldn't stand to have her near."

"It sounds like Tanya recognizes that what she and Matthew did was wrong and is repentant." Reaching across the table, Les put his hand on Tom's shoulder. "If Tanya is repentant, God will help rebuild your relationship. It's going to be painful, but He can give you happiness again."

"If you can bear with me, Tom, I'd like to tell you a story that's just about as sad as yours and Tanya's. Years ago a young man slipped a cog or two one night when he went to a party without his girlfriend. He got into some booze for the very first time and regrettably, ended up in bed with a married woman. It was an uphill battle for his fiancé to forgive him, an even harder task for him to forgive himself. They've been married now for over thirty-five years." There were tears in Les's eyes as he carried on. "God can and will give you and Tanya peace if she's truly repentant. I know. I was that foolish young man."

"It's sad that sometimes we can get off track," Tom interjected. "I know Tanya's intentions were good when she started helping Matthew."

"Unfortunately, Tanya's spiritual guides were both off base." Les continued. "Many so-called Christians don't have a clue what it's all about. We do have to make peace with our Creator, but that's just the start. Take the compassion out of your religion and you've got nothing of value left. That's what Matthew, Tanya and Sandra did. The forgiveness you're showing your wife and the long suffering you're showing Matthew have taken a lot of grit. I know the kind of man you are and the effort it takes to keep from hammering him senseless. I saw Kostich's face after you finished working him over."

"Yes you're right, Les. It's hard not to mangle him, but I know that's not the answer."

"I have a tough assignment for you, Tom. If you can't do it right away, at least think about it. Pray with your wife. Pray tonight if you can handle it. Help her avail herself of God's forgiveness. Pray with your Tanya every night as long as you live. It worked for Beulah and me. I know it will work for Tanya and you too."

"The last thing I suggest will be the hardest. It's probably best to wait a few days on this one, but try to pray for Matthew. I know he hurt you an awful lot, but he's human and he too is hurting. If you can do this, Tom, it will make a giant out of a big man. It will also help Tanya to heal if she can pray for his welfare."

Tom sat in silence, teeth clenched, emotions playing across his face.

"You're dead on about it being a tough assignment," he finally blurted out. "Especially the last part. You're right though. Our love was strong enough to weather the storm. As for praying for Matthew, I'd gag right now, but I know it will do Tanya and me a lot of good if we can manage it."

"I'll be praying for you and your family every day and I'm sure Beulah will too, when she gets home. A last bit of advice, Tom. As you rebuild your marriage, try to help Tanya grow."

Tom shook Les's hand. "Thanks for your help. Your prayers will be much appreciated."

When Tom got back home, Tanya was in tears. "Thank you so much for that beautiful poem," she whispered. "I'll cherish it to my dying day."

Tom took Tanya into his arms. "While I was at Les's place, God gave me peace. I can now say that I've forgiven you and Matthew."

"Thank you so much for giving me another chance," Tanya sobbed. "Thank you for keeping our family together. I'll do my level best to regain your respect and trust."

When they arrived at the folks' place, Betty noticed that both Tanya's and Tom's eyes were red.

"Mom, Dad, I hope you won't hate me, but I've done something awful," Tanya began. "I've been unfaithful to Tom. I won't make excuses for myself. It was with Matthew Schwartz."

"Oh my God," Jed groaned.

With tears streaming down her face, Tanya told them the whole story.

"Without question, the sexual involvement was tough to stomach," Tom interjected. "The worst parts though were Matthew's lies and the insane prayers for my death."

"I don't know why I didn't check Matthew's stories out," Tanya continued. "I guess I'd been brainwashed. He was supposed to be my spiritual mentor. He claimed to follow his Christian beliefs to the letter of the law and I totally trusted him."

Tanya paused for a moment, as she reached over and took Tom by the hand.

"You'll be relieved to know that Tom has forgiven me and we're trying to rebuild our marriage." Tanya couldn't continue. She covered her face with her hands and wept.

"Yes, I've forgiven my Tanya and we're intent on rebuilding our marriage," Tom cried with clenched teeth. "But it hurts. God only knows how it hurts." Between sobs he continued. "I was to be killed by God so that son-of-a-bitch could screw my wife and beat on our kids. It just hurts like hell."

Tom got up and walked over to the kitchen window. Betty followed and put her arms around him. "Thank you so much for being big enough to forgive Tanya and take her back."

Finally Tanya stopped crying. "Mom, Dad, can you ever forgive me?" she pleaded.

"Of course we will," her dad replied, tears wetting his cheeks. "We all make mistakes. Mom and I have made our fair share of them. We're so relieved that your marriage is staying together. No doubt the hardest part for you will be to forgive yourself."

As Betty opened her mouth to speak, emotions were playing across her face. She was unable to get one word out. She rushed over to Tanya. Neither mother nor daughter said a word. They just hugged each other for dear life and cried. Finally Betty regained her composure.

"I guess, Tanya, you and I had to learn our lessons the hard way. How could we not forgive you? We'll do everything in our power to help you out. Always remember, Tanya, you are a gem in God's eyes. Don't ever forget that. You fell, but you are back on your feet again. Even though you've hurt Tom something awful, he still loves you. I realize that both of you would give anything for this not to have happened. Still, I know that you will be better people because of it."

At six-thirty, Tom phoned Matthew. "If it's all right with you, Tanya and I would like to meet you at the teacherage, rather than at the folks' place."

Matthew breathed a sigh of relief. "Yes I think that would be best."

He had put in a long, rough day waiting for his interrogation at the Osmond's. He knew that in the past both Tom and Jed worked a few fellows over. The thought of facing them all brought back the chilling memories of his forced confession at church when Nellie and he fooled around. In his muddled state of mind he was constantly praying for his and Tanya's safety.

A somber threesome sat down at Matthew's table.

"I apologize for letting things go as far as they did," Tanya began. "Yesterday, I couldn't say if I still loved Tom, but now I can, and I've re-pledged my faithfulness to him. I now realize that what you and I did, Matthew, was totally wrong. We have sinned. Further, God had no part in it. I'd like to ask for your forgiveness for leading you along. I also want you to know that I have not been pressured by Tom in any way. You misread him badly and regrettably, I believed you. In the last few hours I have discovered how long suffering and beautiful his love for me is."

While Tanya talked, Matthew sat in stunned silence.

"When you and I first started helping each other, it was kind and pure. Unfortunately, neither one of us was strong enough to control ourselves. Though the physical part of the relationship was wrong, the transfer of my loyalty from Tom to you was far worse. All those fabrications you made about Tom are hard for me to understand. I'm so relieved that they all proved wrong. I don't hate you, but I'm just very hurt. I hope that we can still be civil with each other. You should know I won't be teaching after Christmas."

"When you and Tanya started talking to each other, she told me about your rough upbringing," Tom began. "I encouraged her to help you. When the teacherage burned down, I was the one who suggested you move in with us. What started out as a beautiful thing, turned out so sick. What happened between you and Tanya, you know, the physical things, they're hard to take, but understandable. Tanya is a kind, attractive woman and from what she's told me, she was the one to start the physical part of it."

"Those idiotic prayers of yours for my death though and those bloody tall tales to discredit me," Tom continued, his voice starting to shake. "Really, Matthew. Trying to get God to knock me off so you could have Tanya! I'm mad enough to kick your butt right through your hat, but I've promised you I wouldn't get physical. Let's hear your side of the story."

"Well I guess at the beginning things were alright," Matthew started uncertainly. "I suppose we allowed our relationship to get a bit too personal."

Matthew appeared quite confused as he tried to defend his stories to discredit Tom. His attempt to explain the prayers for Tom's removal was convoluted.

"It seems to me, Matthew, that your stories were a mix of wishful thinking, half truths and lies," Tom shouted. "You were trying hard to completely destroy my credibility in Tanya's eyes."

Sensing that Tom was nearing the point of losing it, Tanya stepped into the conversation. "I learned my lesson, Matthew, and I hope you have too. Now that everything has been found out, I hope that it won't completely destroy you. You're going to have to handle things by yourself this time. Tom and I will have our hands full working out our own pain. Still, I wish you the best."

Fighting back emotion, Tom carried on. "Even though you and Tanya have nearly torn my heart apart, I will not hate you or harbor you any ill will."

Clenching his teeth, Tom reached across the table and shook Matthew's hand. "Please understand this. If we invite you to our house, you're as welcome as you always were, but if I ever catch you there uninvited, I'll break every bone in your body."

Tom beat the table with his fist, and then cupped his head in his hands. He sat there groaning. Tanya got up and put her hand on his shoulder. "Come Tom," she whispered, "let's go."

Although he was grateful for being spared an interrogation at Jed's and Betty's place, Matthew was nonetheless hurting badly. As the night dragged on, he lay in agony, grieving over the loss of Tanya.

"Why did it have to turn out this way, Lord?" he prayed. "I'm sure you brought Tanya and me together. Why do I always have to lose out?"

When Tom and Tanya stopped back at the folks' place, Billy and Grace were already there. Ben and Gail had left again for the evening.

"You both look like you could use a drink of something a little stronger than tea," Jed said.

Tom shook his head. "Tanya can speak for herself, but I'm having enough of a battle with my emotions now. Booze would only make it worse."

When Grandma asked Billy and Grace if they'd like to stay the night, they were ecstatic. After kissing the kids good night, Tom and Tanya left.

As they pulled into their driveway, Tom sighed. "Let's hope we never have to go through another day like this."

Both Tom and Tanya were emotionally and physically exhausted, so turned in early.

"I'd sure like to make love to you, but I really don't know if it will work," Tom said.

"Maybe we shouldn't rush things, Tom. We're both exhausted."

They lay in silence for some time, both of them feeling rough. "I just feel so evil," Tanya moaned. "Oh God, how I hate myself!"

Tom remembered Les's counseling. "I've forgiven you and your folks have forgiven you. Now let's make our peace with our Maker."

Tanya and Tom knelt at the side of their bed.

"Thank you Lord for my Tanya," Tom began. Then biting his lip, he added, "thank you for our love that's seeing us through this tough spot. Help me to be more sensitive to all of Tanya's needs and help rebuild her self-esteem."

With tears streaming down her face, Tanya started hesitantly. "Please dear Lord, forgive me for the wrong I've done Tom and for breaking our marriage vows. Thank you for an understanding husband who still loves me and has given me another chance."

They lay in each other's arms. As the heat started to build between them, they began to caress each other. Their passion grew until neither one could hold back. They ripped off their night clothes and made love with a vengeance, soaring to new heights of emotional and physical ecstasy. It was the best ever for both of them. Afterwards, they lay close, savoring their sweet release, so much in love again, so happy that things were being resolved.

Tom and Tanya discovered the more they prayed for Matthew and the more forgiveness they extended him, the less animosity they felt. They found how impossible it was to hold a grudge or wish ill will to someone you were praying for.

Without question, Matthew was an unpopular person in the community. Over the next few days, he had several angry phone calls and a visit from Roy Jabs. All his fabrications were coming back to haunt him. Recognizing that it would be difficult to continue teaching, he tendered his resignation. With the help of the superintendent, he located a teaching position in southern Alberta.

Matthew spent Christmas with his Aunt Sandra before heading to his new teaching job. He was very distraught over his break up with Tanya and talked to Sandra about it constantly.

"I'm positive it was God's leading that brought us together," Matthew said adamantly. "Why weren't our prayers answered? Why didn't God intervene for Tanya and me?"

"Perhaps our prayers weren't answered because it wasn't God's will," Sandra replied.

"Not a chance!" Matthew responded in an agitated tone. "Not a chance. The more I think about it the more convinced I am that it came apart because my faith in God wasn't strong enough."

As he was driving to his new job, Matthew could think of nothing but the break up with Tanya. One thought kept coming back to him. "Did I fail God? When Tom was in my gun sights, should I have pulled the trigger?"

Although in time Matthew learned to live with the pain of losing Tanya, he was incapable of accepting that their relationship should not have been. Even when he started a new relationship a few years later, his feelings for Tanya did not change.

As Tom and Tanya started anew, they were aware of the Almighty's guiding hand. Glimpses of the dark past would occasionally surface to haunt them, but the wounds did heal in time. Still, there would always be scars to remind them of the painful past.

They continued praying together at day's end for the rest of their lives, always beginning their humble prayers by thanking God for their mate and for their love.

They did have their occasional disagreements, but any differences would be settled before they went to sleep. Tom did his best to help Tanya with her problems and tried hard to be more sensitive. Tanya in turn did her best to toughen up a bit. They had become soul mates.

CHAPTER
20

Jed's and Betty's plans to retire and have Ben and Gail take over the farm were on hold with the young folk in the oil patch. Ben advised his folks to sell out if they got a good offer on the land.

"I wonder if we should buy your folks' land," Tom said to Tanya one evening after supper.

"It's an idea," Tanya replied without conviction. "Do you think we can handle it?"

"I'm working out the angles. It seems to me that expansion is the way to go."

The thought of going into more debt to buy her folks' land terrified Tanya, but she was reticent to raise her concerns with Tom as she still felt beholden to him.

One night when Tanya and Tom were visiting the folks, Tom asked Jed and Betty what their long-range plans were.

"We're kind of at loose ends," Jed replied. "Ben and Gail told us to sell out if someone offered us a fair price. It puts us in limbo though because Ben also mentioned that someday he'd like to return to the farm."

"Well, what about Tanya and me buying you out? We could draw up a sale agreement that would give Ben and Gail the option of buying back the house and some of the land, if they decide to farm in the future."

"Betty and I definitely want to start taking things easier. You guys are pretty well doing all the work now anyway. Are you sure though, that buying us out wouldn't spread you too thin?"

"Tom is confident we could handle it," Tanya replied hesitantly. "Even though I'm not as adventuresome as he is, I trust his judgment. Besides, it sure would be nice for you to have a few dollars for your retirement and be able to stay in your own home."

"Mom and I will **talk** over your offer," Jed concluded.

When Jed contacted Ben and Gail, they were all for Tom's and Tanya's proposal.

Over the next few months Tom spent a lot of time thinking about expanding their land base. In addition to Jed's and Betty's land, Mel Crawford had two quarters for sale. Mel and his wife were also advancing in years and wanted to downsize their operation.

Towards the middle of November, Tom and Tanya dropped in on the local bank manager, Jack Finch. Finch was a balding little wisp of a man. Unbeknownst to Tom and Tanya, he had a reputation of being devious. He was supportive of their planned expansion, even though they still carried a thirty thousand dollar mortgage. They purchased their folks' place for one hundred thousand dollars and the Crawford land for thirty thousand dollars. The twenty thousand dollars they had in savings covered their down payment. All of the farm land and Tom's and Tanya's farm equipment were taken for collateral.

Once Jed and Betty deposited the money from the sale of the land in the bank, it didn't take Ben long to put his designs on part of it. He and Gail wanted to build a house in Calgary and were short on dollars.

After agonizing over Ben's request, Jed and Betty decided to give him twenty-five thousand dollars as part of his inheritance. Too late, they realized a dangerous precedent had been set. Beth and her husband, John, were attempting to buy into a dental firm and were also in tight financial straits. In an effort to keep family relations peaceful, Jed and Betty felt obligated to pay Beth her twenty-five thousand dollar share of the inheritance.

Jed's and Betty's retirement income was now only a portion of what it should have been. To bolster their finances, they sold their small herd of cattle and the farm equipment. They still felt that they could get by on their reduced investment income and Jed's old age pension.

When all the dust settled, Betty asked Jed, "Do you think helping Ben and Beth out is a sign of our generosity or our stupidity?"

Jed chuckled. "Probably a little of both I'd say. It makes one sympathize with the parents of the prodigal son, but at least they only had one who took his inheritance ahead of time."

Tom and Tanya managed to cover their spring land payment, but had to scrape to get enough money to put their crop in. In an effort to save money, they had gambled with the lower floating interest rate on their new loan rather than more secure, higher, fixed rate. Interest rates started an upward trend, dramatically increasing the costs of servicing their debt.

Despite their financial pressures, Tom felt that a good crop would bring them back on top of things. Mother Nature had other plans though. An early frost badly reduced their yields. After selling their frozen grain, they had just enough to cover their expenses and make half of their fall payment. The bank allowed them until spring to get caught up on their loan.

It was a winter without much cheer. Interest rates kept going up, and the market for railroad ties all but dried up. Tom cut a little lumber with Jed's help, but with the frozen crops, there was little money in the rural economy.

When Tom and Tanya met with their bank manager in the spring, the stark reality of their financial plight became apparent. They were faced with a painful choice; try to become current with their fall payment, and pay a small amount on their spring payment, or use the little funds they had to put in the crop.

"I suggest you use your savings to put in your crop," Finch said. "We'll defer last fall's partial payment and this spring's payment until this fall. Hopefully by then, you'll be able to become current."

On the way home from the bank, Tom was glum. "It seems the only luck we have of late is bad luck or no luck at all. I want you to know I take full responsibility for the mess we're in."

"Don't take blame for everything, Tom," Tanya replied. There was also bad weather and poor markets for railroad ties. I'm as responsible as you are, since I didn't do anything to stop you. I love you and regardless of what happens, I always will. We'll lick it together."

Tom pulled Tanya close. "I guess I'd best quit feeling sorry for myself and try to figure out some way we can work ourselves out of this mess."

Once the crop was in, Tom and Jed started sawing lumber again, but with the economy still depressed, Tom didn't get many sales.

On the fifteenth of August, disaster struck again. Hail wiped out eighty per cent of their crop. To help them out of their bind, Tanya went back teaching. Billy and Grace were now in school, alleviating the need for a babysitter.

In the fall, after paying all farming expenses, there was only enough money left over to cover their living expenses for a few months. They had nothing to service their bank loan. When Tom and Tanya met with Finch, he appeared to be understanding.

"Looks like you and Tanya are fighting a rearguard action, but at least you're trying. We can defer your land payments till next spring. Tanya working again is a plus. Notwithstanding this, your situation doesn't look all that rosy. Your floating interest rate is killing you. We won't be able to advance you any additional credit until you become current with your loan."

The visit to the bank left Tom and Tanya stunned. Rather than head home, they drove into Red Deer and stopped in at the District Agriculturalist's office for his help in assessing their situation.

"From my perspective, you have three big problems on your back," the agriculturalist began after getting their input. "Firstly two crop failures, back to back. Secondly, as your banker indicated, the floating interest is really working against you. Thirdly, and in my view most important, I'm afraid you over-extended yourself by more than doubling your land base. Your net worth is a bit shaky, but of greater importance, your cash flow projections will simply not generate enough funds to service your high debt load if interest rates remain high. I think you might squeak by if interest rates would drop back to what they were, but all economic indicators suggest this won't happen soon."

The stark reality of their bleak financial picture proved a bitter pill to swallow and Tanya cried most of the way home.

"To survive, we must stay onside." Tom said, putting his arm around her.

"As long as we love and respect each other, that's really all that counts," Tanya replied between sobs.

Over the next few days, Tom and Tanya wracked their brains to come up with some strategy to get them out of their bind. There was the option of asking help from Jed and Betty, but that was the last thing they wanted to do. Tanya's job helped some, but what they needed was some big money. Tom weighed the option of sawing more lumber, but until the railroad tie and lumber markets improved, that was a no-go. After hearing of Tom's financial plight, his chum Joe Bonner came up with an idea.

"Why don't you and I go into trucking? The oil patch is booming and there's a demand for large trucks. I've been driving a big truck for a guy in Drayton Valley who contracts to large oil companies. He's sixty-five and the other day he said he wanted to sell out and retire."

"He's asking thirty thousand for everything, but he told me all he needs is a six thousand dollar down payment. There's a Kenworth tandem tractor that's four years old. It's equipped with a flat deck, winch and gin poles and a trailer. I can vouch that it's in excellent shape. He has a garage and office. His contracts also go with the business. We could go in on it together. I think I could tap the Old Man for three thousand. If you could come up with the other three thousand, I think we could swing the deal."

"Our finances are flatter than pee in a platter," Tom responded, "but it's a thought. I'll talk it over with Tanya and see what she thinks."

That evening Tom discussed Joe's business proposition with Tanya.

"I'm for it, Tom, but how are we going to come up with our share of the down payment? We won't be able to borrow from the folks. I was talking to Mom today and they just locked all their investment money in a five-year term deposit."

After much agonizing, Tom did what he vowed he'd never do. He phoned his mom and asked her for a short-term loan for three thousand dollars.

"I'm happy to be able to help you out, Tom," Ema said. You kept the farm going when Dad was failing. I have complete faith in you and Tanya."

By early November, Tom and Joe purchased the trucking business. The former owner would carry the balance of twenty four thousand for two years.

When Tom and Tanya stopped in to see the bank manager regarding the trucking venture, he was quite compliant.

"Our bank is always happy with clients who show some initiative, but are you positive you don't have some other source you could tap to bring your loans up to date?"

"I'm sorry, but Jed's and Betty's money is in a five-year term deposit," Tom replied. "Mom had to scrape to come up with the three thousand I borrowed from her and you know that Tanya's and my bank account is overdrawn. I'm sure though, with all the work we have lined up for the truck, we'll be near caught up on our land payments by spring."

"We can't ask you folks to do the impossible," Finch concluded. "Hopefully, you'll have a good winter. Check back with us in the spring before seeding."

"I wonder why Finch goes on and on about whether we've exhausted all sources of help," Tom remarked to Tanya as they drove home. "This must be the third or fourth time he's asked us."

On a Friday morning in mid December just before Tanya left for school, the sheriff pulled into their yard.

When Tanya opened the door he handed her an envelope. "I'm sorry Tanya, but I have to give you this," he said without making eye contact. "It's from the bank in Milden." The Sheriff looked distressed as he quickly headed for his car.

Tanya nearly collapsed after reading the notice. They had three days to pay off their loan, or lose the land!

"How can this be?" she cried, when she got her mom on the phone. "Last month I distinctly remembered Finch telling us he'd give us till spring to get caught up on our late loan payments. My God, what are we to do now? We're going to lose everything."

"This is quite a shock," Betty said, her voice breaking. "Let me sit down."

After collecting herself she continued, "I guess all we can do is to hope and pray that God will help us out. Remember, Tanya, whatever happens, Dad and I still love you and Tom. We have faith in you. We'll support you in any way we can."

When Tanya finally got a hold of Tom, he phoned the bank, but Finch had left for the weekend and wasn't expected back until Monday. In desperation, Tom contacted a lawyer in Red Deer. Tanya got someone to sub and Tom and she drove in to see the lawyer in the afternoon.

"Unfortunately, this is a demand loan," the lawyer began after reading the bank notice. "The bank has the legal right to call it, seeing you're seriously in arrears. Under normal circumstances, they allow you some time to come up with the overdue payments, but this is not required by law. With your type of loan they only need to give three days notice after they call it. Then they have the authority to seize any collateral used to secure the loan. In this instance, that would be all your property and any piece of equipment or building on which they had a lien. Your only out is to pay the bank off by next Tuesday."

"That rotten Finch," Tom bellowed. "There's something fishy going on here! Tanya was with me, two months ago, when he gave us a deferment on our loan payments till spring."

"Now we're getting somewhere. If your bank manager made out a signed document deferring the loan payment, we've got them."

"I'm afraid his offer was verbal," Tom replied, "but Tanya was there with me."

The lawyer shook his head. "I'm sorry, but that wouldn't stand up in court. With nothing on paper, their lawyers would just say it was a misunderstanding on your part and it would be difficult to prove otherwise."

"This is so hard to take," Tanya interjected on the verge of tears. "Our bank manager is taking advantage of us. Is there nothing that can be done?"

"We have the option of writing the regional head office of the bank, but I doubt that would help. I'll phone your bank manager and try to buy a little time. It's a long shot, but it may not hurt to contact another bank for help. If I fail to get an extension, the bank will be removing the farm equipment and you must be off the land on the fifteenth of April. Be careful in any communication you have with the bank, especially if it's in writing. I'm sorry folks, but that's about all I can do for you."

Tom and Tanya left the lawyer's office completely shook. "Its all my fault," Tom said despondently. "What sticks in my craw though, is the way Finch set us up. His lying to us about the deferment has me mad enough to work the snot right out of him, but what good would that do?"

"How are we going to tell the folks?" Tanya cried. "I just don't know how Mom will take the news."

When he finally contacted Finch by phone, Tom shouted, "What the hell's going on? Why did you go back on your word on deferring our loan payments?"

"I'm very sorry, but you and your wife completely misunderstood me. You are seriously in arrears. From our perspective your chances of ever paying us back are slim, so we must salvage what we can. Remember, you have only made one full payment since you took out your loan. It's very upsetting for me to have to take this action, but unfortunately, that's part of my job."

"There will be a day when we'll even accounts!" Tom bellowed. "In my opinion you're nothing but a diseased, mean, low-bred, son-of-a-female-dog!"

When Tom and Tanya dropped in on the folks, Tanya was still crying.

"We're just back from seeing a lawyer in the city," Tom began with tears in his eyes. "I'm sorry, but it doesn't look good. As Tanya told you this morning, that low brow Finch went back on his word and called our loan. Now the lying bastard says he didn't give us a deferment of our loan payments. He said we misunderstood him. It looks pretty bleak. Unless we can come up with a big wad of cash, we'll both lose our homes and all the land."

"I've just got off the phone with that crooked Finch. We're going to see a bank in the city on Monday afternoon to try and get some help in re-financing. I take full responsibility for this whole bloody mess. It may take us some time, but somehow, Tanya and I will make it up to you."

Tanya and her mother were crying as Jed began, his voice trembling. "Let's not throw in the towel yet, Tom. If Mom and I didn't have our investment money tied up, we'd be able to give you a hand. Like Mom said this morning, we have confidence in you and Tanya."

After Tom and Tanya left, Jed and Betty sat in shock. "We're all going to lose our homes!" Betty finally blurted out. "I can't believe this is happening to us."

Tom's and Tanya's lawyer contacted Finch on Monday morning, but the manager said an extension was out of the question.

When Tom and Tanya saw the bank in Red Deer, it was also a deadend. "I'm sorry folks, but since your financial status is shaky, there's nothing much we can do to help you out," the loans officer said bluntly. "Also, as a policy, we're reticent to lend money to individuals who are facing legal action from another bank."

Tom and Tanya left the bank heavy-hearted and headed to their lawyer's office.

"We've been stonewalled again," Tom began in a somber tone. "Getting more credit is a no go."

"I'm sorry to hear that, but I think I've discovered a glimmer of light for you. I've been researching all your old loan contracts. Years before, when you and your folks went into partnership on the land clearing and sawmill ventures, the bank manager sub-divided your yard site off the bank lien and incorporated it as a separate company. The Cat, the sawmill and the building site are still owned by the company and exempt from bank action. As the bank has no hold on these items, you won't be losing them."

"Thanks for your help," Tom continued. "It's not as good as holding on to the land and the folks' place, but it's better than a poke in the eye with a sharp stick."

As Tom and Tanya were leaving the folks' place Tuesday night, Tom was fighting hard to contain his emotions. "I feel like such a fool for what we've done to you. If nothing else, you guys can move in with us, but I vow before God we'll somehow get your house and yard site back. It may take a bit of time, but as I said before, we'll do it. You'll be able to stay here till the fifteenth of April. Remember, our home and yard are yours too, now."

In a last ditch attempt to save Jed's and Betty's home, Tom's and Tanya's lawyer contacted Finch to see what price the bank would need to sub-divide out their house and a few acres of land. Finch told him that it would not be in the bank's best interest to split the land up with a subdivision.

By Christmas, all the equipment and old buildings that the bank hadn't removed were moved to Tom's and Tanya's yard. Jed and Betty decided to stay in their old house till spring.

For the first time since they were married, Jed and Betty didn't put up a Christmas tree. They just hurt too much. The winter months were a time of sober reflection. As the months slipped by, all hopes for a resolution to their dilemma faded. By the first week of April, all of Jed's and Betty's household effects were moved to Tom's and Tanya's place.

"It's so hard to take," Betty sobbed as they drove out their driveway for the last time. "We'll never set foot on our farm again. What did we do to deserve this? I'm trying so hard to accept it, but at times it's just too much to bear."

"We must try to remain positive," Jed replied, tears wetting his cheeks. "We have a home with Tom and Tanya now. That's better than being out on the street I suppose, but damn it anyway, I feel chewed up inside too."

The women wanted to leave the old home place as unobtrusively as possible, but Jed and Tom were not about to leave without raising a bit of hell.

A week before the eviction date, Tom phoned Finch. "Neither Jed nor I are about to slink off like dogs with our tails between our legs. You're going to have to get the sheriff and the RCMP to throw us off."

Jed cautioned Tom to refrain from lifting a hand to anyone. "If it comes to anything physical, let me be the one to get involved. I'm sixty-eight and I'm sure I can mix it up a bit with Finch without getting into too much trouble. Who's going to lay assault charges against a sixty-eight year old?"

Jed forewarned the local police officer, Constable Nader that Tom and he wouldn't leave without being forced off. "If there is to be anything physical, though, it won't be major and Tom won't get involved."

Constable Nader was aware of the unscrupulous dealings of Finch and like the neighbours, was sympathetic to Tom, Tanya, Jed and Betty. He was quite relieved to hear that Tom would be keeping his hands in his pockets. He did, however, feel apprehensive about the possibility of Jed getting physical. Despite getting up in years he knew that Jed was still a lot of man.

News spread fast in the community that the eviction was to take place on April the fifteenth. The day dawned cloudy with snow showers, but by ten a.m. there were over sixty surly neighbours and friends on hand to lend their support to the Parkers and Osmonds.

Finch and the contingent from Milden arrived promptly at eleven. Finch looked very nervous and stayed close to the sheriff. The large crowd of Osmond supporters were restless and a couple of gentlemen standing at the back of the crowd kept things lively. "FINCH IS A FINK," one would shout. The other heckler would call back "HE'S A BASTARD RAT TOO." Finch quickly handed the eviction notice to the sheriff, who in turn handed it to Tom. A hush came over the crowd as Tom read the document, ripped it in two, then handed it back to the sheriff.

"Tell Mr. Finch to take this notice and place it in a spot where the sun doesn't shine!" he snarled.

The crowd roared their approval.

"I would like you folks to know what a crooked little son-of-a-bitch Mr. Finch is," Jed shouted, stepping forward. "He cheerfully lent Tom and Tanya as much money as they needed for their expansion and even encouraged them to borrow more. As you all know, they were having a rough time handling their debt because of two crop failures. They may well have managed to pull through, though, if Finch hadn't gone back on his word."

"Give him Hell, Jed," a heckler called. The crowd cheered and Jed continued.

"Last fall, he gave them a verbal deferment of their late loan payments until this spring. Less than two months later, he called the loan."

"Back where I hail from, we'd have tarred and feathered the likes of you and rode you out of the county on a rail," Jed bellowed as he stepped toward Finch.

Jed carefully picked the site where the eviction notice was to be served. It was adjacent to a big manure pile. There was a large depression beside the pile with two to three feet of manure water in it. The second Jed finished dressing the bank manager down, his hands flashed out. He grabbed Finch by the coat lapels with one hand and by his crotch with the other. Letting out a roar, Jed hoisted the little banker over his head and tossed him into the manure puddle. Again, the crowd roared their approval!

Mr. Finch was completely submersed in the pool. When he crawled back out onto firm ground, he was not a pretty sight and he didn't smell all that sweet either!

"Come on Tom," Jed called out, "we'd better leave before we get ourselves into some real trouble."

"Maybe we should tar and feather the SOB," Tom quipped. "Come to think of it though, that would be just a waste of tar and feathers."

To the cheers and applause of the crowd, Jed and Tom headed down the driveway and off the property.

The most difficult assignment for Constable Nader was not in keeping the peace, but in abiding by professional comportment and not laughing with the crowd. A far harder assignment fell on the sheriff. Since Finch came out to the farm with him, he felt obliged to give his smelly friend a ride back to Milden. Despite the noxious aroma, the sheriff was forced to keep his windows closed and the heater cranked up. Even though Finch was wrapped in an old blanket, he was shivering uncontrollably. Finch never uttered one word all the way back to town and was constantly wiping his teeth off with Kleenex. The sheriff would have to occasionally turn his head away and smile. He suspected that Finch didn't have his mouth closed when he was given his untimely immersion!

Unbeknownst to Mr. Finch, a young newspaper reporter from Red Deer was in the crowd. The picture of Mr. Finch climbing out of the manure puddle, with the accompanying story, hit the front page of the Red Deer paper the next day. It was hardly good news for the bank.

Jed did his best to keep things upbeat, but Tom would not be consoled. The anger he felt was directed mostly towards himself. His zeal to undo the damage he and Tanya brought on the family was understandable and would eventually bring them to better times.

CHAPTER
21

Tom returned to the oil patch and the trucking business while Tanya continued teaching. In spite of inclement weather and a crooked bank manager, they both recognized their loss was mainly of their own doing. Taking responsibility for their mistakes was a necessary step to take before healing could begin. Although hard to stomach, their difficulties were bringing them even closer together.

In her new home with Tanya and Tom, Betty made a concerted effort to be positive. A large part of her life had been ripped away though, and she often found herself reliving the past. Her thoughts would go back to the first time she worked for Jed, the day he told her of his hurtful past, the birth of Tanya, Ben and Beth and watching them grow up. During these times of reflection she would grieve. Although it would take her many months to finally cope with her loss, she was dealing with it.

Each time Tanya urged her dad to talk about his loss, he would dodge and turn the conversation to some other topic. Early one evening, Tanya drove her mom to a lady's meeting and then returned to spend some time with her dad. After making several futile attempts to get him to talk about his feelings, Tanya lowered the boom.

"Now look here, Dad, I know that you're not facing your loss. I vividly remember the day a sixteen-year-old girl was falling right apart because her boyfriend just left for a two year stint in the Army. A big, very dark complexioned man got right after her and helped bring her out of her feelings of despair. His advice worked for the young girl. Now it's time to turn the tables and take some of your own medicine. Where's the pro-active Dad I once had, the Dad who always resolved all our problems coolly and analytically? I know you're crushed and angry."

Jed looked off into space, but made no reply.

"Let's drive over to the home place," Tanya said.

"I guess we could," Jed replied glumly. "There's no use trying to hide my feelings from you. You know me too well. Letting on that all is well when you're really hurting inside is something I learned from my dad. He always said it was a mark of a real man not to show his inner pain. I know now that he was wrong, but it looks like I still have a problem in that area. I really thought I'd gotten a better handle on it."

As yet, the bank had not put up a No Trespassing sign on the home place. Tanya and her dad walked about the yard, each lost in memories. They ended up at the old log house that Jed lived in for the first few years he was on the farm. There was an old chopping block up against the south wall.

"Why don't you sit yourself down for a spell, Dad? I'll run over to the hall to pick Mom up."

From his vantage point, Jed had an unrestricted view of the whole yard. The memories of those forty plus years were gnawing away at him and making him raw inside. To his right was an old rusted fifteen gallon oil drum. Suddenly he leapt to his feet. With an ear piercing roar he grabbed an old steel jack-all handle leaning up against the wall and began beating the oil drum.

"Dirty rotten son-of-a-bitch!" he cried out in anguish, time and time again. He beat the drum until it was completely flat.

Fully spent, he looked down at the doorway of the old house and saw something half buried in the grass. He poked at it with his beating iron until it was loose, then picked it up.

Jed slumped down on the chopping block again and sobbed uncontrollably. In his hand was the small wooden doll that he carved out of a block of birch firewood for Tanya's second birthday. Betty painted it, glued on some hair and made a set of clothes for it. Tanya carried it with her everywhere she went, always sleeping with it at night.

When Tanya and her mother arrived to pick up Jed, he was still sitting on the block. Slowly he got up and handed the doll to Tanya. Neither Betty nor Tanya uttered a word. The look on Jed's face said it all.

All evening Jed paced the floor alternating between roaring and tears. After a couple of hours of ranting and raving, he finally sat down to analyze their problem. He stayed up till one a.m., working out the angles and was at it again the next morning, after Tom, Tanya and the kids left.

Jed was working at the table, when suddenly something struck him. "Damn it!" he cried out. "Why didn't I think of this before?"

"Think of what before?" Betty asked.

"I don't know if it's too late to do anything about it, but something just hit me like a ton of bricks. In the six years since Finch has been here, he's called at least four other loans on farmers in this area. Here's the scary part. In all the foreclosures, the bank sold the land to the same guy. There's a pattern here! Why didn't I see this before? I hope at the very least, we can prevent the bank from selling our old land to the same character."

"I see what you mean, but what can we do at this late date?"

"I'm on good terms with the bank accountant, Michael Cummings. I'll talk with him this afternoon and try to find out if he too thinks there's been some skullduggery going on. I'll also contact John Kerr, the regional head for the bank. You remember John. He was the bank manager here some twenty-five years ago and always treated us well."

"Just what earthly good do you think talking to Kerr will do?"

"I'm not sure, but all the local bank managers must answer to him. I sure wish someone had given me a good kick in the butt when the loan was called and got me going on this earlier."

In the afternoon, Jed stopped at the bank and saw Cummings in his office.

"I'm risking my neck talking about internal bank matters with you, Jed, but in good conscience, I cannot stand by and be party to this dirty dealing."

"Any information I get from you will only be divulged to others with your permission. I also intend to take this up with your regional manager John Kerr."

"Thanks Jed. I have no trouble with that. Including Tom and Tanya, Finch has called the loans on five farmers in this immediate area over the last five years. From what I've been told, in all instances, he used pretty well the same tactics that he used with Tom and Tanya. Here's the scary part. I don't know if you know this, Jed, but in all the previous foreclosures, the bank has sold the land to the same party at substantially below market value."

"It's unreal," Jed said, shaking his head. "This whole scam hit me like a stroke of lightning this morning. Has no one else complained?"

"You're the first one to ring the bell. Now I have no firm proof of this, but it is alleged that Finch got a kickback on all of these transactions. Finch would be far too wily to put his payoffs in the bank, but I know from reliable sources he has a substantial portfolio of stocks and bonds."

"Thanks for your help," Jed said as he got up to leave. "When we meet with John Kerr, I'll advise him to contact you."

"That's okay with me. I think you know where my sympathy lies. The best of luck to you."

As soon as Jed returned from the bank he contacted John Kerr in Red Deer.

Kerr was painfully aware of the whole eviction debacle. He had the newspaper article on his desk and was doing his utmost to distance the bank from the whole messy affair.

"Would it be possible for Tom, Tanya, Betty and I to meet with you to discuss any options that might be open to us?" Jed asked.

"It sounds like our bank hasn't been handling your affairs all that well, Jed. My condolences to you and the family. I'd be glad to see you this Friday afternoon at one-thirty. By then, I hope to be fairly familiar with your situation."

On Friday, Tom and Tanya booked off work and drove into Red Deer with Jed and Betty.

"We must tell it exactly like it is," Jed advised, while they were eating dinner. "Kerr was always very honorable in the dealings Mom and I had with him and he'll appreciate our honesty. We'll also have to remember we're asking for help, not demanding it."

"I take full responsibility for our financial troubles," Tom began when they met with Kerr. "It's hurt Tanya and me a great deal to lose our land, but it hurts us even more that through our screw up, Mom and Dad lost their home. Tanya was with me when Finch told us he'd allow us six months to get caught up on our payments, but now of course he denies saying that. We've heard rumors that Finch will sell our old land to the same guy who's bought the last four farms that the loans have been called on."

"It's healthy to hear both of you taking responsibility for your mistakes," Kerr replied. "It's sad that your folks lost their home. It would have been wise to subdivide their home off the property when they sold you the land, but that's history now. As Jed no doubt told you, we have been investigating all the loans we've called at our Milden branch over the last few years. I've had orders from head office in Calgary to get to the bottom of all the foreclosures, particularly yours. The picture of the bank manager in the manure puddle and the accompanying newspaper article, have caused our bank a great deal of embarrassment."

"This is all very good," Tom interjected, "but will your investigation help us any?"

"I think it will. You should know that what Finch did in calling your delinquent loan was legal. Calling the loan when he promised a deferment though, was totally unscrupulous. I must apologize to you on behalf of our bank for the shabby way we've treated you."

"There are rumors that Mr. Finch took a kickback on the sale of the other foreclosed land, but we have no evidence that would stand up in court. As of yesterday, Mr. Finch no longer works for us. Our bank can't afford this type of exposure. From time to time we'll have to call a loan, but only after we've exhausted every possible option between us and the borrower. Our bank is here to serve our clients, not bully them."

"I hate to interrupt again, but does this change anything for us?"

"I was just getting to that. Head office has authorized me to use my own discretion in handling the land that we took from you. The land will not be sold for the time being. Instead we'll be leasing it for a five-year period. I feel obligated to allow you this period of grace. If you should decide to repurchase your land, this will give you time to do so."

"I can't thank you enough for this break. This gives Tanya and me something to work towards," Tom concluded.

"We're only trying to treat our clients fairly. There will be a number of stipulations though. Number one, for the immediate future, Tom and Tanya, you will not be allowed to borrow from our bank. Number two, Tom, we would not allow you to lease the land back. Finally, when the land is to be sold, we will be using the bid system. We hope we can learn from our mistakes."

Jed, Betty and Tanya also thanked Kerr for his intervention and they got up to leave. As Jed got to the door, John called out after him. "It looks like you haven't changed all that much over the years, Jed. Just between the two of us, if I were as big as you and had been used as badly by a bank manager as you were, I'd have probably given him a manure bath myself."

There was now a bit of light at the end of the tunnel for the first time in months.

By the end of the month, the bank leased the land to the Van Der Blitz's, a family in the dairy business. They had immigrated to Canada from the States with the hopes of expansion.

In early summer, to keep from being on top of each other, Betty and Jed bought a small mobile home and put it next to Tom's and Tanya's house.

****

For the next five years, Tom and Tanya worked with a passion. They had one goal in mind, buying back the land and redeeming the folks' home. Their trucking business was booming and Tom and Joe bought another large truck to keep up.

Tom and Tanya's hard work, plus being in the right place at the right time, soon began to show dividends. As the five year lease was coming to an end, Tom and Tanya were making plans to bid on the land. In February, Joe bought out Tom's and Tanya's share in the company. Tom stayed on with Joe, working for wages.

Three weeks before the expiration of the lease, Tom got an inside lead that the bank's reserve price would be in the one hundred fifty to one hundred sixty thousand dollar range. Tom and Tanya hired a real estate agency to do an evaluation of their old land. Based on the appraised value of one hundred seventy-five thousand, Tom and Tanya felt quite comfortable that with their savings and the money from the sale of their share in the company, they had sufficient funds to cover their bid.

Once the land appraisal was made, Tom and Tanya met with the folks to discuss their bidding strategy.

"We talked to a realtor and he suggested one hundred seventy-five thousand is about as high as one should go. Yesterday we left a bid of one hundred seventy-six thousand at the bank in Red Deer. Tanya and I have an alternate plan if our bid is unsuccessful. I talked with Mel Crawford the other day. He wants to retire and has offered us first dibs on the rest of his land. They don't have all that much land left, but they have a nice house that you could have. Their farm would be a good start for Tanya and me if we lost out on our bid. I know it wouldn't be as good as getting the old place back, but it would be better than a kick in the rump with a frozen boot."

"That's wise thinking," Jed replied. "It will be a good back up. It's very important that it not become common knowledge that you and Tanya have a wad of money at your disposal. I'll be dropping in on the Van Der Blitz's in a few days to get their family history for the Westview History Book. I'll tell them that you and Tanya sold out to Joe and that you're now working for him for wages. Maybe if they think you're out of the running, they won't bid too aggressively."

"I like your thinking," Tom said with a smile. "You're a crafty old fox."

The next two weeks proved very trying for all of them as they waited with crossed fingers. One question haunted them all their waking hours. Would they be able to redeem their land?

CHAPTER

22

If big talk was an indicator of success, Henry Van Der Blitz and his sons, Clem and Bob, would have been the most successful farmers in the country. Henry thought himself an authority on everything that was related to agriculture. No sooner had he signed the rental agreement, than he started spouting off that the bank was going to sell the land to them at the end of the five year lease. The bragging and BS-ing, although annoying, would have been tolerable if it hadn't been for their devious dealings with the neighbours and local businesses. By the Van Der Blitz standards, the mark of a successful businessman was measured by how much advantage they could take of their fellow man. Hard workers they were, but when dealing with the Van Der Blitz's the community soon learned that you had to watch them like hawks.

Shortly after moving in, Clem, the oldest son, got two hundred dollars worth of lumber from Tom to repair corrals. He always had some excuse for not paying. Finally Tom drove over to their place, accosted Clem by the old machine shed and demanded to be paid.

"That lumber wasn't up to snuff," Clem began hesitantly. "Some of the planks were warped, some were dotty."

Tom paused for a few a moments, then grabbed Clem by the coat and rammed him up against the machine shed. "Not only are you crooked, you're a damned liar," Tom roared. "I hand picked all that lumber, just to be sure it was all good. You're a piss poor excuse for a man, Clem. For fifty cents I'd break you in two. I should actually squeeze your head flat. Now are you going to pay up, or do I start beating on you?"

Without uttering one word, Clem pulled ten twenty dollar bills from his wallet and handed them to Tom.

Tom smiled, thanked him, hopped into his pickup and headed for home.

Just before the end of the five-year lease, Jed dropped in on the Van Der Blitz's to record their family's story for the Westview Valley History Book. It was the first time he'd been back in his old house since they lost the land. It was hard on Jed, but he made a concerted effort to be amicable. Seeing he was a former citizen of the States, Jed had common ground with them.

"Well, Henry, we've about covered everything," Jed said as he approached the end of the interview. "How would it be if I finished your story by saying, presently leasing the old Osmond and Parker farms?"

"Couldn't we just say we bought the old Osmond and Parker place?" Henry broke in. "We're damned sure we'll be buying it from the bank."

"Well, we'll just leave that part blank for the now," Jed replied, biting his tongue. "The history book won't be going to the publishers for a few months. By that time you'll know if you're going to buy the land."

"From what I've heard, the bank is figuring on getting one hundred seventy-five thousand dollars for this land," Jed continued. "That's a lot of money."

"Yes, it sure is," Henry said, shaking his head.

Jed was sure that Henry and his family had heard the local gossip that Tom and Tanya might attempt to buy the land back.

"It's hard at times to sit by and watch your kids making mistakes," Jed said, changing the subject. "Both Betty and I regret not having done something to stop Tom and Tanya as they were expanding, but I guess it's all water under the bridge now."

The bait was enough for Henry. "Yes, it's too bad some young people have to learn the hard way. It's a shame their mistakes cost you and your wife your home. How are Tom and Tanya doing, anyway? I know she's teaching. What about Tom's trucking business? How's it doing?"

"Oh, I guess they're making out not too bad. You probably haven't heard that Tom sold out his share of the company to his partner. He's working for him for wages now."

Jed thanked them for their time and promised to be back in touch with them when the final disposition of the land was made.

No sooner had Jed left than Henry phoned Frank Williams, the bank manager in Milden. "I hear tell that the bank's figuring on getting one hundred seventy-five thousand for this and the Parker place."

"I'm quite sure our bank would welcome a bid for that amount, Henry, but we haven't set a reserve price yet. I was just talking with the Regional Office in Red Deer. They'll be doing that tomorrow. The bank's reserve bid or upset price will not be influenced by the rumored value of the land. The figure of one hundred seventy-five thousand is probably a realtor's appraised value. I can assure you, Henry, that the bank has already done their appraisal."

"Well, when will the bank notify us? We sure want to bid on it."

"Our Red Deer office should contact you with our upset price either tomorrow or the next day. They'll also be sending you an information package on bidding procedures."

"Have you guys at the bank heard of anyone else who's interested in the land?"

"No one that I'm aware of and I'd imagine that all inquiries would come through our branch. From my point of view, it may not be the opportune time to put it up for bid. I know of two other farms in the area for sale."

"Tell me, what will happen if there are no bids or if the bids are too low?"

"All those details will be in your bidding package, Henry. If there's no successful bid, our regional office in Red Deer will be getting in touch with you."

The following day the bank notified Henry that the reserve bid on the land had been set at one hundred fifty-five thousand. If a successful bid wasn't received, the bank would ask him to lease the land for one more year.

That night Henry, his wife and the boys got together to decide on their plan of action.

"It would be tempting to hold out," began Henry. "If we knew that there wasn't any interest in the land, we could rent it for one more year and probably buy it for less next year."

"It's just too chancy," Mrs. Van Der Blitz replied. "We have no guarantee there isn't other interest in the land. How do we know that Jed's story of Tom and Tanya having to sell their share of the business to their partner is true? I've heard rumors that Tom might be bidding on the land."

"I'm with Mom," Clem said. "I think we should consider making out two bids. If it looks like we're the only ones interested in the land, we could use a low bid of a bit more than the bank's upset price. If it looks like there's going to be more bids, we could go up to maybe something around one hundred seventy-five thousand. I'm also going to check out Jed's story by phoning Tom's old business partner."

After hashing things over for an hour, Henry finally came onside with his wife and Clem.

At the last moment, Clem decided on seeing Joe Bonner in person. The next day he drove up to Drayton Valley and caught Joe alone in the shop.

"I've heard that Tom sold out to you," he began after introducing himself. "I was wondering if you were looking for another truck driver."

"You're right. I bought Tom and his wife out a month ago, but he's still here working for wages. As long as he stays with me, I won't need any more help, but it wouldn't hurt to keep in touch. Have you any experience driving big rigs?"

"Yeah, I drove a logging truck for one winter."

"Well if you don't find work, give me a holler later on this summer."

When Clem got back from Drayton Valley, he stopped at his folks' place. "Jed's story rings true. "Tom and his wife sold out to their partner, and Tom's working for him now."

The first week of April moved at a snail's pace for Tom and Tanya. Uppermost in their minds was redeeming their folks' home. Finally, the tenth of April arrived. It was a day the Osmonds and Parkers did a whole lot of praying. Tom was too agitated to go to work and Tanya also booked the day off. As the minutes up to the two p.m. deadline ticked by, Tom was pacing the floor in earnest. Tanya made some lunch, but no one was all that hungry. Two o'clock came and went and everyone sat with fingers crossed.

Since the Milden bank manager was home sick for the day, Michael Cummings, the accountant, was handling the bids. At one fifty, Henry arrived at the bank and approached Michael.

"Any bids come in yet?"

"Not a one and with the Crawfords and Blodell's farms for sale, I think our chances of getting a decent bid aren't that good."

"Well alright," I guess we'll buy it then," Henry said in a cocky tone, handing Michael their sealed bid for one hundred sixty-two thousand dollars.

"Thank you," Michael said, biting his lip.

"So now what?"

"At two o'clock, I'll open your bid in the presence of another bank employee. Then I'll phone the bid into our

Regional Office. It looks like yours is going to be the only bid, so if you'll drop in tomorrow morning, we'll make out the Agreement for Sale."

Back at the Parkers' place, Tom's incessant pacing was beginning to grate on everyone's nerves.

"Damn it! I wish the bloody time wouldn't move so slowly," he muttered. "I sure hope they haven't gotten any other bids."

At two forty-five, Tom phoned Reg Stevenson, the bank manager in Red Deer.

"We've just received a call from our Milden branch with another bid, so I guess it's just the two bids. We're still on the phone with Milden, so call me back in a half hour. By then we'll have things finalized."

"Rotten bitch!" Tom growled. "That will be the Van Der Blitz's bid. It would just be our luck if they've out-bid us."

Finally at three forty-five, Tom again contacted Reg Stevenson.

"Well Tom, it looks like yours was the highest bid. Congratulations to you and Tanya! You've just bought your land back!"

For the first time since losing the land, Tom broke down. Tanya had to finish the conversation with the bank manager as Tom was sobbing. The battle to redeem their land was so hard fought! The victory tasted so sweet!

It would have been very difficult to find a more elated four-some! Jed and Betty were absolutely beside themselves with relief. They would finally be going home! Their victory celebration started immediately and continued well past midnight.

The next morning at ten sharp, a very confident contingent of Van Der Blitz's descended on the Milden bank manager's office. Frank had just been updated by the accountant regarding Henry's bid of the previous day. Henry and the boys were so sure that their bid was the only one submitted, they hadn't phoned the bank after the bidding closed.

"Well I guess we've got the land, so now what?" Henry started confidently.

Before the bank manager could respond, Henry barged ahead, relishing all the power he felt he was wielding.

"Now that the land is ours, we'll be borrowing to build a new dairy barn. We've sure managed our affairs better than the previous owner. Now what about a Bill of Sale?"

"Yes, Henry, we'll have to do the Bill of Sale. Before we start on the paper work, though, I'd better phone the Regional Office in Red Deer, just to be sure yours is the only bid."

As Frank listened to Reg Stevenson, a surprised look came over his face. "Damn it, I'm sorry fellows," he said after hanging up the phone, "Regional Office has accepted another bid that was higher than yours. The land's been sold."

"What?" roared Henry. "How can that be? Yesterday your accountant told me that ours was the only bid!"

"Your bid was the only one submitted here, but there was another bid made at the Red Deer branch."

"Did they say who made it, and how much the bid was for?" Henry asked, in dismay.

"The details of the bid will be made public soon, so I see no reason to keep the information from you. The successful bid was for one hundred seventy-six thousand, and it was made by Tom and Tanya Parker."

The next five minutes were a bank manager's worst nightmare. The Van Der Blitz's alternated between blaming each other, the two banks, the accountant and Joe Bonner. They saved their choicest adjectives for Tom and Jed. What hurt Henry most was being sucked in.

Jed, Betty, Tanya and Tom all slept in. They just sat down for brunch when there was a loud rap at the door. Before anyone could answer it, Henry, Clem and Bob stumbled in. After leaving the bank in the morning, they'd been fortifying themselves with spirits and were feeling no pain.

"You, Jed," Henry hollered. "Just what in hell do you think you're trying to pull off, Old Man, lying to me about Tom not having any money?"

It was a poor move for Henry to call Jed a liar. Although Jed would never see his sixties again, he was still stronger than most thirty-year-olds. Jed was halfway to his feet when Tom grabbed him by the shoulder.

"Sit, Jed," Tom barked. "My house. These fellows are my treat."

The Van Der Blitz's were either too inebriated to remember Tom's style, or too inebriated to care.

Tom was on his feet in an instant. Henry was the first on his hit list. "You, Henry," Tom shouted. "Get out of my house, now!"

Henry finally recognized the gravity of the situation just a mini-second before Tom got to him, and made a mad dash for the door. In his haste he stumbled on the porch mat, went head over heels and landed in a heap at the foot of the steps. Clem and Bob didn't need encouragement to leave and raced past their prostrate father. Henry wrenched his ankle and scraped his face. Tom helped him up and steadied him over to his pickup.

Despite the fiasco, relations with the Van Der Blitz's ended on a better note. Tom apologized to Henry for chasing him out of his house and Henry in turn apologized to Tom for barging into his home uninvited, blaming the alcohol for his inappropriate actions.

A few weeks later, Henry and the boys bought a dairy farm some thirty miles to the East. Tom and Jed even gave them a hand in moving, by taking a truckload of their furniture over for them.

During the first week of May, Jed and Betty moved back to their old farm. Beth, Ben, their spouses, neighbours and friends turned up for a homecoming celebration.

As the party was winding down, Ben asked for everyone's attention. "Mom and Dad, we're sure happy to see you back in your home!" he exclaimed. "Gail and I doff our hats to Tom and Tanya. They had some bad breaks, but they got Mom's and Dad's home and all the land back by working their duffs off. In a couple of years Gail and I are going to take them up on their old offer to come back home and farm with them. Let's hear it for the four of them!"

Betty, Jed, Tanya and Tom got to their feet, all fighting hard to control their emotions. "Thank you so much for all your support," Betty finally said, her voice breaking. "A special thank you to Tom and Tanya for all your hard work."

Everyone roared their approval. All were glad that Betty, Jed, Tanya and Tom were given another chance.

CHAPTER
23

A year later, Ben and Gail had enough of the oil patch and moved back to the farm. They bought the last of the Mel Crawford land and a quarter section from Tom and Tanya. Ben, Gail, Tom and Tanya began farming in partnership.

Soon Billy and Grace were both out of school. Billy worked the winters in the oil patch and farmed with his dad in the summer. Grace was in Edmonton taking nurses training. Before long they were both married. Billy married Judy Neufeld, a teacher from Red Deer. Grace married Blake Compton, a university student.

In Jed's eightieth year he started getting chest pains whenever he exerted himself. Being stubborn, he refused to let the pain slow him down.

"You're such a worry to me," Betty said one day when Jed's chest was hurting. "Unless you start taking it easier, something drastic is going to happen to bring you to your senses. If you don't change your life-style, I'm afraid you'll have a day of reckoning."

Finally, Jed gave in to Betty's and Tanya's constant lobbying and made an appointment with a heart specialist in Red Deer.

The doctor diagnosed Jed's chest pains as angina and prescribed nitroglycerine pills. His advice for Jed to slack off heavy work fell on deaf ears though. With Ben and Gail back on the farm, there was no longer any need for him to work. Still, he only felt comfortable if he was rotating. The nitro pills were doing him more harm than good since they enabled him to keep working when the chest pains came.

Jed felt rough all spring, but insisted on putting in a large garden. After a morning of planting potatoes, his chest pains became severe and didn't let up that much with the nitro pills.

"You're hurting Jed, aren't you?" Betty asked.

"Yeah, a little. I've taken two nitro pills though and if I rest for a bit I'll be O.K. I'm sure I'll be back on top of things by tomorrow."

After a half hour's rest, Jed's chest was still hurting. Betty phoned the specialist in Red Deer and he advised her to take Jed to the local hospital immediately. Within minutes, Betty, Jed and Gail were on the road.

Fortunately, Jed was in the hospital when he had his heart attack. Once his condition was stabilized, he spent two weeks in the hospital recuperating and a month at home regaining his strength.

It was starting to sink in that he needed to take life a whole lot easier if he expected to live longer. He occasionally frothed at the mouth when coming up against tasks he knew he didn't dare tackle, but rather than barge ahead, he'd sit down and mutter. "Slow down old man and catch your breath. One close call is quite enough."

As Jed was recuperating, Tanya began feeling under the weather. In late summer, she went to see their family doctor in Milden.

"For the last four or five months I've felt kind of run down," she began. "It's like there's this fullness and aching in my pelvis. The discomfort radiates around to my lower back and I always feel bloated."

"I haven't found anything amiss," the doctor said after examining her. "I'd like to refer you to a gynecologist in Red Deer. I'm wondering if the symptoms you described might be related to hormonal changes seeing you're nearing the age of menopause."

Once harvest was over, Tanya saw the specialist in Red Deer. After going through a series of tests the doctor conferred with Tanya and Tom.

"When I examined your lower abdomen, Tanya, I discovered a firm mass. This concerns me. The discomfort you feel in your pelvis and in your lower back is also of concern. At this point there's no cause for alarm, but I'd like to refer you to the Cancer Clinic in Edmonton for an assessment."

As Tanya and Tom left the office, she blurted out, "I'm just not ready for this. I'm still so young."

"Remember what the doctor said," Tom replied calmly. "He's just concerned about your symptoms. He didn't say anything about you having cancer."

"It's going to be hard, but I have to try to stay calm and not worry too much," Tanya said, her voice quivering. "I'd feel better if we kept this to ourselves until I've been checked out."

On the completion of the tests at the cancer clinic in Edmonton, the specialist, Doctor Ferguson, met with Tanya and Tom in his office.

"I don't want you to be overly concerned Tanya, but I'd like to admit you to the University Hospital for exploratory surgery."

Tanya sat in stunned silence. "Do I have cancer?" she asked, on the verge of tears.

"I have my suspicions, but I'm not positive. The exploratory surgery will help us make a more an accurate diagnosis. I can appreciate your concern, but at this point try not to panic."

"Dear, Lord, why me?" Tanya blurted out to Tom as they left the doctor's office.

Tanya was admitted to the University Hospital for the exploratory surgery. When Ferguson stopped in her hospital room, Tanya was sitting up in bed with Tom standing beside her. It had been a Herculean task for Tanya to keep from falling apart.

"I'm sorry folks, but I have some bad news," the doctor began solemnly. "I'm afraid we've discovered the reason you've experienced discomfort in your pelvis and back, Tanya. You have ovarian cancer."

Tom took Tanya in his arms. She couldn't talk, cry, or even move.

Finally, Tom asked, "How serious is Tanya's case?"

"This type of cancer is always difficult to diagnose. It's often well advanced when we discover it."

"And in Tanya's case?"

Doctor Ferguson looked down. "I'm sorry folks, but Tanya's cancer is fairly well-advanced."

"Are there any treatments I can take?" Tanya asked, her voice shaking.

"There's chemotherapy and radiation of course. Both treatments can slow down the cancer significantly, but as you probably know, there are some side effects. I believe the cancer is too far advanced for surgery."

"How much time do I have left?" Tanya cried.

"It's impossible to accurately predict that as cancer occasionally goes into remission. Based on my experience, though, I'd say with treatment, perhaps upwards of two years and without treatment, maybe one year. Bear in mind, Tanya, these are just projections. They could vary a great deal either way."

"Such a short time," Tanya said. "Oh God, how can I take this?" Tom sat down beside Tanya and they both wept.

"I'm sorry folks," Ferguson said, turning to leave. "No doubt the two of you would like some privacy now."

"I'm awfully frightened dear," Tanya whispered as she grasped Tom's hand. "Do you think God is punishing me for being unfaithful to you and the kids? Maybe God allowed time for the kids to grow up and now He's bringing His justice on me."

"Nonsense! Pure nonsense! When we ask for forgiveness, our wrongdoings are forgotten and never again used against us. Our God is a God of love, not some ogre bent on getting even with us for mistakes we've made. I know of no other person who's so compassionate and supportive of her family and friends. Always remember your mom's words, 'you are a gem in God's eyes.' I'll be with you every step of the way, dear. We'll handle this together."

In the early evening, they phoned the family. Their support helped Tanya immeasurably. Later in the evening Grace came to visit. Crying together helped with the pain and frustration they both felt. Grace promised to stay in closer contact for the remaining time that Tanya had left.

After much agonizing, Tanya decided against chemotherapy or radiation. It helped, that at least in this decision, she had some control over her life.

As the weeks passed, Tanya was slowly coming to grips with the reality of her condition. Tom, however, was still having problems in accepting her illness.

In late November, Tanya and Judy went to Red Deer to do some Christmas shopping. It was the first time Tanya and Tom had been apart since she was diagnosed with cancer.

As soon as Tanya left, Tom went to the mill yard to doze the snow off the landing so the ground could freeze. The more he thought of Tanya's condition, the more wrought up he became. Finally he stopped the Cat and went over to the sawmill carriage. As he sat there, tears streaming down his face, he had flash backs of their life. He recalled the terror in Tanya's eyes as he knocked Kostich off her, the glow of falling in love with her, the warmth of her body as he entered her the first time they made love and the pain on her face when she realized how badly Matthew hoodwinked her and how she'd hurt him with her unfaithfulness. He saw the wild look of passion on her face the first time they were intimate after their reconciliation. Finally, there was that look of hopeless fear when the doctor told her she had terminal cancer.

"Damn it, damn it, damn it!" he cried out in anguish. "I just can't take it anymore."

Spotting an old abandoned car on the edge of the mill yard, he climbed back on the cat with revenge in his eye. Tom dropped the blade and pushed the wreck out onto the landing. He backed up, lifted the blade and drove the Cat right over the top of the car. He crushed and mangled the old car for the next twenty minutes. Tom finally dozed the tortured mess back into the bush.

"Smashing that old car is pretty juvenile," he chuckled, "but it makes me feel a whole lot better."

When Tanya returned from town, she could tell at a glance that Tom had been having a hard time.

"Feeling a bit rough?" she asked, as she hugged him.

"I guess you could say that. I was a fair bit peed off with fate for picking on you, so I vented a bit. You know that old car of Ben's parked at the edge of the mill yard?"

Tanya nodded.

"Well I completely destroyed it with the Cat. There's nothing much left that looks like a car. It's kind of childish, I suppose."

"If it helped, who am I to judge?"

As Tanya prepared for Christmas, Tom was constantly getting in the way as he tried to help her out. He would have cheerfully done all the housework if she'd have let him. Once Tanya picked up on it, she brought it to a quick end.

"By doing everything for me, you're making me feel like an invalid," she said with a wry grin. "I appreciate your intent, but I'm still quite capable and just in case you've forgotten, you're a lousy cook."

It took a moment or two for Tanya's message to sink in. "I see your point," Tom said putting his arms around her. "I'll slack right off."

"Thanks dear. Just treat me the way you did before you knew I had cancer. It will make me feel like a real woman again, rather than a sicky." She gave Tom a slap on his butt and added, "That means in bed too."

Tom smiled. "I think I understand. I promise to smarten up a whole lot tonight."

Tanya, as usual, made enough food to feed the whole community. She asked everyone to treat her as they always had and encouraged them to talk freely about her illness. The love and support she felt from all her family was overwhelming and reinforced how much she had to be thankful for.

While they were opening gifts, Judy told Tanya she just found out she was pregnant.

"What a wonderful present that news is. I'm so happy for you. Wow! My first grandchild! This gives me another reason to keep on going. I promise to still be here when the baby arrives."

As they were washing dishes on Christmas Day, Betty remarked to Tanya, "Isn't life strange? Your dad and I are nearing the end of our lives. Why couldn't God take one of us instead of you?"

"I guess my work here is about done. God must need me somewhere else, but you're right, life is odd. There's one small life in Judy's body being created for living, my body preparing for death."

As the reality of Tanya's illness began sinking in, she and Tom attempted to live each day to the fullest. They made a pact not to dwell on the negative side of things if possible. Both of them recognized that their current goals and priorities had to be dramatically altered.

Right after Christmas, Tanya and Tom began planning their itinerary. Tanya always wanted to find her biological father and it now became a priority. Tom also wanted to take Tanya to visit his relatives in eastern Canada.

On January fifteenth, Tanya and Tom flew to Hawaii for a second honeymoon. They spent countless hours lying close to each other on the beach, absorbing the sun and listening to the tireless roar of the surf. Rather than dwelling on Tanya's illness they were making memories to see them through the difficult days that lay ahead. They were living for the moment.

While still in Hawaii, they met the Montgomerys, a couple from Winnipeg in somewhat similar straits. Clyde Montgomery was terminally ill with Leukemia. This trip would no doubt be his wife's and his last holiday together. The couples spent a few evenings together, sharing their heartaches and their joys. It was just the support Tom and Tanya needed.

After two weeks in Hawaii, Tanya and Tom took a cruise ship to Australia. They rented a car and toured the outback. Traveling the sparse interior, they came upon an old white haired man walking along the road. They stopped and offered him a ride.

"Thank you for stopping. A lot of folk won't. I'm on my way to visit my sister. She lives another twenty miles down the road. I used to drive until I got cataracts."

"We're from Canada. My name is Tanya and my husband is Tom. We farm and Tom has a small sawmill. I used to teach school."

"I'm happy to meet you," the old man said, smiling broadly. "My name is Caleb and my sister is Josie. She has a sickness with her muscles and has been in a wheelchair for a long time. Josie suffers a lot and I try to visit her every two weeks or so."

As they were driving along, Caleb continued talking about his sister. "Josie is very wise. Even though she didn't have much schooling, she's always reading. We are aborigines from the Waramanga tribe. Our uncle Eli had great powers. I think you call people like this a Shaman in your country. We call him a Wirinum. He talked with the spirits. Uncle Eli saw these same powers in Josie when she was a young girl. She has healed many of our people and can look into the past and the future."

Tom and Tanya drove a mile off the highway and delivered Caleb to Josie's door. He thanked them for the lift and insisted that they stop and meet Josie. Although she was confined to a wheelchair, Josie's mind was still sharp and she was soon giving Caleb orders to make tea.

"My married daughter lives in the next town," Josie said to Tom and Tanya. "She looks in on me every few days, but I still get lonely. I'm so pleased that two strangers would be kind enough to bring my brother right to my door. I always look forward to his visits. Caleb tries to come to visit me every couple of weeks, but it's become quite hard for him now with his poor eyesight."

As they were drinking tea, Josie turned to Tanya. "My dear, you are suffering from cancer."

Tanya, nodded, startled by Josie's diagnosis.

"Life is so strange. I have healed others, but I cannot heal myself. The Spirits tell me that my stay on earth is just about up," Josie sighed. "One does not argue with the Spirits."

After talking about their respective lives, Josie turned the conversation back to her special powers. "Most of our people have forgotten our old ways. Many think it was all make-believe."

"Perhaps these people would like you to look into their past or future," Caleb suggested, turning to his sister.

"It is not for us to push our ways on people of different beliefs," Josie replied quietly.

There was an awkward silence before Josie carried on. "I can see that Tanya is afraid of my powers. You need not feel bad my dear. Many of my own people are like that. Some don't believe anymore, some are afraid."

"Tanya's a bit uneasy about her future, with her illness," Tom said, "but I wouldn't mind if you tried to do mine."

Josie was silent for some time. "As you wish sir, as you wish, but first I must meditate. Caleb, could you fetch me our uncle's Womerah?"

Caleb went into Josie's bedroom and returned with the aboriginal spear-throwing device.

"This Womerah was my uncle's," Josie whispered reverently. "He gave it to me just before he died."

Josie was soon rocking back and forth in her wheelchair, softly chanting and passing her hand back and forth over the Womerah. With eyes firmly shut, she raised her hand and touched Tom lightly on top of his head.

"I shall first visit your past, Sir," Josie started in a low monotone. "I see a small boy standing beside a strange looking cart. There is a man in the cart. He has no legs."

Tom gasped in amazement.

"I now see a large man with no trousers on. He falls on a young girl who is also naked. I see a fight, a horrible fight." Josie turned to Tom. "It is you who fights the larger man and knocks him down. It is strange, but I sense that there is a Spirit there with you."

Tom and Tanya shook their heads in awe.

Josie came out of her trance and turned to Tom. "I will now look into your future." She chanted again while stroking her Womerah. Suddenly she started moaning and beads of sweat appeared on her forehead.

As Josie slowly opened her eyes, there was a look of horror on her face. "I cannot tell you what I saw, Sir," she finally whispered.

"Go ahead Josie. Tell me. I insist!" Tom exclaimed. "I've got to know what it is."

"I'm sorry Sir, but I must not," Josie replied firmly. "If I see something frightening in a person's future, I never describe it. If I did, it would cause much fear and might ruin their lives."

Once on the road again, Tom was eager to discuss Josie's vision with Tanya. "It's sure strange how accurate she was about my past, but I don't know what to make of her look into my future. I remember Dad's dream before he died and how Mom made light of it. It makes a person wonder."

"It makes me most uneasy. It's all so frightening. Let's not talk about it."

"Well anyway, I guess it won't do us any good to worry about it." Tom concluded.

As they were flying home, Tanya's uneasy frame of mind returned as she thought of their visit with Caleb and Josie. "I wonder what Josie saw when she looked into Tom's future. It must have been pretty gruesome because she seemed disturbed. Could she have seen my death?"

CHAPTER
24

After a lot of sleuthing, Tanya discovered that her biological father lived in Seattle. She made arrangements to meet him and Tom and she drove down for a visit.

Tanya had mixed feelings about meeting her father, picturing him a weak, selfish, undisciplined loser who always ran from his problems. As they drove up to his house she wondered whether she'd fully forgiven him for abandoning them. The last time her folks saw him was when he burnt down the house, close to fifty years before. She only knew that he stopped drinking and had remarried.

When Tanya and Tom pulled into his driveway, they saw a frail, stooped, balding man in his early seventies coming down the porch steps to welcome them.

Aaron was in tears as he held Tanya close. "Thank you so much for looking up your old dad," he whispered.

Over tea, Tom, Tanya and her dad made small talk. After some lengthy lulls in the conversation, Tanya took the lead. "I feel a bit awkward asking this, but could you tell us your story? So far I've only heard Mom's side of it."

"Alright," Aaron said sadly. "I guess I should start with my childhood. I came from a rough home. My father was an alcoholic and abused our whole family. When I was seventeen, Mother died. I just couldn't take it any longer, so I moved out on my own and found work. Unfortunately, like my Dad, I soon turned to booze."

"Did Mom know about your drinking problem when you first met her?"

"She knew that I drank some, but I don't think she knew how bad it really was. After we married, I managed to stop drinking for a bit, but soon the pressures started to build again. Your mother was headstrong and insisted that we move to the farm. I became frustrated, as I knew absolutely nothing about farming. Your mom was trying her best to help me out, but I felt so uptight I began drinking again, this time, with a real vengeance."

"I know what you're talking about when you say Mom was headstrong. She's a wonderful lady, but at times she can be quite stubborn."

"I shouldn't be blaming her. I was at fault. I really have no excuse for abusing your mom, or for drinking for that matter. I might as well be honest and come clean. I was just weak and selfish without the guts to face up to my problems."

"We've all made mistakes," Tanya sighed. "I have parts of my life I'd like to live over. I guess as long as we learn from our errors. That's all that counts."

"You're right on that one. You see, I was brought up to look down on blacks. First, a black man gave me a sound thumping for abusing my wife and then he seemed to be making a play for her. When I burned the house down, I had no idea that you and your mom were in the bedroom. After Jed broke my back, I was so down that I even tried to kill myself in the hospital. Before my back was broke, I had a glimmer of hope that we'd somehow get back together as a family."

"In the Rehabilitation Centre, I got to know Cornelius, a man who was paralyzed from the waist down and confined to a wheel chair. He was worse off than me, but still the most cheerful man I'd ever met. I couldn't figure out why he was always so positive. We chummed around for a few weeks before he blasted me right out of the water."

"I can still hear his voice, as if it were yesterday. 'Aaron, you've got to smarten the hell up or you just plain won't make it. You have three problems. First, you only talk about the negative. Number two, you've got to learn how to give yourself a good stout kick in the ass. You really need that. Third, quit feeling sorry for yourself and start reaching out to others. Remember, Aaron, there's lots of people out there worse off than you. It's not going to be easy, but unless you change your ways, you're in for some heavy sledding.'"

"I started applying his advice. He was right about it not being easy, but at least now I was moving in the right direction. It made a tremendous difference for me when I found out that Jed paid for all of my medical expenses. I guess Jed thought like Cornelius did."

"Yes, Jed has a big heart." Tanya interjected. "He's treated me like his own daughter. How did you manage to straighten out your life?"

"After I left the Rehabilitation Centre, I joined Alcoholics Anonymous. I met Marge, a divorcee when I started going to church. By reaching out to her, I started healing. The more I looked out for her, the better I felt about myself. After a year or two, Marge and I got married. Did your mom tell you about our marriage?"

"Yes she did. I remember Mom reading your letter to me. She was really happy for you and told me she hoped your new marriage would work out. When Tom and I got married, I wanted to send you a wedding invitation, but had no idea how to contact you. We lost touch with you over thirty years ago. You said your wife's in the hospital?"

"Yes, my poor Marge has Alzheimer's Disease," Aaron replied, looking downcast. "We had a good life together, and then two years ago her memory started to go. I kept her at home as long as I could, but last month I finally played out. I still feel guilty, even though our doctor says it's best for both of us. I try to spend four or five hours with her each day. She still recognizes me, most of the time anyway. I love her dearly. It's hard to see her so helpless."

With tears in his eyes, Aaron reached out his hand and rested it on Tanya's shoulder. "As for a family, just you. Marge and I had a son, but he only lived a few days. Marge had no children from her first marriage, so for all these years, it's just been Marge and me."

"Now, tell me about your family."

"I'll show you some pictures of them," Tanya replied, as she opened a photo album she'd brought with her. "I had a good childhood. Here's a picture of me trying to hold my half brother Ben and half sister Beth on my knee on their first birthday. Ben and Beth are twins. Here's one of Mom and Jed standing in front of Tom's Cat. Tom and I farm. He has a sawmill, which keeps him busy in the off seasons. This is one I took of our kids riding to school on horse back. I don't know if you knew that I was a school teacher. I taught full time before the kids were born. Now I just sub the odd time. Our children, Billy and Grace are both married. As yet there are no grandchildren, but Billy's wife Judith is expecting. Mom remains in good health. Jed had a heart attack last year, but he's made a good recovery. They'll be happy to get an update on you."

After going through the pictures Tanya closed the album. "Now, the bad news," she said, her voice growing husky. "Last fall I got the grim news that I have ovarian cancer." Tanya paused. "Just when Tom and I could start taking it easier, this came along. Your wife suffering with Alzheimer's and me with cancer. It makes you wonder about life, but I guess as long as we love and support each other, that's all that counts. Tom is a tremendous help. Both Marge and I are so blessed to have mates who support us. It's sad that it takes a calamity to bring folks together. We should have done this a long time ago."

As the hours slipped by, Tanya's original assessment of her dad faded into the background. She found in its place a re-born man, a man who loved and supported his wife, a man who yearned to meet his daughter, but lacking the strength to go against his wife's wishes.

"I'm sorry I took the line of least resistance," Aaron said as Tanya and Tom were leaving the next morning. "It should have been I who looked my daughter up. I'm so glad that you're stronger than I am, Tanya. Thank you so much. I now feel complete."

As Tanya hugged her dad goodbye, they were both in tears. "If we don't meet again, Dad, I can now die at peace with myself," she whispered.

They got home from visiting Aaron just as seeding was about to begin. Ben and Billy wanted to do it all, but Tom vetoed their plan. With everyone bearing down, they were soon finished.

Despite her increased discomfort and loss of strength, Tanya's medications kept her discomfort to a minimum. She put in a small garden, feeling it would be good therapy.

Tom and Tanya rented a motor home, and by the middle of June, were on their way to eastern Canada. In Moncton, they visited with Tom's Uncle Sam, his dad's oldest brother, now in his late eighties. Tom last saw him when they visited their farm when he was ten years old. Sam's mind was sharp and he was soon recalling the past.

"I'll never cease to marvel how your dad managed without legs. And that work cart he invented! When we were growing up, he was always inventing something and building it out of nothing. I remember chains he made for his bicycle so he could drive in snow. The darnedest thing was that his ideas always seemed to work."

Tom told his aunt and uncle about his dad's last years, his ongoing fight with infection, and his death.

Sam remained silent for a few moments. "You know, Tom, I was out in the back yard, splitting wood the afternoon your dad passed on. I got this odd feeling that he was there with me. It became so powerful that I just stopped and sat for a spell. It was strange, but the feeling went away as fast as it came. The next day we got the telegram of his passing. As near as we could figure, he passed on about the same time I felt his presence. It's one of those things you can't prove, but you still know there's something to it."

"I had a similar experience when I was sixteen," Tom replied, recounting the incident of his dad coaching him when he fought Ruben Kostich.

"I heard Dad as clearly as I hear you now. If it hadn't been for his coaching, I'm sure I would have lost the fight. Don't ask me for a logical explanation. All I know is that Dad was there with me."

After spending a few more days visiting Tom's relatives, they headed down the eastern seaboard, then west through the central States and back home.

As fall turned to winter, Tanya's condition steadily deteriorated. Tom was constantly by her side, even staying with her when she was hospitalized for a week. Her pain was now becoming more acute. She had lost thirty-five pounds and was very weak.

When she visited the Cancer Clinic, Dr Ferguson again encouraged her to admit herself to the hospital before the pain became unmanageable. Tanya said that she wanted to stay at home as long as possible.

Tom bought Tanya a hospital bed and enlarged the bedroom door. During the day, she would be out in the kitchen or front room in the thick of things. Tanya and Tom spent countless hours lying beside each other, holding hands, reliving all the years they spent together. It was a time of spiritual growth. Family and friends constantly dropped in to give them support. Tom watched Tanya like a hawk and if he noticed that she was getting tired or was in too much pain, he'd tactfully suggest she needed some rest.

One of Tanya's visitors was Mary Gunther, her colleague from teaching days. They spent an enjoyable evening reminiscing about old times.

"Last week I was talking to Molly Compton, a teacher from Red Deer," Mary said. "We were listing all the old rural schools that had been closed in the area. I was sure surprised when she mentioned that her former husband, Matthew Schwartz taught at the Stella School west of Milden."

"We heard that he was married and that his wife left him within a year. Did Molly say anything about their marriage?"

"I was just getting to that. I told Molly that I first met Matthew close to twenty years ago and that he was a bit of a different sort."

"Molly chuckled and said that Matthew was half cracked. She was widowed with a young daughter when they met. After they got married Matthew insisted that she quit teaching and look after the house. Molly said he was always going on about wanting a large family. One morning he was reading the Bible at the table before breakfast and her little girl couldn't sit still. In a fit of anger, Matthew grabbed Stephanie and started spanking her hard. Molly tore right into him and threatened to call the police if he ever lifted a hand to Stephanie again. Matthew's excuse for disciplining Stephanie was that, young as she was, she had to be taught to revere the Bible. Molly said that shortly after this, she and Stephanie pulled out."

"According to Molly, over the years he's had difficulty in keeping a job."

"It sounds like he hasn't learned from his mistakes," Tanya said. "The winter he stayed with us he tried to convince me to use corporal discipline on Billy and Grace. It looks like he's still in the same rut. Wasn't Matthew hospitalized after his marriage came apart?"

"That's what Molly told me. I guess he's been in and out of Psychiatric hospitals a number of times. The last she heard, he was teaching somewhere up north on an Indian reservation."

After Mary left, Tanya turned to Tom. "The news about Matthew sure brings back some haunting memories. Thank God it's all in the past."

"You can say that again. It sounds to me like he's still got a head full of cob-webs."

In early October, Judy had a baby girl. It was Tanya's dream to be there with her for the birth, but she was just too sick to manage. She was thrilled when she learned that Judy and Billy named their baby girl Tanya Judith. Once Judy and baby Tanya Judith returned from the hospital, they spent a lot of time at Tom's and Tanya's.

Christmas was a precious time for the whole family. In her hospital bed, Tanya stayed in the middle of the action. Although overjoyed to have her family around her, it was hard for her to lie in bed and watch helplessly while her mom, Gail and Judy prepared the meals.

On Christmas Day, Tanya spent the day on her bed holding Baby Tanya. "This is the best Christmas present I've ever had," she remarked to Judy. "The Lord has been kind to spare me until wee Tanya was born."

By the twenty-seventh, all the company had left. Tanya slipped a lot in the last couple of days. It seemed to Tom that she held on to celebrate Christmas with the family. On the thirty-first, despite taking the maximum dosage of medications, Tanya's pain was becoming unmanageable. Tom phoned Billy and Grace to come home and then made plans for an ambulance to pick Tanya up the next afternoon to take her to Edmonton. As the pain allowed, Tanya phoned as many of her friends and relatives as she could, to say goodbye.

Billy, Grace, their spouses and wee Tanya spent New Year's Eve with their folks. It was a close time for the family. They laughed together, cried together, and shared their love and support for each other. It was family tradition to be together to do the count down for the New Year. Tanya refused to let her pain change that. Shortly after they brought in the New Year, the young folks left to spend the night at Billy's and Judy's.

With her pain so intense, sleep was impossible for Tanya. Tom sat beside her bed, holding her hand. Sometime in the wee hours of the night, he crawled into his bed. Try as he may and exhausted as he was, sleep would not come. After tossing and turning for a long time, Tom finally drifted off into a troubled sleep.

He dreamt that Tanya and he were being pursued by a shadowy figure. No matter how hard they tried to get away, they were always found. The scene changed and they were being attacked in an old shed. Then Tom found himself outside the building. As he stepped back inside, a man came towards him. He looked closely at the figure and realized he was looking into his own face. He gasped in horror when he saw that the eyes were those of a dead man. Tom awoke with a start.

It was five a.m. and Tanya was moaning in agony. Tom just couldn't take it anymore. He got up and gave her twice the maximum recommended dosage of pain medication.

"What other alternative do I have? Please God, give her some relief," he whispered.

They lay side by side in silence for an hour. With the pain easing some, Tanya turned to Tom. "When I go, dear, I want you to feel free to remarry."

Tom rolled over and looked at Tanya. She lay there gasping for breath, tears glistening in her eyes. Tom reached over and took her hand.

Finally Tanya added in a whisper. "I'm sure it won't be long now. I'm so tired and I hurt so much." Tanya caught her breath again. "I love you Tom. You've been so good to me, but I worry about how you'll manage when I'm gone."

There were now tears in Tom's eyes as he replied. "Thank you so much, dear."

Tanya's condition had deteriorated a lot during the night. Tom was glad that the kids had been over and that she made her phone calls to her friends. He made breakfast, but all that Tanya wanted was a little weak tea.

"Do you think you can manage without me for a few minutes?" Tom asked. "We're about out of wood. I should go to the mill yard and get a pickup load."

"Go ahead," Tanya whispered, "I'm feeling some relief now. I'll try to get some sleep. If I need you, I'll ring the bell."

Before leaving, Tom wheeled Tanya's bed into the front room and pinned the mill yard buzzer to her pillow.

Ben asked to borrow his chain saw, so before heading to the wood pile, Tom stopped at the shop for it. After trying it out, he decided that the chain needed sharpening. "I'll do that later in the house," he thought and put the saw in the cab of the pickup.

It was now at the tail end of a mild spell. Although still fairly warm, the Chinook arch was slipping from the southwest to the west northwest, a sure sign that winter would soon be returning. As Tom gazed at the western sky he wondered if this would be the last Chinook Tanya and he would share.

CHAPTER
25

"HAVE FAITH IN ME AND I WILL MAKE YOU WELL," a voice called out.

Matthew Schwartz leapt to his feet. It was late June and he was sitting at the table in his small teacherage doing his school year end reports. "That was God's voice!" he exclaimed. "What does God mean, 'have faith in me?'" Matthew sat down and pondered for a few moments. Suddenly the answer came to him. "If I have faith in God rather than in the medications I'm taking, I will be healed."

Matthew jumped to his feet again and headed to the medicine cabinet. "As a show of faith, Lord, I'll get rid of all my pills," he cried out. He scooped all his pills into a bag and threw them in the garbage.

Matthew's mental condition rapidly deteriorated. In late July he was forced to spend two weeks in hospital to get stabilized. Matthew's doctor told him he had no choice but to go back on his medications.

****

Several years passed.

In late August, just prior to beginning the new school year, Matthew visited his aunt Sandra and learned of Tanya's illness. Over the next few weeks, his thoughts were again becoming fixated on her and he was starting to feel depressed.

One night in late September, Tanya's voice woke him from a deep sleep. "I'm in so much pain, Matthew," she moaned. "Why did our relationship have to end?"

The next afternoon, after school was out, Matthew went for a walk. Suddenly the hair stood up on the back of his neck.

"YOU HAVE FAILED ME MANY TIMES BEFORE," a voice thundered. "WHY DID YOU NOT BELIEVE ME WHEN I SAID I WOULD HEAL YOU? TAKE YOUR MEDICATIONS AND BURY THEM. BELIEVE THAT I WILL MAKE YOU WELL AND IT WILL HAPPEN."

The minute Matthew got home he cleaned out his medicine cabinet again and buried all his medications in the back yard.

By Christmas he no longer paid any attention to his personal hygiene and was growing a beard. His normally mild demeanor had become very aggressive and belligerent. The superintendent was forced to intervene in a couple of donnybrooks he had with students and parents. He was constantly prevailing on Matthew to get medical help. Finally, just before the Christmas break, the superintendent dropped in on him.

"Matthew, I'm afraid we have to come to grips with the way you've been conducting yourself at school. I've been getting pressure from both parents and the band council.

Unless you get medical help over the Christmas break, I'll have no choice but to put you on mandatory sick leave until you do something about it."

"Everyone else is out to get me so it doesn't surprise me that you're joining in too," Matthew replied acidly, his face growing red.

On December 23, Matthew came to spend Christmas with his younger sister Freda and her husband Neil on their small farm a few miles out of Red Deer. Freda and Neil had not seen Matthew since the previous Christmas and were taken aback by his slovenly appearance and hostile comportment.

Freda tried to put him at ease, but Matthew was soon ranting and raving about his superintendent and how their disagreement was negatively impacting on him.

"Have you thought about talking things over with your psychiatrist?" Freda enquired. "Maybe we should make an appointment with him."

"He'd be the last person in the world I'd want to talk with!" Matthew hollered. "What good has he ever done me other than making me addicted to all those rotten pills? If I'm not welcome here anymore, just say the word and I'll be on my way."

"You're always welcome," Freda replied. Over the next few hours she made a concerted attempt to calm Matthew down.

The next afternoon, Matthew drove into the city to visit his Aunt Sandra. When they met, she too was taken aback by his slovenly appearance and hostile attitude. After a half hour of listening to Matthew tearing his superintendent apart, Sandra grew tired of his rhetoric and turned the conversation to Tanya's illness. "You know, Matthew, I can't help wonder if having to live with a self-centered man like Tom isn't contributing to Tanya's sickness."

"Why does that devil still have to haunt me?" Matthew exploded, bringing his coffee mug down hard on the table. The cup shattered, cutting his hand.

Like Freda and Neil, Sandra was concerned with Matthew's irrational behavior. After patching up his hand, she also suggested they go to see his Doctor. "You too!" he shouted. "Whose side are you on anyway? You're no different than Freda!"

After he left, Sandra immediately phoned Freda.

"I can appreciate your concern for Matthew," Freda said. "I'm afraid his mental health is nearing the crisis point, but he refuses to take his medications anymore. The more I try to talk to him, the more agitated he becomes. He maintains he's okay and scoffs when I offer him any help. Neil and I are at a loss as to what we can do for him."

On New Year's Eve, Matthew got into a heated exchange with a guest and Freda was forced to intervene. By eight thirty he was exhausted and headed for his room. As he lay on his bed, his thoughts returned to Sandra's comments. "She did say that with Tom gone Tanya would be healed, didn't she?"

Matthew awoke with a start. He saw a dim light in his room.

"YOU FAILED YOUR ASSIGNMENT YEARS AGO," a voice boomed out. "I'M GIVING YOU ONE MORE CHANCE TO REDEEM YOURSELF. DO NOT FAIL THIS TIME. REMEMBER, YOU HAD THE CROSSHAIRS OF YOUR GUN

ON TOM'S CHEST, BUT YOU DIDN'T PULL THE TRIGGER. TOM IS EVIL. HE'S KEEPING TANYA IN BONDAGE. THAT'S WHY SHE'S DYING. TOM IS ALL THAT STANDS IN THE WAY OF HER BEING HEALED."

Matthew shook uncontrollably. He lay awake for the rest of the night making plans to carry out God's directive. His mission gave him new boldness.

At six a.m. he quietly dressed and stepped outside. His pickup was in a shed a fair distance from the house and he had no trouble starting it without waking the household.

As he headed west to Milden he was constantly praying for wisdom and boldness to do God's task. A few miles from Tom's and Tanya's place, he pulled to the side of the road. He flipped the truck seat ahead, got his 12 gauge, single shot shotgun out and then put a hand full of shotgun shells in his pocket.

"God has given me new courage," he kept repeating to himself. "This time I will obey him. I must always remember that Tanya loved me before and with Tom out of the picture, she still will."

Matthew drove the last half mile with his lights out, then turned off the motor and coasted into the driveway.

Tom finished loading the pickup with wood. As he was getting into the truck he felt an overpowering sense of Tanya's presence, even smelling her perfume. He whirled around and called out. "Is that you, dear?" but there was only silence.

"Are you losing it Tom, or what? How could she get out here?" Suddenly a feeling of panic swept over him. "Damn it, is Tanya okay? Is she somehow trying to contact me?"

Tom sped for the house, grabbed the chainsaw and ran up the porch steps. "What am I doing?" he said under his breath, as he got to the back door. "Maybe it's all in my head. I'd better calm down and not wake Tanya up if she's sleeping." He quietly opened the kitchen door, put the saw down by the kitchen table and tip-toed into the front room.

"Tanya," Tom whispered. "Are you alright dear?"

"I guess so," Tanya moaned, "but I'm awfully scared. It feels like there's a ton of weight on my soul. I'd have rung the buzzer, but it's fallen to the floor. Help me stand up. That might help some."

Tom turned on the front room light and helped Tanya to her feet.

Matthew was walking up the driveway, shotgun in hand, his heart beating wildly. To his horror, he noticed a light in the house come on. "Tom must be up," he mumbled. "Oh well, here goes." With a surge of adrenalin, Matthew climbed the steps. "God is with me," he whispered, as he banged on the door.

"Yeah, who is it?" Tom hollered out. "I can't come to the door. I'm helping Tanya."

The sound of Tom's voice rekindled Matthew's hatred. Enraged, he threw the door open.

For a moment Matthew stood in the doorway in shock. "I can't believe that's Tanya," he muttered in disbelief. At the far side of the room he saw Tom supporting a frail, emaciated old woman with sunken eyes.

As Tanya glanced up, she saw an old man with a scraggly white beard, disheveled dirty clothes and wild, bloodshot eyes.

"My God!" she thought. "Could that possibly be Matthew?"

Eyes flashing venom, Matthew screamed in a voice full of hate, "I'm here to carry out the Lord's orders! Your time has come, you Godless infidel, you rapist! God has instructed me to do away with you. Your satanic influence has caused Tanya's sickness. If it wasn't for you, she'd be healed and we'd be together."

Tom was taken aback, but only for a moment. "I should have broken you in two, years ago!" he roared.

With a macabre grin, Matthew loaded the gun.

"Don't do this, Matthew," Tanya cried out. "I've never really loved you! I've only loved Tom."

The brutal words ripped into Matthew's soul. "You've brainwashed her too," he cried in agony as he pointed the gun at Tom.

Tanya lurched in front of Tom as the shot rang out.

The shotgun blast hit her in the chest, killing her instantly. As Tom was right beside Tanya, he was in the line of fire and part of the blast caught him in the chest. Tom reeled backwards, badly wounded but still on his feet.

"Oh my God I've shot Tanya!" Matthew shrieked in horror. "You Devil! You pushed her in front to save yourself!"

The impact of the shotgun blast may have stopped a lesser man, but not Tom. Now he was fighting for his life.

"You low-bred dog!" he bellowed and dove for his chain saw. His hands were a blur, his moves all instinctive. As Tom rolled to his feet, the chain saw was snarling full bore. Blood was squirting from his chest with every heartbeat, but he was totally focused on stopping this madman.

Matthew was desperately trying to reload his shotgun to get off another round. In his haste, he dropped the shotgun shell.

"Damn this gun anyway!" were his last words.

Matthew just had time to place another cartridge in the breach when Tom got to him. He rammed the snarling saw up between Matthew's legs, brutally and effectively emasculating him. Tom continued lifting up on the saw, ripping into Matthew's belly. With a scream of agony Matthew collapsed, dead in a pool of his own gore.

As Tom glanced down at Matthew, he shook his head and muttered, "You poor hapless idiot. You never could get it through you head, could you?"

Tom shut the saw off and staggered back to Tanya. Though much weakened from the loss of blood, he dragged her over to the front room couch. Tears were streaming down his face as he sat down beside her and put his arm around her to keep her from slumping over.

"My Tanya, my Tanya," he sobbed. "Why did you fall in front of me? Why did it have to end this way?"

Blood was still oozing out of Tom's chest and he was coughing up large clots of blood.

"I'd better get help!" he gasped.

He crawled over to the phone and called Jed.

Once back with Tanya, he whispered, "I wonder if Jed will get help in time. With my darling gone, I hope he doesn't." He held his mate close and silently wept for the loss of his lover.

"I don't think I can last much longer, dear," he whispered. "I'll be joining you soon."

There the two sat, propped up against each other, one dead, the other dying. Tom's thoughts drifted back over the last thirty-five years.

"It's been a beautiful love affair. I'm so glad we won't be separated for long."

Tom was slowly losing the battle. As his lungs filled with blood his coughing became worse and his breathing more shallow and laboured.

"It's getting late. It's starting to get dark," he gasped. When he glanced at his wrist watch, he saw that it wasn't yet nine-thirty a.m. "I guess I must be getting close to the end."

He was still fighting for air, but it had become impossible to breathe. Suddenly, that wonderful feeling of peace and well-being descended on him again. Where a second before he was fighting for breath, now, miraculously, he had no more desire to breathe. The light grew fainter still.

"So this is what Josie saw," Tom whispered as darkness enveloped him.

Tom's phone call shook Jed so badly he had to take a nitroglycerin pill and sit down for a minute or two. While Jed was trying to get his chest pain under control, Betty phoned for the ambulance and the RCMP.

Within minutes, Jed and Betty were at Tom's and Tanya's place.

Betty raced up the porch steps, past Matthew and into the living room. "Oh my God, I can't believe this," she screamed. "Dear Lord, our darling girl is gone, but we've got to check on Tom."

As Jed walked past Matthew, he growled, "you lowbred son-of-a-bitch."

Jed checked Tom for vital signs, but found no pulse.

"Damn, we didn't make it in time to save him," Jed cried in desperation. Although Tom was gone and his eyes were glazed, he had a peaceful expression on his face.

Jed glanced down at the coffee table, picked up a piece of paper and read aloud:

Dear kids and little Tanya. Mom was killed by Matthew Schwartz. He tried to do me in. She jumped in front of me. I'm badly wounded. Got Matthew with my chain saw. Hard to breathe now. Mom's not suffering anymore. Split everything equally. Look out for each other. When Tanya's older, tell her Grandma and Grandpa went to be with God. Jed and Betty are coming. Will soon be with Mom. Love   Mom and Dad

As Jed read Tom's note, tears were slipping down his wrinkled old face.

"Damn, damn, damn," he whispered hoarsely. His hand, now shaky, reached out and rested on Tom's shoulder.

"My son, my son," he cried in anguish, "God rest your soul, my son."

Betty sat down beside Tanya and held her daughter's head on her shoulder. As she stroked Tanya's face, she sobbed, "my little girl, my darling little girl." Looking upward, she cried, "Why not me, God? Why couldn't you have taken me instead of them?"

Jed turned to his daughter, his whole frame racked with sobs. He reached out both hands and cupped Tanya's head.

Holding her head gently, he repeated the same words he spoke forty nine years before on the day she was born.

"Tanya, my little Tanya."

EPILOGUE

Tanya's and Tom's stories were not at an end. With the pulling of the murderous trigger, all pain ceased for Tanya and she found herself rising up from the floor. As the room faded from view, she heard a roaring sound like a jet taking off and felt herself being swept into a mist-filled tunnel. When she peered ahead, she saw a light.

When the light faded for Tom, he also heard the roar and found himself in the dimly lit tunnel. As he moved towards the light, he became aware of a presence in the tunnel with him. Although he could not see anyone, he heard a voice he knew so well.

"Welcome home, Son!"

"Dad, is that you?" Tom called out.

"Yes it is."

Like Tanya, Tom came out into the most beautiful, brilliant light. It radiated warmth, love and a feeling of well-being. Tom stood in awe.

Then Tom saw his dad! Bill didn't look a day over thirty and as he ran to meet Tom, he did a couple of dance steps!

"Dad," Tom cried out as they hugged, "you have your legs back!"

"Yes, we are all renewed when we come into this life."

"Thanks for always being there for me, Dad."

Bill nodded. "Ever since I came into this dimension I've been looking out for you. When Matthew had the cross hairs of his gun on your chest, you didn't fall into the creek, I pushed you. I've been waiting for you for years. I'm so proud of you, Son."

Now off behind the Light, Tom saw a beautiful young woman. It was Tanya! As Tom raced towards her, two strange things happened. First, his trick knee was working properly again and, wonder of wonders, his eyes had straightened so he no longer saw double! Then they were in each others arms, laughing and crying for joy.

They were soon joined by all those who had come to greet them. As they glanced about, Tom and Tanya found themselves in a beautiful, park-like country where every tree and flower gave off their own phosphorescent light.

As they walked hand in hand, Tom kept repeating, "my Tanya, my Tanya, my Tanya."

TANYA'S AND TOM'S EARTHLY LIVES HAD COME TO AN END. THEIR NEW LIVES IN THE NEXT DIMENSION WERE JUST BEGINNING....

Printed in the United States
128219LV00001B/189/A